THE RAT REVEREND CLANCY & THE SEVEN DEADLY SINS

DAVID L. CARTER

APOCRYPHILE
PRESS

Apocryphile Press
PO Box 255
Hannacroix, NY 12087
www.apocryphilepress.com

Copyright © 2022 by David L. Carter
Printed in the United States of America
ISBN 978-1-958061-00-8 | paper
ISBN 978-1-958061-01-5 | ePub

Please join our mailing list at www.apocryphilepress.com/free
We'll keep you uptodate on all our new releases,
and we'll also send you a FREE BOOK. Visit us today!

*This one is for my big brother, Chip—the most
kindhearted, Bojangles loving 'sinner' of us all!
With love and inexpressible gratitude.*

CONTENTS

☙ I ☙
IRA (WRATH)

S TANDING AT THE ALTAR, GAZING down at a
dwindled and lackadaisical congregation, Reverend
Doctor Silas DeBassompierre of St. Aloysius Episcopal
Church in Morehead City, NC, felt his gorge rise ominously.
This forced him to pause at the end of his meticulously practiced but uninspired homily, close his eyes, and swallow hard to
keep down his breakfast. Of course, this gastric distress was less
the result of his indignation at the laxity of his members than it
was the natural consequence of the six Bloody Marys he'd
consumed the evening before at one of the seediest dives to be
found on the waterfront. He knew that as a clergyperson it was
unseemly for him to drink in public, but sometimes one simply
has to break the rules.

Gritting his teeth against the nausea, he asked himself if this,
celebrating a Sunday service to a handful of geriatric parishioners, was what he'd gone through all the twists and turns and
challenges of doctoral level theological education to arrive at?
Hell no! No, by this point in his career—after all he was almost
35 years old—he should have been well placed in a tenure-track
position in one of the Episcopal Seminaries. But of course, in the
church as in all other human institutions, it is usually the scum

that forms at the top... how he'd ever imagined that it would be any different for him was still a mystery. He took a deep breath through his nostrils and exhaled slowly. Oh, God, he petitioned, just let me make it through this service and I'll never touch another Bloody Mary...

A tentative coughing sound, recognizable to him as coming from his administrative and pastoral care assistant Grace Holbach, who was seated in the front pew, prodded him out of his preoccupation with his own discomfort, and he opened his eyes and genuflected, as if to signal that he'd been praying. And in a sense, he consoled himself, he had been. Petition, he decided, was a perfectly appropriate form of silent prayer, and particularly appropriate for a priest about to proclaim the General Confession.

Raising both hands in the obligatory gesture of blessing, he closed his eyes and opened his mouth.

"Let us humbly confess our sins unto Almighty God..."

৩৯৯

"LET us humbly confess our sins unto Almighty God..." squeaked Clancy, addressing his own congregation. Clancy had observed countless services presided over by the young and handsome Reverend Silas DeBassompierre from a hiding place beneath the Hammond Organ in the sanctuary of St. Aloysius. He was obliged to stay hidden, for although he too was a member of the Christian clergy, he was not a human being, but rather a rat who had been raised by his not so recently departed and deeply mourned Great Aunt November in the cellar of that church. He had received, in a nocturnal vision not long after dear Aunt November's demise, the call from God Almighty to spread the Gospel of Jesus Christ to the various creatures who inhabited or passed through the churchyard of St. Aloysius Episcopal Church and the surrounding environs. Since then, he'd managed to bring together various species to form a small but growing and vibrant congregation. They met for worship every Sunday morning at ten a.m., careful to begin and conclude while the human congregation was inside attending to the service presided over by the human Rector, the Reverend Silas DeBassompierre who, little did he know, was the Rat Reverend Clancy's paradigm for ministry and inspiration.

Thrilled beyond measure to provide his little flock with spiritual food, he gave them a moment to recall and repent, in the privacy of their own consciences, of their sins and transgressions. Then he consecrated the offerings that each had brought in accordance with their vastly varied dietary restrictions and offered them back as the Body of Christ. That done, he clambered back on top of the green plastic vermicomposter, which served as his lectern, and prepared to make a few announcements prior to pronouncing the dismissal.

"Bless you all for coming!" His voice was high and keen with natural ebullience. "And this Sunday, I want to let ya'll know that, just like Reverend DeBassompierre, I encourage any member of my church to come visit me at any time if there is something weighing heavy on you that you feel like you need to give up to God. I don't want anyone to think that you *have* to tell me what you might be doing or have done that isn't nice, but it does help, sometimes, to say out loud what you aren't very proud of, and you can be real sure that I won't tell a soul. That's one of the rules of being a reverend. I'm not allowed to gossip, especially about my members and whatever sins ya'll might have committed..."

The gathered members of St. Aloysius Jr. Church of the Urban Wildlife each regarded their reverend with varying degrees of affectionate puzzlement. Of course he had mentioned the General Confession at some point in every service, but none of them having any real concept of sin, none of them had taken that literally. The reverend himself was fond of saying, after all, that all they had to do to be a Christian was to love Jesus, an invisible but ever-present human figure whom he described as being very kind and helpful and possessing the valuable skill of resurrecting the dead. Wasn't that enough? And tricky enough, too, given that He was one of those humans, and they only really knew anything about Him through the word of Clancy's mouth.

"Only thing weighing on me are all these young'uns!" vocalized Ometa, an opossum who was relatively new to the community. "You gonna take 'em off my paws?!" And, jiggling with amusement at what she perceived as a witticism, she caused the nine baby opossums clinging to her sides to squeal in alarm. "Don't you worry, babies. Mama's just kidding."

Clancy was, as a matter of fact, prepared for some resistance to the idea of private confession. His parishioners, after all, were all relatively recent converts. They hadn't had the advantage of being raised, as he had been, in the Church by a good Christian she-rat. "Well, Ometa... you do have a point, I guess. I know that it can be hard, when times are tough, the way they are for most of us, just living paw to mouth, to always do the right thing, and God understands. I don't think God means for us to feel bad about anything we do just to get by... but sometimes we go too far, and we ought to feel bad about some things..."

"Like what, Reverend?" said Bertram, a grotesque looking and strong smelling buzzard, who had become, over the course of a tumultuous catechumenate, one of the pillars of the church.

"That's a real good question too, Bertram. I think it depends, but most of the time if we do anything that hurts ourselves or anyone else, we've been sinful."

"What have *you* got to confess, O Holy Rodent...?" Came a faint, gravelly voice from within the bowels of the vermicomposter, as muffled by being surrounded by soil as a voice from a grave. "That's what I wanna know..."

Clancy was taken aback. It was unusual to hear a peep from the earthworm Hertz during a service, for Hertz professed to find Clancy's liturgies meaningless and boring. Nevertheless, Clancy loved the irascible invertebrate dearly for, not long after Aunt November went to be with the Lord, he'd encountered

Hertz half dead on the cold wooden floor of the sanctuary of the human church, having been trodden in clinging to the toe of one of Reverend DeBassompierre's wingtip shoes one muddy evening. Clancy had restored the worm back to health by depositing him in the soil of the potted fern that hung suspended above Grace's desk in the administrative suite and checked on him every day. It was while Hertz was recuperating in the fern pot that Clancy, who had never ventured beyond the walls of St. Aloysius, discovered through his new friend that not all creatures knew of the love or even the existence of their Creator. Not yet feeling called to ordained ministry, Clancy nevertheless felt led to evangelize and eventually baptize his friend, even though the worm's skepticism regarding the Gospel seemed to increase along with his health. When the steering committee of St. Aloysius purchased the materials needed to institute a community garden/vermicomposting program, Hertz convinced Clancy to move him to the composter so that he could take advantage of that career opportunity. Clancy knew he would miss his friend, but he knew as well that he mustn't stand in the way of the worm following his own path. And so the bond between the rat and the worm was deep and abiding, while not without friction. At one point, for example, Clancy had become impatient with Hertz's reluctance to make a profession of faith and had baptized him in the toilet of the men's room of St. Aloysius in a fit of temper that he would never cease to regret. So he was generous to a fault when it came to Hertz's occasional digs.

"Hertz! You are absolutely, positively right! Before I start thinking I can forgive anyone else's sins, I have to take responsibility my own..." and, as usual when he felt uneasy, Clancy reached for his tail and gnawed on a kink near the end of it, an unconscious self-soothing habit carried over from a sometimes lonely childhood.

Clancy searched his soul as he gnawed his tail, and resolved to model the transparency he felt his parishioners should adopt. *I'm supposed to set an example.* "Now, let's see... I wished this morning I could preach as good as Reverend DeBassompierre... that's greed...or maybe it's envy...or maybe it's pride...oh, I always get them so mixed up..."

"Oh, for Heaven's sake!!" came a voice from above. Then, descending from the electrical line connected to the church building with a flutter of wings and a soft, chuckling vocalization, Ottoline, who was one of a pair of pigeons who had also been among Clancy's earliest converts, intervened. "Reverend, don't let this worm browbeat you. You don't have to bare your soul in front of the whole congregation! It seems to me, given what you've told us about Jesus, anything that might come between ourselves and God has been washed off us in our Baptism..."

"Ottoline's right," said Bertram the buzzard, who very much admired the matronly pigeon. "That's what you said when we all got Baptized!"

"I guess you're right, Ottoline..." agreed Clancy. "But Reverend DeBassompierre says that Baptism doesn't make us perfect, just forgiven... "

Hertz the earthworm was not a little annoyed. Here the rat was on the edge of making himself predictably ridiculous, and these birds had to come along and ruin it. "Amen!" the worm said, not uncynically. "I think that human was right for once. After all, you baptized *me*, didn't you, and I'm no angel..."

Ottoline's soft grey breast expanded, indicating she had more to say to this, but Clancy did not seem to notice, for Hertz's words had hit their mark. "You're right, Hertz," he said. "You know, I believe you're exactly right. I'm no better than any of the rest of you, but that doesn't mean that as a Reverend I shouldn't set a good example. And that means I must try to stay on top of my bad habits. I've been snacking too much, for one thing. And that's not a good witness. Why, just this morning I had to squeeze harder than I ever have before to get out of the basement! I know I need a good breakfast to get through the day, but I *could* skip lunch, and I don't have to take Little Debbie Cakes out of the food pantry just because they've been sitting there for months. And I should start exercising again too. Thank you, Hertz. I can always count on you to help me stop fooling myself. Well! It's good to get that settled! I'm going to watch my diet. And when I feel like eating something I don't need... well then, I know I need to pray!" And with that, Clancy, in one of his characteristic bursts of spontaneous affection, leaned over and kissed Hertz right on the tip. "See ya'll tomorrow!" He said, "I'm going to get me some steps in right now!" And he was off around the cornerstone of the church to the plywood crawlspace door, one corner of which was gnawed away just enough to admit him into the cellar where he and his great-aunt had once made their fusty lair. Ottoline, Bertram, and the others all turned to regard Hertz, who instantly disappeared into his own muck.

"Come back here, sir," warbled Ottoline sternly at the composter. "Not so fast. You should be utterly ashamed of yourself. Why must you constantly antagonize the Reverend! You always take advantage of his sweet nature and his regard for you, and I for one am sick and tired of it! What's the matter with you?!"

Hertz responded to this upbraiding with all the boldness that comes with being concealed, protected and out of the reach of someone who is in any event a basically nonaggressive opponent. "Nothing's the matter with me! And what do you know?! Maybe I want what's best for him just as much as you do, you ever think of that, featherbrain? And besides, he *is* getting too fat!"

Ottoline gritted her beak. She wondered if she'd ever in her life known anyone as ill-natured as this worm seemed to be most of the time. "Now, just a minute, sir. While you may have a longer acquaintance with the Reverend than the rest of us, that certainly doesn't mean you have a proper perception of his character or his intelligence or his appearance, for that matter. Your eyesight is quite rudimentary, like not a few other things about you. You may think that you're more worldly-wise, but I can tell you one thing—the Reverend, while he may be very impressionable, has integrity. And what better example of that can there be than his kindness to you in spite of the fact that you belittle him and point out his shortcomings... which are very mild... every chance you get. And to what end? Why are you so critical? If you can't find it in your heart... if you even have one... to *appreciate* the Reverend and all he does for you and the rest of us, why not simply let him be?!?"

Ottoline, mild and maternal by nature, waited for a response, and when there was simply silence from within the composter, she wondered if perhaps she'd been too harsh. But then the image of the Reverend kicking himself for nothing came to her mind's eye, and once again her pigeon breast swelled with indignation.

Safe within the composter, Hertz fumed. He dared not respond to Ottoline, lest she perceive that her words had hit a nerve. Why *didn't* he just leave the rat to his foolish notions? Why *did* he bother?

Well, I won't any more! he vowed. I give up trying to get that silly squeaking creature to look at how he comes off. I'm done!

And with that he made his way to his chamber in the deep dark labyrinthine interior of the compost.

"WELL, I lost my temper. I'm so sorry you all had to witness that," said Ottoline to the creatures that remained. "That worm certainly knows how to ruffle my feathers sometimes!"

"That's okay, Miss Ottoline," said Bertram. "You just gave it to him straight. That old worm needs to be nicer, especially to the Reverend."

Ottoline blinked, taking this in. "Well, I do stand by what I said. I appreciate your support, Bertram. I just wish I had more patience."

"That worm would try the patience of Jesus Himself," said a squirrel by the name of Elwood, who, like Ottoline, felt very protective of their Reverend. Following the tragic and untimely death of Elwood's son Timmy as the result of a vehicular hit and run on the busy boulevard in front of the church, Clancy had ministered awkwardly but with sincere compassion to his grieving parents. "Don't worry about him. He'll get over it. Or he won't. Who needs him, anyway?"

"WHO NEEDS THEM ANYWAY?" grumbled Hertz, tossing and turning and coiling and squirming, trying to get comfortable. He couldn't get the pigeon's words out of his mind. "*I* don't. I have enough to worry about, running this colony, making sure every worm does their share, without wasting my time with a bunch of overgrounders. Let them have their Reverend, and their stupid church. I really don't give a damn." And he tossed and turned and stretched and coiled, but he still couldn't settle his uneasy mind. "Damn it," he said. "Now I can't sleep."

For a while he contemplated leaving the chamber and going up to the lid to find something to munch on, but after having criticized the rodent's appetite, he decided he wasn't going to give in to that kind of indulgence. No, he knew how to get by on next to nothing, unlike that spoiled rotten rat, unlike that snooty pigeon, or any of the rest of those silly creatures. He knew what it was like to be on his own, without any help from anybody, ignored by his own parents, tricked by the elders of the colony he'd been born into, abandoned on the surface to dry up in the sun or get munched up by some stupid robin. No, he was a survivor... he was the one, after all, who had made both the composter and the garden what they were. Every single worm in the colony was descended from him; he had his figurative hands full. What did he need with any other animal! He was doing real work, he was helping the planet, by Ground! What were all those silly animals out there doing with their prayers besides deluding themselves that there was any justice in the universe! And of all of them, the most deluded was Clancy.

That damn rat. Hertz wished he'd never met him, never mind that the rat had saved his life, or said so. "He doesn't care about me any more than I care about him. Who needs him!" And, repeating this last phrase like a mantra, the malcontented worm eventually lapsed into an uneasy sleep.

OVER THE NEXT FEW DAYS, the Rat Reverend Clancy threw himself heart and soul into his new diet and exercise regime. It seemed to him that even after skipping lunch for just one day, he was seeing... and more importantly, feeling... a significant difference. His pelt felt softer and smoother to his tongue, he had more vim and vigor. He wasn't one hundred percent sure, but he thought he might be having a slightly easier time squeezing himself in and out of the gnawed-off corner of the crawlspace door of the cellar. "Lord," he said to himself. "I praise Your Name, for giving me such a dear good friend in Hertz. Sometimes what he says hurts my feelings, but deep down inside, I know he cares a lot. Lord, I just ask that You bless him, and show him that You love him, because I'm not sure I do a good enough job of explaining Your ways to him. Because after all, he's a whole lot smarter than me. And he had a real hard time growing up back in his old colony, and that can make it not so easy to trust. Help him find his way to You, Lord... In Jesus Name, I pray. I promise, I'll help any way I can...."

OTTOLINE CONTINUED to feel uneasy about the way she'd spoken to Hertz the worm. She shared the incident with her spouse, Steven, a pigeon like herself, though Steven possessed a far less outgoing, more placid character. "I'm afraid I may have caused a rift in the congregation, Steven..." she worried. "He can be so unpleasant, but I should keep in mind that he is the Reverend's oldest friend. And like it or not, he's a part of our community. If the Reverend doesn't object to the way Hertz talks to him, who am I to criticize?"

Steven, as was his way, didn't answer. He simply sat alongside his wife within the ornamental belfry without a bell that topped the roof of St. Aloysius Sr. Church. That was where they made their home. He knew that his dear wife would answer her own concerns. He was, among other things, her sounding board. She burbled on:

"I suppose that even if there is a rift, I shouldn't feel overly responsible. If that worm is entitled to his opinion about the Reverend's behavior or appearance, then at the very least I'm entitled to my concerns about how the Reverend is being treated. I just wish I could find some way to interact with that worm without letting him get under my feathers." Ottoline fell silent, and wondered how it was that she had not, after all their years together, absorbed any of Steven's natural placidity. She supposed that the two of them, as compatible as they were, were simply wired differently. "Perhaps..." she murmured to herself after some time, as much to herself as to Steven, "... perhaps that's the discipline that I should adopt, now that we're being encouraged to examine ourselves... maybe I should spend more time with the worm. Maybe that's how I can become more patient of and understanding toward him. It certainly isn't anything I really care to do... but apparently that's the point of penitence."

৩৯৩

HERTZ COULD HEAR the pigeon calling his name. He could hear her beak tapping out a tattoo, at first tentatively, then more impatiently, against the forest green plastic casing of the composter. He wasn't deaf. Let her tap and gurgle till hell freezes over, he told himself. He wasn't going to give her any satisfaction. He'd made his decision, and he was going to stick to it. He needed that rat and the rest of them like he needed a hole in his tip. He had his pride, by Ground!

But when the tapping and the warbling of his name ceased abruptly and, to his mind, prematurely, moments later only to be replaced by that male pigeon's voice sounding far more urgent than normal, Hertz's curiosity won over his spite, and he burrowed his way to the ventilator slot in the green plastic composter casing to find out what was going on.

⚜

"Poor Bertram," Ottoline was saying. "He's going to be torn. It's terrible that his father should die without their having some... reconciliation."

"It's too bad," agreed Steven. Hertz thought about interjecting his observation that the young buzzard's father had been a royal sonofabitch—he had shown up at Bertram's baptism ceremony with the sole intention of spoiling it by making a stink, just because he was unhappy with Bertram for taking up with Donna, an elegant, aloof and troubled vulture with a tragic past with whom the young buzzard had once been madly in love. Among the avian members of St. Aloysius Jr., Hertz found Bertram to be the least objectionable, so out of the slim degree of respect of which he was capable, the worm held his peace.

"How did it happen, Steven?" asked Ottoline. "How did you find out?"

Steven related the following: He had, as was his custom, flown off to Bertram's roost in the woods to spend some time with him before they reported back to the churchyard for choir practice, and was a little surprised to find that the buzzard wasn't home. Steven wondered if perhaps Bertram had gone to visit Donna, for whom he stilled harbored strong feelings, so he was just about to wing his way to the municipal water tower, underneath the tank where Donna had her own nest, when a familiar gargling salutation interrupted the pigeon's reflections. It was the voice of Bertram himself, descending from high above the treetops. "I thought I smelled you down here!" Bertram landed with a flurry beside Steven on the limb and enveloped the smaller bird with his strong, acrid aroma, which was nauseating until you got to know him. "I bet you think I went to go see Donna..."

Steven chuckled.

"Well... I wish that's where I was. But tell you what, I've been run ragged scavenging for my mama and granny and my sisters because... well, my daddy died yesterday, Steve."

Steven's narrow beak fell open.

Bertram went on. "Yep. I sure was surprised myself. My little sister Sudie Mae came by last night to let me know, said he just didn't wake up from his nap after breakfast yesterday morning. Said he'd been just fine up till then; they think it must have been his heart. Anyway... course my mama and them need some help now, so that's what I've been doing... matter of fact, I guess I've pretty much moved back to the old place for now. I bet Daddy'd be having a fit if he knew. But someone's got to feed all those females..."

The young buzzard inclined his long neck toward the smaller, older bird, as if to indicate exhaustion... a need to rest his head on some accepting and accommodating flesh. But then he contracted it back again. "I guess Daddy never thought about what might happen to them if he...." And here the full impact of what had happened finally hit the young buzzard. He gritted his powerful beak but could not hold in a swelling outburst of complicated grief. "Damn it, Daddy!" he cried. "Why'd you have to be so mean!"

Steven the pigeon, whose own father, long dead, had been an important and positive presence in his life, felt helpless. He remained silent. The two birds, so dissimilar in size, features, diet, temperament, and experience simply sat together on the bough until Bertram, reluctant to subject his friend to another outburst, spread his wings. "I better check on the girls before practice. Tell Miss Ottoline for me, would you, Steve? And the Reverend? And tell them not to worry about me... Daddy's been worse than dead to me for a long time now."

And with that Bertram took off to see to his family's needs, and Steven returned to the church to inform Ottoline.

"It's very sad," said Ottoline. "Bertram is going to have a hard time coming to terms with the end of a significant relationship that was so fraught with discord. You know, it's all the more reason why I was hoping to patch up the quarrel between myself and Hertz. You never know when you might lose the opportunity to make peace with someone you've injured. But he doesn't seem to want to reconcile... I've been calling and tapping, but he hasn't answered..."

Oh, for Ground's sake, Hertz grumbled to himself deep within the compost. *I suppose if I don't let her apologize now, she'll never leave me alone...*

And so, at last disposed to respond to his adversary with his grudging forgiveness, Hertz uncoiled and began to tunnel his way to the composter casing, but when he finally surfaced it was too late. "I suppose he just needs more time," Ottoline had warbled, then she and Steven had taken off.

ॐ

As it turned out, choir practice was something of a balm to Bertram's distressed spirit that evening, for it helped him to put the memory of the night before aside for a while! But as soon as practice was over and he made his way back to the family roost, it all came back to him. It was as if, in order to face the future and all the changes it held in store, the recent past had to be put into a more sober perspective.

He remembered how he had found out about his Daddy's death. On that day, he had already been feeling a certain uneasi-

ness even before returning from his evening scavenge to his solitary roost in the forestland between the church and the
neighboring subdivision. But when he found his middle sister
sitting in his nest with her usual air of guardedness, his appre-
hension turned into alarm. "Sudie Mae!" he croaked. "What're
you doing here? You know Daddy'll raise hell if he finds out
you've come to see me!"

"Oh no he won't," said the young female buzzard with
conviction. In the dim light of dusk, her dark, sharp, red-
rimmed eyes gleamed, but whether with joy or sorrow, Bertram
couldn't discern. "Daddy's done died, Bert. He died this morning." And Sudie Mae watched her big brother closely for his own
reaction.

Bertram's beak loosened and gaped. His father... dead? It had
to be a mistake... or a trick. "Sudie Mae!" Bertram cried, but in a
hushed rasp, as if he was terrified the subject of their conversation could somehow hear them. "Don't say that!"

Sudie Mae, while young, nevertheless had enough insight into
the convoluted and unhealthy dynamics of her family to realize
that her outcast brother was expressing reasonable fear. She
knew well that her father wouldn't have been above taking
offense at the suggestion that he was dead, even though it was
true.

"He really is, Bert," she said, and when she spoke next her
voice was softer, less abrupt, and the strange gleam of excitement at sharing the news had left her eyes, which were now
dark, dull and somber. "He just didn't get out of his roost this
morning. Mama tried calling him, she tried pecking at him, but
he was just as stiff as week-old possum meat. Mama said it must
have been his heart. He hadn't been right all week. Granny's real
tore up. Won't eat. She says there ain't nothing left to live for
when your only son is gone..."

Bertram's beak fell open. Sudie Mae went on. "Granny's
crazy, but Mama's scared to death too. Mama said if you don't
come help us out, she doesn't know what'll happen to us. You

know Daddy never let us do anything for ourselves, so now look at us..."

Bertram felt a sudden cold course through him, as if he'd swallowed a shadow. "Did Mama send you to come get me?" he asked.

"No," said Sudie Mae. "But I know that's what she wants. She wants you to come home, Bert, and help us. She never wanted Daddy to make you leave before. She tried to tell him he was just spiting himself and the rest of us, being so stubborn, but you know how he was. He never listened to nobody, except his own daddy. Now he's gone and left us without anything. But he can't have it all his way now, Bert. He can't tell you what to do, not if he's dead! So if you want to help us, you can. If you don't, well... I guess I'll have to figure it all out..." And Sudie Mae, regarding her brother now, could not help but see, from his stricken expression, that he was truly anguished. She had never felt emotionally safe within her family. She had never had the chance to develop the capacity to consider the feelings of others apart from how their feelings might affect *her*. So it was as if she were seeing her brother now for the very first time without the blinders of self-protection.

"Bert, even if you don't want to stay... I know you have your own friends now... but even if you just came back for a while, just to show us... or me, at least, how to get by... well, that would be a real big help. If you could just come back for a little while, Bert, I promise I'll learn real quick. I know I can. Will you come home for just a while, Bert?"

Bertram, still feeling the cold shock of death, how it denied any possibility of reconciliation with his father, heard his sister's plea as if from a great distance. *Let 'em starve*, a bitter, familiar voice within him said. But that voice sounded like a cheap imitation of his father, and he shook his head violently as if to shake the voice out of his skull. "Alright..." he said when the dizziness subsided. "Tell Mama I'll be by after a while. I'm gonna go find ya'll something to eat."

And for the rest of that night, which seemed to last a life-time, Bertram was occupied with the practical contingencies of providing for the immediate needs of his suddenly helpless female relatives. Except for his thoroughly grief-stricken grand-mother, they all welcomed Bertram's return with raucous grati-tude if not outright affection. Of all of them, only Sudie Mae—who had always been the most independent—seemed to remember why he'd been away in the first place. "Oh, if only you'd have come back sooner," his mother said. "It would have made your daddy so happy."

Sudie Mae caught her brother's weary eye and rolled her own in shared understanding.

CLANCY SQUEEZED himself out of the gnawed-out corner of the crawlspace door of the cellar to listen in on the choir practice. While he too loved to lift his voice in praise, he'd discovered early on in his career as the pastor that both singing and preaching at every Sunday service put a real strain on his voice, so he stepped aside when Bertram joined the church. He watched from the ground in the pleasant, if strongly odorous shadow of the composter, while Ottoline, Steven and Bertram cooed and gurgled on the rim of the nearby birdbath that some-times served as a baptismal font. The hymn that they had chosen, "I'll Fly Away," was among his favorites, though there was scarcely a sacred song that he knew of that he didn't like, some more than others. He scampered over to the birdbath to let them know he approved.

"Oh, I love that song! I believe I'll try to work it into my sermon this Sunday... I'm not sure how, though, I'll have to think about it. This week I'll be preaching on the Prodigal Son..." Clancy was fortunate in that his unwitting mentor the Reverend DeBassompierre always rehearsed his own sermon every Friday morning in front of Grace, who would then unsparingly critique his delivery, though rarely his message. "Maybe I can say that the Prodigal Son tried to fly away too soon... Oh, I don't know... "

"Who's the Prodigal Son?" asked Bertram, who possessed a refreshing curiosity about things of the spirit. "Someone in the Bible, I reckon?"

"Yes!" proclaimed Clancy. "Well, sort of. He's someone in a story that Jesus tells us about a young man who doesn't respect his father's wishes and who runs away from home and gets into trouble and when he comes home his father is so happy to see him—even though he was disobedient—that he throws a great big feast! Reverend DeBassompierre says that all the stories that Jesus tells in the Bible are to show us how much God loves us. So I think this story is saying that God loves us just the way a father loves his son, even when the son isn't really doing what he's supposed to. That's why Jesus tells us that when we pray, we should pray to our Father in Heaven, because God is just like that Father in His story, who forgives us and always wants us to come home!" And with that Clancy stood and spread his forelimbs, as if he himself were welcoming back a Prodigal Son with open paws.

The three birds were then peculiarly silent. Clancy, caught up in his own rapturous vision of a Heavenly Banquet, took a moment to realize this. Slowly he lowered himself back onto all fours and regarded his choir members. "Doesn't that make sense? Or should I forget it and preach about something else?" he asked uncertainly.

The three birds looked at one another. Bertram's odor seemed to thicken, as if to signal his discomfort. "I was going to tell you after practice anyway, Reverend," he said. "But I might as well tell you now. My daddy died yesterday."

Clancy felt his tail, ears and whiskers stiffen... this was a shock. "He did what?" he cried, and to his own horror he almost didn't stifle the impulse to follow up with "Praise the Lord." For after all, he had had his own unpleasant run-ins with Bertram's daddy. He reached for his tail, twisted it, then he dropped it and reached for Bertram's tough feathered wing. "Bertram....I'm sorry."

"Thank you, Reverend," said the young buzzard. "I know he wasn't very nice to you, but he was my daddy. I still can't believe he's really gone."

Clancy, whose Great-Aunt November had been far from the tyrant that Bertram's father was, but in her own way had still maintained a decided grip on Clancy's sense of self, understood the young buzzard's ambivalence more than he cared to admit. It was hard not to rejoice over the fact that the old buzzard had gone to meet his maker.

"Perhaps..." Ottoline ventured tentatively, "We might somehow remember him in this Sunday's service?"

Bertram brightened. "Could we do that? Reverend? Maybe say a little prayer? Would that be all right? Even though he was kind of..." Bertram's brightness dimmed a bit. "...Mean?"

Clancy thought mean was a mild word for the old dead buzzard, who had forbidden his high-spirited son to have any friends outside the species, and who had banished him apparently without a scruple. *Evil* seemed to Clancy to be a more apt term. But of course, it wasn't Clancy's place to judge. "Of course we can," he responded.

"Oh, good," said Bertram. "I'll see if my mama and my sisters want to come. I hope they do!"

৩%৩

SUDIE MAE, having accompanied her brother to the St. Aloysius churchyard Sunday morning, was not a little discomfited by the presence of so many disparate creatures in one place. Once they arrived she stuck as close as she could to her brother's side, and could only nod shyly in greeting when he introduced her first to the two pigeons, Ottoline and Steven.

"It's so nice to meet you, Sudie Mae," said the ever-gracious

Ottoline. "Bertram's told us a lot about you. We were so sorry to hear about your father's death."

At this Sudie Mae could only nod again. She was aware of, and ashamed of, her aloof manner, but she couldn't help herself. She had never seen so many of these animals alive before, not so up close and personal. It was particularly strange to have so many squirrels scampering around. She'd always loved squirrel meat, and it made her feel funny to have real live squirrels just looking at her as if she was just like one of them.

Ottoline, sensing Sudie Mae's discomfiture, knew that she should stay close to support the poor thing. "Our Reverend should be out soon to begin the service. I know he's looking forward to seeing you, Sudie Mae. If you like, you are more than welcome to just stay near us. Just stand with the choir, though I don't know if you enjoy singing like your brother. Well, whether you want to join in or not, do feel free to stand with us. I remember the first time I attended one of Reverend Clancy's services. I had no idea what to expect, and I don't know what I would have done if I hadn't had Steven with me, to help me feel not quite so out of place..."

Sudie Mae felt her ruddy face warm with gratitude, and she managed to nod.

"Oh, good," said Ottoline. "Now, following the service, we will have a time for fellowship, a more informal gathering, so if you have time to stay for that, I'm sure Bertram would love to have you meet some of the other members... Oh! Here comes the Reverend now! Right this way...."

And Ottoline ushered Sudie Mae over to the side of the composter, where Bertram and Steven already stood at attention, as Clancy wriggled himself with more ease than ever through the chewed-out bottom corner of the crawlspace door. Looking neither to the right nor to the left, he proceeded with as much solemnity as a rat could muster towards the multilevel green plastic composter that served as his altar and lectern.

"The Lord be with you." He squeaked as he assumed his place above the gathering.

"And also with you," said a smattering of congregants, those regulars and members of long standing who knew the routine responses. Sudie Mae responded as well, a beat behind the rest, and blushed.

"Amen!" proclaimed Clancy. "Thank you all for being here this beautiful Sunday morning that the Lord has made. Today is one of those days that is so pretty it's hard to believe that anything could go wrong or that anyone could be sad. And we ought to be grateful for our own good fortune always. But it's real important to remember that sometimes things aren't so good for those around us. As Christians, we can't let our happiness ever get in the way of helping someone who is sad. So I have to tell you, if you haven't heard about it already, and maybe you have, that one of our members just the other day lost a parent. Our Bertram's father passed away unexpectedly, and we were so sorry to hear that. Let us all take a minute and pray for the repose of his spirit, and for peace in the hearts of those he left behind. Those of us who can, please bow your heads...."

Sudie Mae watched, wide-eyed, as the congregation of diverse creatures all responded as one body to the little rodent's instruction.

"Dear Lord," Clancy began, "We ask your blessing for the soul of Bertram's Daddy, a buzzard created in your own image. And just like all the rest of us, he—Bertram's daddy, that is, not you Lord—made some mistakes. Lord, have mercy on Bertram's daddy and welcome him into the Heavenly Banquet. Send Your Holy Spirit to comfort his family, specially Bertram and his baby sister Sudie Mae, who has joined us here today to pay her respects to her daddy's memory..."

Sudie Mae had never felt so mixed up in her life. She knew that her brother was involved with a bunch of new friends of different species, and that they all got together once a week or so for something called Church, where they talked about someone called Jesus and his father, but she hadn't realized that these figures were considered to be so important and powerful and able to—it sounded like—feed the dead. She looked at Bertram beside her and tried to see if she felt as uneasy as she did. But he looked, as far as a buzzard *can* look, perfectly content. Sudie Mae wanted to fly away. How could Bertram be so calm? The last thing she wanted was for their father to still be in some sense alive and thus presumably still able to impose his imperious will upon her. She couldn't believe that Bertram wouldn't feel just as horrified. Had her father been right about this rat reverend after all? Did it have Bertram under some sort of spell?

"...and Lord," Clancy continued, "We know that You know best. We know that You know our hearts and our minds—and even our bodies—better than we do ourselves. You know what was in Bertram's Daddy's heart when he was here on earth, and You know that he just wanted to do what was best for his family. Even if he didn't always do the right thing, and even if he didn't want Bertram to know You as his Heavenly Father, I think his heart was in the right place. So Lord, comfort Bertram and Sudie Mae here, with the knowledge that their Daddy, with all of his good and bad parts, has been granted eternal life. All this we ask in Jesus' Name, Amen."

"Amen" came the response, in a chorus of squeaks, chitters, coos, clicks and hisses. All but Sudie Mae, who felt as if a tide was rising within her, a slow swelling of a swirling emotion that was the point at which rage and fear become indistinguishable.

"No!" she screamed, a wrenching, gurgling, keening buzzard banshee scream. "Don't you dare bring him back to life! I'll kill him!" And with that she spread her wings and opened her beak and craned her neck in the instinctive defensive posture of her species, inadvertently knocking Steven over. Steven righted himself and moved a safe distance from Sudie Mae, who now confronted her aghast older brother. "Don't let him do it, Bert! Don't! You don't know how bad he got after he made you go! I can't stand it, Bert! I can't!"

"Sudie Mae!" Bertram moved toward his sister, but in her distress, she seemed to perceive even this slight advance as an aggression and took to the sky. "Sudie Mae!" Bertram called. But if his sister heard, she did not heed. Soon she was above and beyond the forest, lost to even her brother's sharp and concerned gaze.

"I better go after her," he said. "I'm sorry, Reverend. She's real upset."

Atop the compost bin, gripping and twisting his tail as if to break it, Clancy couldn't help but feel relief that Sudie Mae was gone.

"Bertram," said Ottoline. "Let me come with you. I may be able to... be of some use."

"If you want to, Miss Ottoline," said Bertram. "But Sudie Mae's pretty hard to talk to when she gets upset."

"Then I'll just listen," said Ottoline. "Let's go."

And the buzzard and the pigeon were off.

Clancy, still twisting his tail, regarded what remained of the gathering from his perch atop the composter. What in the world?! How had this happened!? He'd been in ministry long enough to know that the loss of a family member could easily give rise to erratic behavior at a memorial service, but this was something else. Sudie Mae had as much as said that she opposed her father's very salvation! Surely that was not how a Christian ought to feel.

"Hey Reverend." A voice rose from the congregation, the irrepressibly plainspoken voice of Ometa the opossum. "We just gonna sit here forever?"

"Oh, Lord, I'm sorry," said the Reverend Rat. "Now I've gone and forgotten my whole entire sermon. Let's just skip it and go on to Holy Communion, I guess."

BERTRAM AND OTTOLINE found Sudie Mae in the very first place Bertram thought of to look—the makeshift roost that Bertram himself had inhabited throughout the time he'd spent banished by his father. He'd figured Sudie Mae would go there before she'd go home, as it was the only place away from the rest of the family that she knew she would be welcome. "Sudie Mae!" said Bertram as he landed on the branch just beside her. "What's the matter with you? The Reverend was just praying for Daddy to rest in peace!"

Sudie Mae, hunched and glowering and as motionless as if she were a gargoyle carved out of stone, did not respond. The only indication that she was even aware of her brother's presence was in the subtle darkening of the crepey skin of her face, neck, and head.

Ottoline, noting this, extended a wing to gently nudge Bertram. "Bertram, pardon me, but maybe you could dash back to the church and let the Reverend know that we've found Sudie Mae, and that she's alright? I would appreciate that so much."

Bertram was surprised and relieved by Ottoline's willingness to be alone with such an upset Sudie Mae. "You want me to go back, Miss Ottoline?"

"Would you?" said Ottoline, as if the suggestion had been Bertram's and not her own. "Oh, I think that would be so helpful. I can stay here with Sudie Mae, and we'll join you back at the church as soon as we're ready. Thank you so much, dear." And Bertram took off toward the churchyard, leaving the two female birds alone at his bachelor roost. From the lower branch that she'd lighted upon previously, Ottoline hopped up to perch beside Sudie Mae. "My dear." She warbled after a few moments of silence, in which the distant chatter of a gathering of starlings could be heard in the distance, reassuringly inane. "I'm sure Bertram is just concerned. Of course you are perfectly right to be upset. The Reverend's prayer didn't really take your feelings into account, did it? But he was only trying to help... I can promise you that."

Sudie Mae did not stir a feather. She continued to perch and glower into space. But with Bertram gone back to the church-yard and the small, calm presence of Ottoline beside her, the turmoil within her, as well as the flushing warmth in her face and head and neck began to lessen. She didn't understand much of what the pigeon was saying, but she was glad to hear that pretty low voice continuing to coo.

"As far as I know, dear—and I have been around for a long, long time—no one who has died has ever managed to exert any power over the living. According to the Reverend, a human named Jesus did come back to life, but that was a very special and unique case that hasn't been repeated. And it was only possible because this Jesus was so very nice. Now, in light of what I suspect about your father, I don't think you need to be concerned about his exerting any control from the beyond. I can't imagine that the God that the Reverend speaks of as being Our Heavenly Father would allow that." Ottoline paused and seemed to listen for something in the cool breeze that for a moment was sweeping through and stirring the pine needles all around them. "He wasn't very nice to you at all, was he?" the pigeon murmured sadly.

Sudie Mae could only moan.

"Oh dear," said Ottoline. "I'm so sorry."

The two birds perched for some time in silence as the morning sun grew higher and stronger.

"He's dead, dear," said Ottoline eventually. "If there's any bright side to death, it's that it brings an end to the worst as well as the best things in life."

"But what about when *I* die?" Sudie Mae cried. "I don't want to be around him again!"

"Well, that's a reasonable concern," said Ottoline. "But I'm sure there's a way that everyone can be taken care of."

❧

"REVEREND," said Ottoline later that week upon joining Clancy in his usual evening stroll around the garden area. "Is this a good time?"

"Ottoline!" Clancy cried. "I don't believe I've even seen you since Sunday!"

"I know, Reverend, and I'm so sorry. I suppose I ought to have shared my concerns with you earlier. But at any rate, I've been spending a good bit of time with Sudie Mae. As I'm sure you're aware, her father's death and—I think—our remembering him in prayer during the service on Sunday has stirred up some... uncomfortable feelings. So I've just been trying to support her. She really is a lovely young bird, a little rough around the edges, perhaps, but so good-hearted."

Clancy, for better or for worse, had forgotten all about Sudie Mae's outburst. It was, after all, not the first time a congregant had become upset during a memorial service. No doubt it wouldn't be the last. "Oh, Ottoline, I'm so glad. I've been thinking about her, and I've been meaning to try and check in with her and Bertram, but I've just been so busy."

"Of course," cooed Ottoline with perfect diplomacy. She paused to preen a wing and put her thoughts in order. "Maybe that's for the best, anyway. Sudie Mae is... I think very reasonably... wary of authority figures... particularly male ones... and so for that reason, I took the liberty of... counseling her. And at the risk of seeming boastful, I do think that my visiting with her has had some positive effect. She does seem less... volatile. And she's even indicated that she would be interested in becoming more involved with our community. She even... and this is what I wanted to speak with you about this evening, Reverend... she even mentioned the possibility of meeting with you, if you would be willing... to discuss some questions she has regarding... well, I suppose the simplest way to put it would be the afterlife. I just don't feel qualified, as a *laybird,* you see, to help her with questions beyond my sphere of expertise. So I suggested..."

"Oh!" Clancy was immediately delighted and excited, so

much so that his whiskers stiffened. "Oh, of course! I'd be happy to, Ottoline! Well, I should have known that maybe poor Sudie Mae might be worried about her Daddy's soul... especially since he was so... different. Does Bertram want to come?"

"I don't know," said Ottoline. "I'm sure he would be interested. And Reverend, even though Sudie Mae is feeling less... fragile, I do think it would be best if we met all together— if I came along to lend a female perspective?"

"Oh, sure!" Clancy said. "Why, I could see if everyone in the church can come! It could be... well, it could be like one of Reverend DeBassompierre's Tuesday evening seminar series!"

Ottoline felt a bit like she was being swept up in a strong prevailing wind. She took a deep breath. "Oh, that would be wonderful, Reverend, but for right now, I think we should keep the group rather small. Sudie Mae is new to us, after all, and some of her concerns, I think, may lead to some... delicate matters, that she might not want to discuss around too many strangers. You do understand?"

Clancy did not understand, but he did have confidence in Ottoline, particularly when it came to understanding the ways and internal dynamics of other birds. "Oh, sure!" he said. "Oh, praise the Lord. You tell Sudie Mae that I can't wait to talk to her about Christian eschatology!" And with that, delighted not only by the opportunity to lend comfort to a grieving parishioner, but also by the opportunity to pronounce a newly learned theological term that had just entered his vocabulary upon overhearing the Reverend DeBassompierre practice his most recent monograph, he threw his little forearms around Ottoline's satiny neck.

◌◌◌

THE ESCHATOLOGY SEMINAR WAS HELD, like just about everything to do with St. Aloysius Jr., at the composter. Clancy was very excited, though he felt not a little daunted—for, as he was unable to read, his knowledge of scripture and doctrine was limited to what he overheard and observed throughout a career spent in the cellar and the nooks and crannies of the senior St. Aloysius Church. Of course, his eschatology was informed in part by personal experience and intuition—it was inconceivable to him that, for example, the strong and indomitable spirit of his Great-Aunt November had been utterly snuffed out by the expiration and eventual decomposition of her flesh. After all, he was reminded of her presence daily, often through hearing, in his own thoughts, her familiar and often repeated exhortations to upright behavior.

He was in fact recalling her frequent admonition to never forget that he was her precious angel, and to conduct himself angelically, when those members of the community who had expressed interest in having the discussion began to join him. The first to arrive were Ottoline and Steven, with Sudie Mae and Bertram descending shortly afterward. Then the two squirrels, Horace and Mildy—who had lost their only son Timmy in that tragic collision with an automobile on the boulevard that ran before the church some time before—were the last to arrive.

"Welcome," Clancy began. "I'm so glad to see you all. I've been looking forward to this all week. I think it's real good for us to have time together where we can share our questions, especially about things that are so hard for creatures like us to understand. I'm not going to preach at you, or anything like that. No, whatever you want to ask, just ask me, and I'll answer the best I can. And if I don't know the answer, well, I guess I'll have to just take it to the Lord in prayer. So. Who wants to go first?"

"I just want to know—" blurted Sudie Mae without preamble, "—is my daddy dead and gone forever, or what? Because if he ain't, I don't think that's right. He was mean and ugly, to me and to Bertram specially, and I don't know about Bert, but I couldn't wait for him to die. Nasty old thing." And with that she snapped her beak shut and glowered.

Clancy was visibly uncomfortable with such blunt antipathy,

but he did his best to not respond out of judgement. "Well, Sudie Mae..." he said, "Let me just say, I understand how you feel. It can be hard, and we can have some mixed-up feelings when someone dies, especially if they haven't always been nice to us. On the one paw, because we're Christians, we never wish ill on anyone, of course, because God wants us to love our enemies. On the other paw, God doesn't like nasty behavior any more than we do! So God knows He's asking an awful lot of us, when he asks us to forgive. But don't worry, Sudie Mae, God will help you."

"I don't need help, if he's dead," said Sudie Mae. "But if he's not, he'll need help! 'Cause I'll kill him!"

What followed that extraordinary statement was a very awkward silence. Clancy felt he couldn't let a threat of violence, even one as fantastic as this one, pass without at least a mild reproof, but of course he was reluctant to put poor Sudie Mae on the spot. "I think," Ottoline mercifully murmured, "and correct me if I'm mistaken, Sudie Mae, that what Sudie Mae is concerned about, Reverend, is the possibility of her having to... endure certain aspects of her father's unacceptable behavior in the here and now as well as in any future state. I think she'd like to be reassured, that someone with... a history of inconsiderate behavior...can't continue to cause problems for survivors after death. Sudie Mae feels—I think with ample justification, Reverend—that her father can't be trusted."

"That's right," said Sudie Mae. "He's a liar on top of everything else."

Clancy wished he hadn't suggested the seminar format for this discussion. He felt, not for the first nor last time in his career, that if he didn't come up with a good answer, and quick, he was giving God a bad name. "Sudie Mae..." He spoke to, but found he couldn't look at, his newest and most innocent parishioner. "I know it's hard to imagine that God could forgive someone like your Daddy, who did not treat others how he wanted to be treated, but..."

"Oh, cut the crap." A low, gravelly, muffled yet discernible voice arose seemingly out of nowhere. It was only after Hertz extended himself through the ventilation slot in the green plastic casing of the composter that the other attendees of the seminar became aware of his presence. "You and your forgiveness. You just want to have your little Debbie Cake and eat it too. All that lovey-dovey forgiveness is easy for you to preach! You've never had anyone really double-cross you the way I have. Listen, babe —" Hertz inclined his tip towards Sudie Mae, who was regarding him with such astonishment that it was as if the composter itself was speaking to her. "The rat's a softie, don't listen to him. He's not telling you the whole story. Not that *I* believe anything those humans say about God and Jesus and all that garbage, but one thing they do talk about, that sounds pretty good to me, is that if you don't watch out, you can always end up in Hell, and that's the last place anyone wants to be. Fiery pits, and the worms eat your flesh... Ha! that's what you get for being a bad daddy! And it goes on forever and ever, at least that's what they say in that book of theirs. I've heard 'em say it!" And with that Hertz laughed his gravelly little laugh, which sounded to the rest of the gathering as if something inside the worm was grinding against itself.

"Is that where Daddy is?" cried Sudie Mae with evident relief. "Hell? Is he getting eaten up by worms?"

That particular image of divine wrath had always made Clancy uneasy. He hated to think of his dear friend Hertz and Hertz's kind as devourers. "Well," he began, "I don't think anyone here"—he looked pointedly at the gleeful worm—"Can say for sure. Because after all, the Bible says, we mustn't judge. Jesus says that loud and clear. But the Bible does say too that when we die, God can tell if we belong up in Heaven with Him and everyone else who loves Him and loves one another, or if we belong in Hell, to be with the Devil and his demons and everyone else who is selfish and evil and doesn't want to share the good things they have with their friends and neighbors. But you don't have to worry about Hell, Sudie Mae, because I know you're a Christian, and Jesus died to save you from your sins, and that means you do love God and love your neighbor... so..."

"I ain't worried," said Sudie Mae. And indeed, Hertz's vision of Hell had plainly lightened her heart. "As long as I don't have to be around Daddy ever again, I'm gonna be happy. And I'm real glad to know there's a Hell for him to go to. I hope it's as bad as this here worm says it is!" And Sudie Mae spread her tail-feathers, bent her legs and rested on the ground, for the first time since the seminar began, assuming a relaxed posture.

But this breezy relegation of another soul to the everlasting torments of hellfire and eternal separation from God, even a soul as besmirched with evil and unruliness as that of Bertram and Sudie Mae's tyrannical daddy, was more than Clancy could bear. "Oh, Sudie Mae!" he cried. "You don't know what you're saying! Hell is so awful you wouldn't want to wish it on anybody! It's just full of terrible suffering, and the Devil loves to make everyone there wish they'd never even been born, he doesn't want anyone to be happy."

"Then he sounds just like Daddy," blurted Sudie Mae. "Don't he, Bert? They'll get along real good!"

Clancy felt his tender heart not so much sink as shrivel like a slug doused with salt. What could he say about the mercies of Heaven that could compare to the justice of Hell? He wasn't at all sure now even of his own anointing, as the pillars of his church gathered around the composter listening intently to Hertz' fulminations as he poked through through the ventilation slot in the composter casing like a disproportionately tiny, slim, yet irrepressible phallus. This was not the first time that Hertz, with his incorrigible, mischievous penchant for playing the devil's advocate, had undermined Clancy's intent to bring hope and healing to a fraught relationship. And yet he had to admit, Sudie Mae now seemed at peace. Clancy couldn't bear to listen anymore to Hertz's description of crackling flesh and running sores, or to see any longer the expression of vindicated relief on

Sudie Mae's countenance. So he turned like Lot's wife to the comforts of home. He made his way towards the crawlspace door. He was still a bit too stout to squeeze easily through, so before he was all the way in he heard the buzzard call his name and felt obligated to squeeze himself back out into the open again.

"She just needs more time, Reverend," said Bertram *sotto voce.* "We can't all be as good as you..." And here Bertram spread his wings, as if to express in the flesh the expansive qualities he perceived in his pastor. So for a moment Clancy's view of the gathering around the composter and the protruding worm was blotted out.

"Oh, Bertram, I'm not any better than anyone else," said Clancy with true modesty, but he was wonderfully flattered nonetheless. "You're right. Sudie Mae just needs time."

"I don't, though," said Bertram. "I don't mind if Daddy is in heaven, as long as he behaves. What's heaven like, anyway?"

"Oh, Bertram... no one really knows too much. But I do know, because I've heard Reverend DeBassompierre preach about it, that lions lay down with lambs, and we all help each other be the best we can be. No one gets eaten by anyone else, and everyone learns how to get along, because they have all the time they need to work out their issues."

❧ 2 ❧
ACEDIA (SLOTH)

"OH, GOD, WHY ME???!!!" cried the Reverend Silas DeBassompierre, MDiv, ThD. He gaped at the computer screen on the desk before him, closed his eyes, shook his head, then buried his handsome face in his hands. For a longish moment he held this pose of absolute forsakenness. Then he lowered his hands, clenched them into fists, and then, with one index finger pointing rigidly downward with dramatic fury, he pressed the button on his desk phone to summon his parish administrative/pastoral assistant. "Grace!" he cried. "Get in here quick!"

That done, he turned his attention back to the computer screen and muttered to himself the content of the email message he'd just received from the suffragan bishop of the diocese, a woman of insufferable, overfunctioning cheerfulness. It was only a moment until the door to his office, which had been only slightly ajar, opened wide to admit Grace. She stepped up to his desk, put her arms across her chest, and sighed. "What do you want, Silas?" she asked. "You know I'm right in the middle of formatting that damn service leaflet. This better be life or death."

"It is!" The clergyman insisted. "Grace, she's killing me! My

God, if Marge springs one more thing on me, I'm going to go back into inpatient treatment! If she wants me to be the designated diocesan intellectual, then when in the name of God is she going to give me some time to revise my chapter on Methodius of Olympus! Oxford University Press is breathing down my neck!!!"

Having heard the basic premise of this rant numerous times before, Grace Holbach responded merely with a slight arch of her left eyebrow. The young priest was too absorbed in reviewing the email of his discontent to register her lack of empathy, but that lack wouldn't have surprised him in any case. It was Grace's maternal imperviousness to his moods that made her invaluable to him, along with her willingness to bear the brunt of St. Aloysius' pastoral care concerns. "Look at this, Grace! Just look at it!" And he swiveled the screen of his desktop computer as far as it would go on its base and pushed it across the desk in her general direction. Then, before Grace could take in any more than a passing glance at the words on the screen, he swiveled it back to face himself and began to read, in an unnatural, mocking voice several pitches higher than his own and dripping with the molasses of a Tidewater Virginia drawl: " Dear Silas—An outreach and engagement opportunity has come up, and given your expertise in Church History and Patristics, I thought of you first thing. The North Carolina Council of Churches is hosting a panel discussion on Christianity in Conflict that's going to be taped before a live audience in early May and broadcast live as well. The other clergy participant will be Pastor Rusty Blattery of Christ's Radical Apostolic People. The moderator is going to be Mason Bland—recently retired from the six o'clock broadcast of Channel 7 News, who, as you know, is a Presbyterian Deacon and a dear dear friend of mine. His 'moderating' presence as a mainline Protestant (get it?) will help to balance, I think, the progressive outlook I know you will represent against what I think you and I would both agree is the retrograde theology of Pastor Blattery. As one of the best educated priests in the diocese, you are the perfect person to help promote a peace-loving, justice-seeking, welcoming and accepting Christ-centered and Spirit-led Anglican ecclesiology to the general public using this platform. We're counting on you, Silas, to knock 'em dead—with the Love of Jesus. Just let me know when you're free to meet, and we'll hash out all the logistical details. Thanks for all that you do! Yours in Christ, Bishop Marge +."

Reverend Silas DeBassompierre, having groaned out the signature line of the email, looked up at his assistant with as much anguish as if he'd just read to her his own death warrant. "A month! A month to prepare for a televised debate! She's trying to drive me insane, Grace! I swear to God, she is! I knew I shouldn't have voted for her at the General Convention! But it was between her and that ass Trip Mullholland."

"Oh, Silas, take it as a compliment. Cause that's what it is. She's right. There's no one around here that can touch you when it comes to church history and systematics. And it seems like a pretty lightweight topic, if you ask me. Christianity in conflict? You can handle that with your hands tied. That's easy!"

"Easy!" The young priest closed his eyes and shook his head from side to side slowly as if refusing medication. "In a sane world, maybe it'd be easy. But this isn't a sane world, and you know it, Grace. This is Eastern North Carolina. And she's throwing me to the lions! That idiot wannabe televangelist Blattery! Who has actually advocated from the pulpit the stoning of homosexuals! A complete cretin, for sure, but he *does* know the Bible chapter and verse. He could come up with a proof text for picking his ass! And when he can't, why, he just trots out a poor defenseless fetus." The Reverend pressed the heels of his hands into his eye sockets. "Why me, Grace! Why me!"

"Because you're the only priest in town with a doctorate, Silas," she said. "Like it or not. You're the designated egghead. And you can't fool me... you're flattered... admit it!"

"I am not!" The reverend cried, as indignant as if he'd been catcalled. "Maybe I *would* be if they gave me adequate time to prepare and put me up against someone with half a brain. Surely they could have found one of the more reasonable evangelicals! But that dinosaur Blattery! Who doesn't even *believe* there were dinosaurs! Oh, *God*!" And the priest leaned back in his leather upholstered swivel desk chair and jibbered as if he were on a cross being pelted with stones.

"A month is plenty of time to bone up on your Bible, Silas," Grace said. "I promise, I'll keep your calendar as clear as I possibly can. It'll all work out. And just remember how you feel right now the next time you ask me for a budget breakdown ten minutes before a vestry meeting." And with that she went back to her desk, leaving the young Reverend to enjoy his suffering.

⚜

IN THE CORNER of the rector's office, curled up leisurely on the horsehair cushion of an antique prie-dieu above which an icon of the Virgin and Child hung as an object of contemplation, a tabby cat called Macrina came to full consciousness from a light, restorative slumber. The Reverend's initial outburst had semi-awakened her. As the priest's pet and confidant, no one knew better than she how intensely if unreasonably the young priest felt overburdened by the expectations of his congregation, his bishop and himself. Macrina felt a typically diffident feline affection for her keeper, but often, especially when he had one of these petulant outbursts, she felt he needed a good scratch to snap him out of his self-absorption. Like most human beings, he had no idea how good he had it. However, Marina wouldn't dream of scratching the priest, and in her time as the unofficial church cat of St. Aloysius, she'd come to the awareness that Grace could always be counted on to put the huffy priest in his place and get him off his duff. This time was no different. At Grace's final statement, the Reverend DeBassompierre's eyes narrowed and his nostrils flared like a caged animal that had been tossed some scrap of meat. Then he stood and stalked over to the enormous set of bookshelves that took up nearly the entire western wall of his office. He drummed his fingers on his cleft chin as he scanned a shelf near the top, reached for one thick volume with his free hand, and returned with it to his desk, where he began to read aloud in a subdued but audible mutter. Macrina could sense that he was now, in spite of himself, inspired.

☙✻❧

THE RAT REVEREND Clancy made sure he was tucked well out of sight behind the bookcase when the human clergyman approached, but as soon as the Reverend DeBassompierre was back at his desk and absorbed in his reading, Clancy knew it was safe to peek around the corner. His presence in the office was well known by Macrina, who, having been left at the church one evening when the Reverend DeBassompierre was out of town, had come upon Clancy filching communion wafers from the cabinet in the sacristy. Considering herself accurately to be far too domesticated and refined a creature to sully her paws with violence toward even a thieving rat, she'd nevertheless upbraided him thoroughly, an encounter which had ended with the two hashing out their prejudices and then sharing a meal and getting to know one another. Marina and Clancy shared a mutual admiration for the handsome young priest, though of different levels of intensity and ardor to be sure, and she always enjoyed listening to the rat's stories of his own ministry to the outdoor creatures under his watch, idiosyncratic as it necessarily had to be.

"Poor Reverend DeBassompierre!" said Clancy to Macrina when the Reverend DeBassompierre and Grace left for lunch. "He seems tired."

"I don't know why," said Macrina. "He does basically the same sort of thing here as he does at home—read and write. But it's true that he hasn't been sleeping well lately, so he probably is tired."

This thought, that Macrina enjoyed the privilege of observing the Reverend in his natural habitat, living with him in such intimacy that she could observe his sleeping habits, made Clancy feel such a tangle of complicated emotions that he had to pause and take deep breaths. "Being a reverend is a lot of responsibility," said the rat. "Believe me."

"He can always say no," said the cat reasonably. "And so can you."

In that the cat was not, despite Clancy's efforts, a declared Christian, and thus unable to imagine the joys and sorrows of a call to ministry, Clancy didn't bother to explain. "It's not always that simple," was all he said. "But I'm sure it will all work out. Grace is right about one thing—Reverend DeBassompierre is the smartest human being in the world!"

"Maybe so," said Macrina. "But I have a feeling he isn't going to be too easy to live with over the next few weeks. I may have to stay here at night for a while... we'll see!"

Once again Clancy was overcome with conflicting sensations in his heart of hearts. He loved Macrina, now that he'd gotten to know her, and would not begrudge her her access to the Reverend's private life and the freedom of being known to him. But why should humans find cats acceptable as housemates, but not rats? It was an injustice that he found hard to come to terms with.

"We'll enjoy having you," said Clancy. "But won't he miss you?"

"Not when he's in one of his moods," replied Macrina. "He just goes to bed and forgets to change my litter."

"Poor Reverend DeBassompierre," said Clancy. "He has so much on his mind."

Macrina marveled mildly at the rat's indomitable naïveté. Then she yawned and returned to the prie-dieu for another nap.

❧

OFTEN, after the Wednesday afternoon Vestry meetings which they both, though for different reasons, dreaded and endured, the Reverend DeBassompierre would follow Grace in his Fiat to the home she shared nearby with her nineteen-year-old son Tommy, and the three would have supper together. The Reverend was hesitant to admit, even to himself, how much he'd come to look forward to these weekly evenings of comradeship —comprising as they did the near entirety of his social life, espe- cially since the breakup of his most recent romantic entangle- ment. This had been a short-lived relationship to be sure, awkward and not without a frisson of desperation, with a woman by the name of Mercedes Hernandez, whom he'd in fact met through Grace, as Ms. Hernandez had been her divorce attorney and later best friend. Reverend DeBassompierre was as taken with Mercedes Hernandez as he ever had been with any woman, but it had not taken long before he came to realize that the feeling was far from sustainable. Attractive, intelligent, and vehe- mently agnostic, Mercedes Hernandez was in a variety of ways too much work for the perpetually exhausted priest. The two remained friends, but that was largely because they both cared for Grace.

"Hey Preacher!" said Tommy Holbach when his mother and the priest walked into the kitchen, where he was standing at the counter inhaling with appreciation the stream from the baked ziti he'd just pulled out of the oven. Tommy was enrolled in the culinary arts program at the community college, with the inten- tion of one day opening his own food truck. "Hey Mom! Right on time. We just have to let it cool off a little. Salad's already on the table."

"It smells delicious," said Grace. "I'm going to change. You guys go ahead and start. I'll be right back." And she took the stairs of the split level up to the second floor, leaving her boss and her son, the only two men in her life at the moment, to themselves.

Reverend DeBassompierre took what he'd come to consider his seat at the round dinner table, directly across from Grace's usual seat, and he regarded Tommy, who was dividing the deep dish of ziti into eighths. Although Grace had only worked for St. Aloysius for the past few years, it still seemed to Silas that to some degree, he'd watched Tommy—whose father had not been very involved even before the divorce—grow up. And even though Tommy didn't seem to take life very seriously, and in the Reverend's opinion spent far too much time in a pointless activity he referred to as *gaming*, it was in a way this very unreflective embrace of modern life that the Reverend admired. Tommy might not change the world, but he was a good kid and didn't give his single mother a hard time. Silas found him as agreeable as he found any young person—which wasn't saying much, but it was enough.

"How are your classes, Tommy?" he said, to make conversation.

"Depends on the class," said Tommy. "I like culinary arts, obviously. Probably going to flunk calculus. I hate English. Psych is all right."

"You hate English?" The Reverend was horrified. "Why? What are you reading?"

"Something the prof wrote," said Tommy. "Says it's his MFA thesis. It's a snooze."

"That is educational malpractice!" The priest's voice rose like a missile. "Have you told your mother that? That instructor needs to be fired. I'm going to contact the department head!"

Tommy shrugged and laughed. "It's better than high school."

The reverend's indignation detumesced in the presence of such affable nonchalance, and he too shrugged. He loosened his clerical collar. Down came Grace, wearing shorts and a polo that Tommy's father had left behind, noting maddeningly when she'd offered to send it to him that he'd lost a lot of weight and it fit her better anyway.

"Jesus, it's hot in here," said Grace. "The price I pay for a kid who can cook. I'm going to have a beer. Want one, Silas?"

The Reverend thought it would be unseemly as a member of the clergy to indulge in alcohol, even just beer, which he loathed anyhow, in front of a minor, so he shook his head in a quick, furtive sort of way, as if to signal to Grace that she should have more discretion. But if she caught the message, she ignored it blithely. "I'll fix you a lime spritzer, then, how about that?"

Silas DeBassompierre closed his eyes and rested his chin on the heel of his hand. He took a deep breath through his Levantine nose, absorbing the atmosphere in the kitchen. The air was warm; the baked ziti had a very garlicky odor, rather overpowering, yet gratifying, like the enthusiasm of a very outgoing companion. Suppers with Grace and her son were unlike any other meals of his experience. The family dinners of his youth in the upper middle-class suburb of New Orleans had not been precisely formal, but they had hardly been relaxed occasions. He couldn't help but wonder what it might have been like to have had a family like this, without the sort of low-key prestige, notable heritage, and connections and opportunity that came from being a DeBassompierre. Would he still have taken his haphazard but privileged path from the most renowned Catholic Prep in New Orleans, to Tulane, to Harvard Divinity School, then to a short-lived novitiate as a Franciscan Friar, and finally, after an eye-opening trip to Vatican City, to ordination in the Episcopal Church? Or would he have been, as a young man, like Tommy, content with the prospect of a future in which the intellect would be of use, but not figure prominently? How much of his history, what he thought of as the conditions that created Reverend Silas DeBassompierre, MDiv, ThD, was really essential to his sense of self?

Grace placed a sweating glass on the sunflower placemat in front of him and pulled him thus out of his revery. "Penny for your thoughts," she said. "Thinking about your television debut?"

"Do what?" said Tommy from the counter. "You're gonna be on TV, Sy?"

Silas DeBassompierre winced. "I *wasn't* thinking about that farce-to-be," he said somewhat sulkily. "But now I am. Thanks, Grace."

Grace rolled her eyes. She turned to Tommy. "Silas has been asked... without any malice on anyone's part, as far as I can see, to take part in a televised debate about religion and social policy. It's actually a great opportunity for him, but he'd rather feel sorry for himself that he has to put a little effort into something new."

Silas glowered, not directly at Grace, but at the seltzer she'd fixed for him.

"But that's great, Sy!" said Tommy. "You could go viral!"

Now the Reverend glowered directly at Tommy. "I don't want to go *viral!*" he said. "I want to go *postal*. This is nothing but a publicity stunt for the bishop, and I resent having to participate. My so called 'opponent' in this debate is a charlatan and a grifter and has about as much critical intelligence as one of the earthworms in the community garden composter. He's an utter simpleton, but he's got the bible memorized, and that affords him the delusion that he knows what he's talking about."

"But that's great!" said Tommy. "You're a genius. You'll own him in front of everybody and come out looking like a boss." He put a pair of mismatched potholders on his hands, brought the tray of baked ziti to the table and sat down between the priest and his mother. "Dig in," he said. He reached for a fork, then froze with a stricken expression as his mother reached over to still his hand with her own. *Wait*, she mouthed silently, with a nod towards the priest.

"Oh!" said Tommy, louder than he meant to, and bowed his head.

"Father of Souls," the Reverend DeBassompierre had already

begun to intone. "We thank You for the nourishment we are about to receive, and for the skill that You have, in Your providence, gifted to this young man as a means by which he can create not only delicious meals for his mother and guest, but a future for himself in the restaurant industry. We thank You also, Heavenly Father, for providing us the respite of fellowship in the midst of strife, for the opportunity to refresh body and soul with food and open dialogue. Grant us, along with these Your gifts, the strength to endure until such time as all of our trials will have passed, and we will once again come together in the fullness of Your Presence at the Heavenly Banquet, where all who are heavily yoked are set free of their bonds and given Rest. All this we pray, in the Name of Your Son Jesus Christ, Amen."

"Amen," said Grace noncommittally.

"Wow!" said Tommy. "I didn't understand half that, but Amen."

For a while the three munched in companionable silence. Reverend DeBassompierre, as if picking up the thread of a lapsed conversation that he'd perhaps been having internally, set down his fork, wiped his mouth, and spoke. "It's not just that I don't have the time," he said. "I really do think I'm being set up. It would be one thing if this was going to be an honest debate, but it's not. And I don't believe for a second that the bishop has any illusions about that. She knows as well as I do that Blattery is fundamentally—pun intended!—intellectually dishonest. I'm sure he thinks he's the True Christian, but he's really a gnostic in drag, full of false dichotomies and a conflict-based eschatology. He worships the Bible at the expense of Divine freedom. He thinks God Almighty is bound by cultural contingencies..."

"I don't know what that means, but it sounds great," said Tommy through a mouthful of pasta. "Why don't you just say that!"

"Because *nobody* will know what it means!" barked the priest. "At least no one who will be watching that circus. What passes for Christian formation in this godforsaken backwater of a state

is the theological equivalent of television itself. Crude sensation-
alism and pat conclusions. The sort of mindset that Rusty Blattery was born to exploit. All he'll have to do to please the rabble
is trot out his proof texts and rant and rave about unborn babies.
All I have to offer is nuance and reason... and that isn't sexy. Oh,
it's going to be a nightmare..." He gritted his teeth. "Why doesn't
she debate Blattery, if she's so gung-ho? Why ME?"

"I bet it's your movie star looks," said Tommy without a hint
of sarcasm, for it was true that with his chiseled jaw, cleft chin,
large melancholy eyes and sculpted features, the Reverend
DeBassompierre was, especially at first glance, a knockout.

The Reverend waved away the comment as if it were a fly,
but even as he did so he discerned in the young man's remark a
sickening ring of truth.

"I hate to say it," said Grace, "But I bet Tommy's on to something. I wasn't going to admit it, but I agree with you that the
whole thing seems random, and I don't understand why Marge
doesn't just take on the debate herself. But Silas, you are relatively young, and face it, telegenic. At least you'll have that going
for you. Rusty Blattery is no heartthrob, God knows."

"That makes it even worse!" Silas DeBassompierre cried. "I'm
being pimped!"

"Silas Magdalene!" Grace shook with her own wit.

The Reverend scowled at Grace with real anguish and her
laughter lapsed into a smile that expressed genuine if exasperated sympathy. "I know it really is probably going to be a big
waste of time for you. I know how people think around here.
They want someone to reassure them that they have all the right
answers, and you're too honest to do that. But you know what,
Silas, there's no reason you can't turn this whole thing into something that works for you. You've got your dissertation coming
out, you're always looking for a tenured teaching position; why
not let this be your chance to show what you're made of? If you
want, I'll put together a press release... I'll send it out to the
AAR, the SBL, the presiding Bishop, Episcopal News Service,

and all the presidents of the seminaries. If you play your cards right, you can make a case for yourself as the lone progressive voice crying in the wilderness of the Bible Belt. Silas, this could be your golden ticket. Let me play this up. What can it hurt?"

Silas DeBassompierre did not cease from scowling at Grace from across the dinner table, but the slight thoughtful narrowing of his Byronic eyes indicated to her that her sensible suggestion had made a dent in his carapace of fatalism.

"Grace," he said, "you may actually be right this time. I've been set up, prostituted, put in an impossible position, but if you look at it another way, I've got nothing to lose." He picked up his fork and, brandishing it like a crozier, he lifted his chin. "Maybe this'll teach Bishop Marge not to mess with someone with a ThD! *Sic semper tyrannis!*" And he stabbed his ziti with gusto.

"What does that mean?" asked Tommy.

"It means: no more mister nice priest!"

☙❧

BECAUSE THE REVEREND and Grace did not go out for lunch on Tuesdays, it was late afternoon before they left the building free for Macrina and Clancy to exchange views. "He's in an atrocious mood," said Macrina blithely. "He threw up about five times last night. Of course, he's been drinking a lot of those things he calls Bloody Mary's, and sometimes they make him do that. He's very mad about that debate he's going to have this Friday. He says he's got a thousand times more brains than the man he's supposed to be debating, but that other man knows something called the bible cover to cover even though he doesn't understand what most of it means. He says he'll never be able to memorize all the chapters and verses he wants to reference in time for the debate. He says there's no point even trying. He says it's the Catholic Church's fault for overemphasizing neo-scholastic thought in his early religious training."

"Oh, he's just being humble!" cried Clancy. "I don't know how anyone could know the Bible better than Reverend DeBassom-pierre, because he reads some of it every single day, and he preaches from it every Sunday just like I do, except he can read it himself and I have to hear it from him when he practices his sermons on Fridays. No, I'm sure Reverend DeBassompierre knows the bible better than anybody. He's just nervous."

Macrina wasn't so sure, and her silence indicated as much, and the effect of this was to at once fortify and undermine Clancy's assurance of the Reverend DeBassompierre's command of Scripture.

"He just has to have faith in himself. That's all. Oh, I wish I could help him, but it's up to you, Macrina. You have to find some way to let him know that he's going to be just fine."

Marina, well aware of the futility of getting across anything apart from the most basic ideas to even the most perspicacious of human beings, simply returned to her nap, leaving Clancy to his only known means of supporting his mentor emotionally—he closed his own eyes and began to pray.

⚜

"Hello?"

"Silas? It's Mercedes... surprise!"

"Good morning, Mercedes. I knew it was you. Your name came up on my phone."

"Well, then, for God's sake, why didn't you say "Hello, Mercedes?" like any normal person would have done..."

Silence.

"Never mind. Silas, Grace told me about the debate coming up, and I just wanted to let you know that I'm happy to help you any way I can. Now... before you get huffy, I know that you know your theology and all that stuff, but just keep in mind, I'm a lawyer, and a damn good one, and I've won a lot of cases where all the odds were against me. And that's because I know how to argue a case. Now, it seems to me that that's what you need to do here... it's one thing to spew a lot a bunch of information no one knows or cares about, it's another thing to *present* that information, that evidence, that argument, in a way that will be convincing to a jury... which in this case is bound to be hostile to whatever it is you have to say from the jump. People don't like to hear inconvenient truths. So, if you're going to get anywhere with the deplorables, you're gonna have to go after the other guy with both barrels... it's the only way. You're going to have to be the prosecuting attorney, is what I'm telling you, Silas. Otherwise, he'll come after you. Don't let him. I know you don't like conflict, Silas... God knows I know that! But you can do this if you just knuckle down. Now, what you want to do right off the bat is establish motive... just like in a murder trial. What does this guy and his ilk get out of getting people to believe in his fairy tale? Obviously, it all comes down to sex and money. You need to research this guy, Silas, and find out everything he's trying to hide. And I can help you..."

"Thank you, Mercedes. It's nice of you to offer. But I'll pass."

"I knew you'd say that. And here's exactly where I prove my point: that you can only win by taking the offense... Silas, if you don't let me help you with this, you're no better than any other so-called Christian. Here I'm giving you the tools you need to expose a charlatan and present a halfway reasonable way to think about religion, and you won't take them and use them because you'd rather not get your holy hands dirty. Well, that's just lovely. There's no such thing as an innocent bystander, Silas, and you know that as well as I do. Silence equals death, remember?"

Silence.

"Silas!"

"Like I said, Mercedes. I appreciate your offer. But I'm a priest, not an attorney, and this is my problem, not yours. I am not going to assassinate my opponent's character, no matter how much he might deserve it. I am going to present my interpretation of the Christian tradition on its own merits, not on the demerits of some other interpretation. And let the chips fall where they may."

"You mean you don't want to make even the slightest effort to try something different and stop being above it all. You're not fooling me, Silas. I know how you are. You love to make it look like you've been thrown to the lions. Well, when you get chewed up and spit out, don't come crying to me."

"I wouldn't dream of it."

"Oh, you passive aggressive piece of shit. If it wasn't for Grace, I'd..."

There followed a female growl of inarticulate exasperation, then the silence of a dead line. Reverend DeBassompierre hung up his own phone and leaned back into his chair, as spent as if he'd wrestled an opponent or made love. He had no idea that he was smiling.

෴

THE GREAT DEBATE was to be held, like most local events of any size larger than a church service, in the auditorium/gymnasium of the very local community college that Grace's son Tommy currently attended. Silas DeBassompierre found this arrangement to be yet another piece of evidence of the utter futility of his participation in the whole charade, for this would give his opponent an even greater advantage, in that he would be sure to pack the place with like-minded vulgarians, whereas he, the Reverend DeBassompierre, could scarcely fill the pews of his own little parish on a major holiday, so learned was his preaching and so swaddled in the quotidian was the transcendence he proclaimed. Still, the young priest told himself, there was nothing for it but to get it over with. He was glad, at least, that he'd appealed to Grace to attend, and to bring along with her, if at all possible, Tommy and maybe a couple of his friends. "I know they'll probably be bored to tears..." said the Reverend, "but just knowing they're there will help me remember to keep it as short and simple as I can. And it'll just be nice if there are at least a handful of people there who don't think Blattery is the next best thing to Jesus."

"Don't worry," said Grace. "Me and Tommy will be there for sure. And so will Mercedes."

Silas tried to effect nonchalance. But in fact, he felt very pleased that Mercedes would be there to support. Overcritical though she was, she was still on his side, and that would matter.

"Well," he said after a moment. "I'm going to go get my hair cut. And then stop at home to take a shower. So you'll meet me there? And you'll bring my books... remember, the Greek Interlinear, the first two volumes of the Ante-Nicene Fathers and my Hebrew Concordance?"

"Jesus, Silas! You want me to lug all that! On top of everything else? You know I have other things to do... the church hasn't stopped just because you—"

The young priest looked pained. "Please, Grace... I'm already late for the barber, and you know how much I sweat when I'm nervous... and carrying all those books in this heat, with the cameras on me... I'll be a mess. And I want the books, if only to have some physical symbol of the fact that *scriptura sola* is simply insufficient... there are necessary tools of interpretation. I'm telling you... if I can get even one person in this godforsaken viewing area to see *reason*... well, this whole nightmare might be worth it."

"All right, all right." Grace shook her head. "Just go. Leave it to me. Go get freshened up."

With a hint of a sheepish smile, the Reverend DeBassompierre ducked his head as if duly chastened, and then he was gone.

CLANCY FELT he had to be there. He knew it was a foolish, if not outright suicidal prospect, but it was as urgent a need as defecation. He just had to go, or he would feel he'd missed out on something that could bring him closer to God, to the Reverend DeBassompierre, to destiny. The question, of course, was how? How could he possibly attend an event halfway across town, in a room full of perhaps hundreds of humans, who would just as soon see him dead as take the time to get to know him? It wasn't until he saw Grace come into the office with a big dun-colored plastic tub, and begin to fill it with volumes that she pulled from the bookcase he was at that very moment hiding behind. Then it struck him that he too was dun-colored, at least apart from his inner ears and his underside. Maybe... just maybe...it was a sign from God. The eager rat waited. And soon—as if the Almighty itself had dialed her number—the telephone on Grace's desk in the administrative suite began to ring.

"Damnit!" she said. "It never fails."

And with a grunt she rose to her feet and stepped out of the room to her desk. Then she could be heard clear as day answering the telephone with unapologetic impatience. "St. Aloysius, Grace Holbach speaking. What do you need?"

A pause. "Oh, Mercedes. Thank God. Yes, he just left. Listen, he's driving me nuts, I'll be so glad when this is over with, you have no idea. We'll have to go out for a drink. You're still coming, aren't you?"

Another pause. "Good. Why don't you just meet me here, then, and we'll pick up Silas— he's home getting a shower—and we'll all drive over together. Tommy's going to meet us at the auditorium after his afternoon class. You can help me lug all these books. I swear to God, Silas wants me to pack up half his office, you'd think he'd be embarrassed."

Clancy strained his ears, but the volume of Grace's voice lowered to a mutter, and he could hear the squeak of the tension spring as she lowered herself into her desk chair. Feeling fairly confident about her absence for the time being, he scrambled up the side of the plastic tub, perched for a moment on the rim as if preparing to take flight, and he slipped down to huddle in the rounded corner of the container against the smooth, thick and conveniently dun-colored library binding spine of Volume I of the Ante-Nicene Fathers.

From the far corner of the office, from the tongue-colored horsehair cushion of the prie-dieu, Macrina observed the reverend rat's maneuver and was not unconcerned. It wasn't diffi-cult to guess what the rat was up to, but Macrina wouldn't have expected the rather nervous little creature to be quite that nervy. Glancing out towards the administrative suite where Grace was still seated at her desk nattering into the telephone, Macrina padded over to the bin and peered within.

"Are you trying to hitchhike to the debate?" the cat asked. "Because I don't think that's a good idea."

"Oh, Macrina!" Clancy lifted his snout, so that in the dark-ness of the storage bin what little light there was seemed to shine from his eyes and his two prominent orange incisors. "I know it's crazy... but I've got to go. I've got to be there, to hear what the Reverend has to say. I don't know why... but I just have to. Macrina, I don't know if you pray, but if you do, please pray for me. I *am* kind of scared. I've never done anything like this before. But I have to. I just have a feeling...just a feeling...that maybe I can learn something I need to learn. Macrina...if anything happens to me...If I don't come back tonight, will you tell Ottoline...tell her she can take over the church, if she wants to, with my blessing? Oh, maybe I shouldn't do this after all...I have responsibilities."

"Scat!" said Grace from the doorway. "What are you doing! Get out of that bin, you crazy cat! The last thing we need are any surprises." And with that she fitted the plastic lid on top of the tub and prodded it with her foot into the administrative suite, where she could keep an eye on it until Mercedes arrived.

THE GYMNASIUM of the Community College was set up for the event but otherwise empty when the contingent from St. Aloysius arrived bearing the plastic storage bin packed with learned theological tomes and a petrified rat. Clancy was wedged against the side of the bin with the corner of Volume One of the Ante-Nicene Fathers poking him in the rear, but he dared not move a muscle lest he give himself away. He sucked on the tip of his tail, which had the effect of shoring off panic, but could not keep his mind's eye from seeing the many probable ways in which his existence could be at once discovered and extinguished this very night. Never before, he figured, had he put himself in such a fix. He just couldn't believe he'd been so foolish as to climb into the bin. And yet, the impulse had been so overwhelmingly strong... it was as if a will beyond his own had taken over... he'd done it without thinking, and by the time he had, with Macrina's help, begun to think, why, by then it was too late. Oh, he scolded himself silently, sucking his tail like a dud teat, how could I be so dumb!

But even as he berated himself, he knew that his current predicament was not so much the result of stupidity or even lack of thought, but of an impulse as familiar as it was unmanageable. It was faith that drove him to these extremes. It was by faith that the conviction that he must start the church had been ignited by a vision in the night, and it was by faith that he had been compelled, when he was just a little rat, to accept Christ as his Personal Lord and Savior upon his Great Aunt November's sharing with him the story of the Gospel. It was by faith that he'd crawled into this book bin. Never before had he regretted, or even questioned, anything he'd come to by faith. But he wasn't sure he might not regret it before the night was done. How in the world was he ever going to make it back home? How could he hope to avoid being detected and, more likely than not, killed, or at least chased away with screams and swats, and left behind with no idea how on earth to get back to the church? Never in his life had his faith led him to where he was so utterly trapped and doomed. And he had no one to blame but himself... though a part of him couldn't help but blame Grace for allowing this to happen!

⚜

"GRACE! There you are! Do you have my books?"

"Nice to see you too, Silas. Yes, for God's sake, they're right here in the bin. You can thank me and Tommy for lugging them in here. And Mercedes. Now, where do you want us to put these damn books?"

"I don't know..." The priest looked around wildly, as if he'd just emerged from a trance. Towards the front of the room was a long table, across the front of which hung a large cloth skirt banner announcing the event.

"Just put it..." the frazzled Reverend DeBassompierre said, "...just put it under the table, next to my chair, so I can reach it when I need it. How am I supposed to know where everything goes? Why do I have to make all the decisions?"

⚜

"GOOD EVENING, Crystal Coast! And welcome to WMCB Action News 7's Community Conversations special episode. As you all know, Action News 7 is committed to bringing you not only breaking news, weather, traffic and sports coverage, but also providing in-depth discussions around the issues that matter most to coastal North Carolinians. This evening's live broadcast of Community Conversations is brought to you by WMCB in cooperation with Carteret Community College's Fellowship of Christian Athletes and the North Carolina Council of Churches, and the topic will be, "Christianity in Conflict: Which Way Forward?" I'm former evening news anchor Mason Bland, your host and moderator for tonight's discussion, and before we get started let me just remind our live audience, our television viewers and our panel that, in keeping with our mission to provide balanced viewpoints on the controversial issues of the day, during the first half of the program, equal time will be given to each panelist to address questions posed by myself, your moderator. Then, during the final half, they will address questions from selected members of our live audience. We expect questions...and answers...to be in keeping with the stated topic of the program, and encourage everyone participating to abide by these discussion guidelines. When necessary, agree to disagree respectfully and without *ad hominem* attacks. Given the distinguished and venerable positions held by our two panelists tonight, I think we can rest assured that tonight's debate will be a peaceful one."

Reverend DeBassompierre, his expression as pained and pursed as a salted slug, bit the inside of his hollow cheek so hard he tasted blood.

"Now, it's my pleasure to introduce our two expert panelists. To the right we have Pastor Rusty Blattery of Christ's Radical Apostolic People, Eastern North Carolina's largest nondenominational church, with satellite campuses in Morehead City, Beaufort, Harker's Island, Havelock, and a brand-new campus under construction in Atlantic Beach. To the left, Reverend Silas DeBassompierre..."

Silas DeBassompierre's jaw muscles twitched as he bit down even harder on his cheek in order to stop himself from shouting out *Reverend DOCTOR!*

"... . Rector of St. Aloysius Episcopal Church, located at 1413 Bogue Boulevard. Gentlemen, let's just begin with a brief statement from each of you regarding what you consider, in your educated opinion, to be the essence of the Christian faith to which you have both dedicated your lives. Pastor Blattery, why don't we start with you..."

"Jesus!"

Underneath the table, hidden from the camera's eye and the audience by the thick fabric banner skirt across the front, pinioned by Volume One of the Ante-Nicene Fathers against the hard plastic corner of the storage bin, Clancy himself had to suppress a squeak, for the Lord's name as shouted out with such unexpected vehemence by the human called Blattery really startled him. He'd heard Reverend DeBassompierre shout out the name of the Lord like that, but only when he was angry. Clancy couldn't help but wonder what Blattery could be angry about so early in the discussion.

"Jesus!" the pastor of Christ's Radical Apostolic People bellowed even more vociferously. Then, as if for good measure, he said it again: "*Jesus* is the essence of my faith, because *Jesus* is the *Way*, the *Truth* and the *Life* and no man comes to the Father but by *me*! John, 14:6. Yes, friends, while worldly values may change and the world may tempt us into compromising our faith in the name of convenience and being woke, as long as we cling to the Name of *Jesus* and his Holy Word we will never go astray. That's why at Christ's Radical Apostolic People we preach and teach and live and love *Jesus* as revealed by the Gospel as our only hope...Amen!"

"Amen!" Clancy squeaked, forgetting himself in the novelty and the excitement and the sound and fury of such unabashed praise. He remembered himself soon enough, however, and froze in terror, and for many moments was so sure of imminent detection and death that he lost control of his bladder and slightly wetted the spine of the Ante-Nicene Fathers Volume One. But after the moment passed it was clear that he wasn't—yet—given away. He thanked the Lord, that this Blattery person, whoever he was, had such a loud voice and so much to say.

"Now friends..." the voice, high but husky with enthusiasm and southern charm continued, "...I know that the times we live in are evil, and the Enemy is hard at work sowing discord, and that these days people come from all walks of life, and it can be real challenging to walk that narrow way between being godly and being 'tolerant.' And at Christ's Radical Apostolic People, we praise God that we've been blessed with a guide and keeper that will help us stay the course, and that's God's Holy Word— the Living Bible. Christ's Radical Apostolic People isn't a Baptist Church, it isn't a Methodist Church, it isn't a Pentecostal Holiness Church, it's not a Protestant or a Catholic church, it's a Christian Church, a Bible Church, with the Bible as its cornerstone. And that means we stand on the bedrock solid Foundation of God's Word. We believe that the Bible is Spirit-filled, God-Breathed and without error, and with that assurance we never compromise our Christian principles. That's not to say we're perfect—for all have sinned and fallen short of the Glory of God, Romans 3:23; but it means that we know we are sinners, and that we are saved through Grace alone. And that, friends, is the essence of the Christian faith, as proclaimed by Jesus, His Apostles, and the Holy Scriptures. All else, as the Good Book says, is but as dung, Philippians 3:8. Amen?"

With that, the voice came to a halt, as if in anticipation of some response, which was soon gratified by a sound that reminded Clancy of a sudden summer rainstorm, or the opening in unison of innumerable cellophane snack wrappers. For never before in his lifetime of hearing sermons and hymns and various other performances of worship and praise in the Sanctuary of St. Aloysius Church, had he seen or heard the curious phenomenon of applause.

"Thank you, Pastor Blattery," said the moderator smoothly. "And now, Reverend DeBassompierre... your response?"

Clancy held his breath out of an amalgamation of lingering fear and anticipation, for as compelling as the enthusiasm and conviction of the other clergyman had been he was no match, Clancy was certain, for the brilliance and erudition of the one and only Reverend DeBassompierre.

The silence that immediately followed was lengthy to the point of awkwardness, and finally ended when the young priest cleared his throat. "I would agree with...Pastor...Blattery, that what is particularly distinctive about Christian faith and worship would be the centrality of the figure of Jesus Christ, and the understanding of His life and work and his continuing presence in the Paraclete as a unique and essential revelation of Divine Love. I would caution all Christians, however, to avoid the projection of what are often our very human qualities and preoccupations onto the divine, which have the effect of restricting our understanding of Revelation to a very literalist interpretation of Scripture, an interpretation that is always indisputably incoherent. It's important to keep in mind, when discussing the concept of revelation, that no single aspect of any form of divine communication should be taken without regard to its particular context. The Hebrew and Christian Scriptures, I would agree, are without a doubt essential to any understanding of God's will for humankind, but they can't be considered without reference to a tradition of interpretation that is part and parcel with the very process of their canonical status. All of that is to say that we mustn't assume we have all the answers...though I would suggest that it is safe to say that we have some."

Silence followed, and though Clancy listened for it, there was no corresponding rainstorm of applause. Only a single voice rose from somewhere within the crowd, a male voice, human, expressing its lack of comprehension with three words: "Do what, now?"

After an awkward silence, the smooth voice of the moderator said, "Thank you, gentlemen. That was a wonderful introduction to your particular points of view and brings us naturally to our next question. What do you see as the role of the church in the arena of public policy? Pastor Blattery, we'll start again with you."

To the right of Clancy's dark container came a scraping sound, which puzzled Clancy until the Pastor began to speak, and the slight elevation of his voice indicated to Clancy that he'd stood up, scooting back his chair to do so. As he spoke his voice reached Clancy from alternating directions as the speaker paced across the stage.

"The United States of America..." he began, "...is, no matter what you might be told in your government-run schools or hear from the liberal mainstream news media, a Christian nation, founded on Christian principles by Christian men dedicated to following the will of God. We may have, in our Constitution, the separation of Church and State, but the Church is *not* God, but *under* God, just as we are one *nation* under God. There is no separation between *God* and state! Never has, never been, never will be! Why, ever since the Pilgrims landed on Plymouth Rock, even in that godforsaken state of Massachusetts, God has led and guided men and women of faith into positions of leadership, not just in government, but in business and industry, which is the backbone of our country's strength. If it wasn't for God's favor, would we be the richest, most powerful nation in the history of the whole entire world? If it wasn't for God's favor, would we enjoy the freedom to speak our minds even when we don't agree, like we're doing right here? Friends, don't be fooled by the politicians and the elites and the false prophets of the age. America has a special, God-given role to play in the world, to set the captives free—Luke 4:18—in the name of Jesus, and anyone who calls themselves a Christian, and especially if they call themselves a shepherd, who tells you that America isn't Spirit-Filled and Spirit-Led...is a 'deceiver, and the truth is not in them'—Matthew 12:16. Be wary, friends, 'be watchful and vigilant, because your adversary the devil walks about like a roaring lion, seeking whom he may devour'—1st Peter 5:8; we've seen what happens when God abandons a nation. No friends, America is God's country, and like the Prodigal Son—Luke 15:11-32—our nation will return to God, and repent, and receive God's blessing. I just pray it isn't too late..." And on that note, the chair to the right scraped against the floor again, and there came the sound of the Pastor's buttocks settling with a soft short hiss into the vinyl cushion of the folding chair.

"Reverend DeBassompierre?"

Following upon the Pastor's passionate and exhaustively referenced exhortation, the tone if not the substance of Clancy's mentor's rebuttal, which followed a deep sigh, seemed as unleavened as the mass-produced communion wafers he consecrated and transformed into the Body of Christ each Sunday and major feast day. "Mister Blattery makes the very common and debatable claim that it is possible and in fact necessary to attribute to the Founding Fathers of this nation a Christian provenance to the values they claimed to advance and uphold in their establishment of a new government for the thirteen original colonies, of which this state was one. Any honest look at the facts, however, belies such a claim. The Founding Fathers were, with a few exceptions, Deists, whose general attitude towards Orthodox Christian teaching was one of scorn. As for Mr. Blattery' assertion that the United States even today enjoys what he sees as a special blessing, I would think that any clear-eyed observer of our turbulent and bloody—if not to say genocidal—history, and the present conditions of staggering inequality, racial and ethnic tension, crises of homelessness and access to adequate medical care—along with a crisis of meaning—would question his values. If such conditions of injustice—from which I fully accept that I benefit—constitute a blessing—one might be forgiven for preferring to be cursed."

From the large space before the table came a swelling grumble audible to Clancy, like the sound of distant thunder. Soon enough it subsided, but it left Clancy with a deeply unsettled sensation. This was compounded by the fact that he could not understand how two human beings who were clearly fellow Christians could disagree so thoroughly. What's more, he couldn't help but feel that the Reverend DeBassompierre wasn't being as nice to his fellow pastor as he could be.

"Well..." said the third voice, the smooth voice, the voice of the moderator and anchorman. "Let's move on to our next question, submitted by a member of our studio audience. The question is: If God is good, why does he allow innocent people to suffer things like rape, torture, cancer, murder, genocide and kidney stones? Pastor Blattery: Your response?"

"Thank you, Mason," said the husky high voice to Clancy's right. "You know, Mason, I get this question a lot, from folks who have been broken, who have been hurt in some way, who feel let down by God, and feel that God doesn't love them. I want you to know, that in a world so fallen and full of sin and brokenness as this world is, God understands why sometimes it's hard to see His footprints in the sand. Amen? And I want everybody to know that God loves each and every one of us, and never gives us more than we can bear. Even when it seems like we're completely on our own, God is standing right beside us, even when we feel like He's abandoned us. Now, suffering isn't easy, and no one knows that better than God, who 'gave His only begotten son' —John 3:16—and God never wants us to suffer in vain. He wants us to *use* these periods of darkness and chastisement to bring us closer to Him, because God wants us to 'be perfect, as Your Father in Heaven is Perfect'—Matthew 7:19. You see, friends, God is a God of Love, but He is also a God of righteousness. Think of it this way, when you feel like God has turned away from you, keep in mind that "God is the same, yesterday, today, and tomorrow—Romans 5:31—so whether you realize it or not, *your* sins have turned *you* away from God! Not the other way around! And God wants to put you on the *right* path, even if it means reaching right down and snatching you around to get you there. If your little girl or your little boy was running out into traffic, wouldn't you yank their arm right out the socket if that's what it took to keep them safe? And wouldn't you want to teach them a lesson by smacking their behind? Friends, the Love of God doesn't mean we can do as we please in this world. God's love and God's wrath go together like biscuits and red-eye gravy. And don't let any so-called Christian ever tell you any different. They may mean well, but as they say, the road to Hell..." A pause, and then the unmistakable sound of laughter from the audience. Clancy wished he knew what was so funny.

The moderator cleared his throat. "Reverend DeBassompierre?"

Another awkwardly long silence. Then Clancy's mentor took a deep breath through flaring nostrils and began to speak with what struck even himself as snidely exaggerated patience. "The question is an important one, and in many respects, presents—to my mind—the only serious challenge to the goodness, if not the existence of the God of the Abrahamic tradition. For the suffering of the innocent—quite apart from the matter of unbearable suffering in general—calls into question any meaningful correlation between divine and creaturely conscience. Consider the suffering of animals, for example, who haven't, so far as we know, the capacity to make sense of their pain; or the suffering of the planet, or even the suffering of the knowledge of our own mortality—it's certainly tempting to bypass all of this with an appeal to mystery, or to God's sovereignty. These facile explanations do not respect the capacity of suffering to absolutely crush the human spirit along with the will to live and the ability to love. The only responsible theodicy—and I use that term advisedly—and the book of Job will bear me out on this, along with the work of the celebrated systematic theologian and analytical philosopher of religion Marilyn McCord Adams—is to posit that it is within the capacity, and it is the desire of the Almighty to provide not merely a satisfactory explanation for unbearable suffering, but also to provide adequate compensation and explanation of some kind. In short, I think it's safe to say that Christian Theology must hold God accountable for God's part in our situation as creatures ontologically vulnerable to unbearable suffering." And with that, Reverend DeBassompierre fell silent. And again, from the audience, a lone and audibly aggravated voice. "What the hell's he talking about, Pastor?"

Clancy, who ordinarily found himself uplifted by Reverend DeBassompierre's orotund and Latinate language, felt at once protective and bewildered. What on earth *was* the Reverend saying? It seemed to Clancy that he might mean that God had some explaining to do. Clancy could only imagine with queasiness what Aunt November would say to that.

"Thank you, Reverend DeBassompierre," said the moderator, whose voice, though smooth, betrayed some bewilderment. "Our next question is—"

"Hold on just one red hot minute!" the high and husky voice to Clancy's right protested. "Let me get something real straight here. You mean to tell me you think *God* owes something to *man*? 'Cause that sounds like the devil talking to me!"

An abbreviated but intense rainstorm of applause followed. Another lone voice, this one ostensibly female, shouted *Amen*! Clancy was possessed, suddenly, urgently, literally, by the need to see what was happening. But how to see without being seen? This was, of course, for Clancy, with regard to Reverend DeBassompierre, a perennial question. But never before in his memory had the situation been so fraught with risk.

Reverend DeBassompierre's voice, brittle yet somehow strong, interrupted, and for the moment calmed his desire. "Mr. Blattery..." he said. "You certainly have an impressive command of chapter and verse, but I would encourage you to keep in mind —as I've indicated before—the context of each chapter and each verse that you lift up. You may feel justified in imputing to me demonic motives, but even a surface reading of the Holy Scriptures as a whole should suggest to you that, in fact, to interrogate the ways of the Almighty is entirely Biblical, and thus by your reckoning, Christian. Didn't our father Abraham contend with God to spare the righteous men of Sodom? And in the original Hebrew, doesn't the very name of Israel translate as 'he who wrestles with God'? Now, should anyone—yourself included, of course, Mr. Blattery—care to confirm any or all of the scriptural or linguistic references I've made, I recommend to you the following interlinear translations available through various university presses..."

And before Clancy could gather his wits about him, the lid was lifted from the storage bin, a blinding light from above flooded in to temporarily blind him, and a hand reached down and touched him.

Never having made much physical contact before with any human whatsoever, much less the Reverend DeBassompierre, Clancy upon reflection was distressed to recall that his initial, immediate instinctive impulse was to bite! The warm, stiff, hairless fleshy appendage that was the Reverend DeBassompierre's index finger, as it touched the base of Clancy's rough, dry tail, felt so foreign, and yet so alive and unpredictable, that Clancy's conflicting desires—to at once both escape and submit to that contact and pressure—was concomitant with the impulse to seize, to pierce, to draw blood.

It was a truly remarkable feeling. The touch of the Reverend's hand was as brief as a heartbeat, for the priest withdrew his hand from the bin as if from a burning bush. Clancy heard a sharp intake of breath and knew this was his last chance to do something to save his skin. With all his strength he leaped up and scrambled up the side of the bin and over the edge onto the cool shellacked wooden floor of the gymnasium just as Reverend DeBassompierre pulled the bin out from under the table and peered inside. The priest reached in again, brought out the large thick hardcover book that he called the Septuagint, then neatly pushed the bin back under the table. Clancy, finding to his relief that he wasn't exposed, that he was still hidden from view by the heavy dark tablecloth banner hanging almost to the floor across the front of the table, could not resist another risk of exposure. He poked his snout through the half inch or so of light—and was astonished by what he saw.

Never, not even at the Christmas Midnight Mass at St. Aloysius Sr. had Clancy ever seen so many human beings all in one place. In the front row Clancy could make out the familiar face of Grace sitting between her son Tommy and another woman, unknown by sight to Clancy, but who he just somehow knew was undermining Reverend DeBassompierre's confidence. She must be that uncompromising creature by the name of Mercedes Hernandez. All three of these faces were watching the stage with wide-eyed, uneasy expressions.

Suddenly, abruptly to Clancy's right there was the sound again of chair legs scraping against the floor, and now of course Clancy could see that the preacher named Blattery was on his feet again, and that those feet were shod with brand-new brightly colored sneakers, not unlike the type of garish neon footwear that Grace's son Tommy and his friends wore. The sneakers retreated, then Clancy could see them and the legs that ended in them go around the side of the table, to stand between the table and the audience. And now for the first time Clancy could get a full view of the man, albeit from behind. What he saw rather puzzled him, as he had never before seen an adult human male attired so similarly to one of the juveniles of the species. His trousers were as dark and close fitting as some of those that Tommy sometimes wore, and his shirt too was form-fitting, and short sleeved as well, revealing bulging biceps and forearms that were curiously darker in hue than the deeply creased back of his neck, and as smooth and hairless as a woman's. Above that pale, creased and lengthless neck the man's hair was silver and cut very short. Overall the effect was of a person well into middle age, despite his adolescent clothing and ruggedness of shape. "Folks..." he said again, raising his high, husky, hortatory voice. "When we have our Bible, do we really need any other book? When we have Jesus, do we need any other savior? I say no. We can rest easy in God's Word like in our own beds. Can I get an *Amen*?"

Before Clancy's beady black eyes the crowd seemed to come to a boil, with only a few stragglers remaining seated. Most audience members stood up upon hearing the preacher's amen. Many shouted in response and then began clapping. Some, including a large woman near the back row with a frowsy cloud of yellow hair, stood swaying from side to side with her face turned upwards to the vaulted auditorium ceiling and her arms held out and forward, slightly crooked at the elbows and with her palms held up and open as if to receive some manna from heaven that she fully expected would descend. Clancy watched her hold this swaying pose for a long, long moment while the applause slowly dwindled, until at last, having swayed a bit too far to the right she lost her balance, dropped her arms and faced directly forward with an expression of wide-eyed alarm before steadying herself and lowering herself back into the metal folding chair. Clancy's attention was then drawn to the three individuals in the front row who were the only persons in that row who remained seated. Tommy, Mercedes, and Grace looked very ill at ease, and as Clancy watched they clasped one another's hands in what seemed to be an instinctive protective measure. The sight of that affected Clancy like an uncomfortably nearby lightning strike. Ambivalent as he felt most of the time about Grace, whom he considered to be an efficient but insufficiently emotionally supportive helpmeet to the Reverend, she was, after all, part of the St. Aloysius family, as was her inoffensive and cheerful son Tommy, and even sharp-tongued Mercedes. Now all three of them looked terrified. Clancy wished he had the nerve to peek up at Reverend DeBassompierre to get a sense of how he was feeling, but he didn't dare.

"Friends—" The young old preacher raised one hand, index finger extended, and a respectful hush fell over the crowd. "Now, if the Reverend here wants to set me straight about how to come to know the Lord outside His Holy Word, why, maybe we ought to let him have his say. After all, it's still a free country...for *now*...."

With that, the crowd cheered, the Preacher turned to regard his opponent's reaction, and Clancy for the first time could see his face, which was remarkably smooth and shiny, like that of an infant, especially when compared to the deeply creased skin on the back of his neck. His eyes seemed to be the same flat color as his hair and his perfectly square white teeth were bared in a triumphant grin. He rubbed his palms together, making a sound like the chafing of dead leaves against one another, and as Clancy stared, he winked, presumably at Reverend DeBassompierre.

The Reverend stood, scooting back his folding chair forcefully. And Clancy beheld those familiar shining black wingtip shoes that seemed to be the only shoes the Reverend owned.

"Mister Blattery, if you're not going to be respectful of my perspective as a scholar who has devoted years of my life to the study of the scriptures in their original languages and their explication by towering theological minds throughout the history of the church, I'm not going to waste my time or yours trying to convince you of anything. Some people, as I'm sure you know, prefer, like dogs, to return to their own vomit. Care to reference *that* scripture passage for me? I can't be bothered. I GIVE UP! To *hell* with you and *anyone* in here who would rather listen to you and your capitalist Manicheism than to reason." And Clancy could not see, but he could not help but imagine, the flush and the throbbing veins on the young priest's face, as he'd seen so often before during Vestry meetings. *Oh Lord*, thought Clancy, *Grace needs to take him outside now.*

But before Grace could do anything, the audience reacted. The woman who had been standing and swaying cried out the name of Satan, and this was followed by a general hostile murmur. The preacher Blattery, back in his seat, must have made some gesture that commanded silence, because suddenly a hush fell.

"Now folks," the preacher said, in as remonstrative a tone as anyone could wish. "Let's not forget we are Christians. We are called to bear patiently the world's scorn—Matthew 6:19—and be slow to anger, quick to forgive—Hebrews 20:12. The Reverend here may not love us, but that doesn't mean we're not called to love him, to love him in the Lord, to pray for his Redemption, and not his Damnation..."

But even as his silver-haired, bronze-skinned and sneaker-wearing opponent endeavored to bring the crowd under his control, Reverend Silas DeBassompierre stood and pointed at the swaying blonde woman towards the back of the auditorium, fixed upon her his blazing dark eyes, and responded to her accusation with all the withering scorn that he normally reserved for his Vestry.

"Satan?" Reverend DeBassompierre repeated the loaded term with affected injury, but his tone instantly shifted back to its previous loftiness. "You're calling *me* satanic? Well...as 'Pastor' Blattery has, I've no doubt, informed his followers, the term *Satan* means, quite literally, in the original Hebrew, *the accuser*; and in the cosmology of ancient Israel, the figure of the accuser, Satan, played a key role in the Heavenly Court of Yahweh as a means by which the God of Israel deepened the understanding of His Divine Nature among His Chosen People. *Satan*, in this view, was then instrumental in discerning and naming hypocrisy and shallow faith, and given that contextualization, I am not unwilling to accept... with pride... that designation. If pointing out where 'Pastor' Blattery is full of you-know-what makes me a Satan, then so be it!"

And with that he reached for the book before him, lifted it up, held it open before himself with one hand as he sometimes did the Gospel when the acolytes were absent, and he began to recite aloud in a curious, rasping staccato language that Clancy could not understand but recognized from slight acquaintance as Hebrew.

The audience went wild. Clancy saw it with his own two eyes: nearly every person in the rows of folding chairs stood up as if the metal seats had suddenly become red hot. Only Tommy, Grace and Mercedes in the front row remained seated, and they looked terrified. Amidst the general uproar, Clancy heard a number of terms of approbation hurled towards the Reverend, among them, *Satan*, *Judas*, *libtard*, and one term new to Clancy that the swaying woman hurled with a particular vehemence: "*Faggot!*"

Once again, the sneakers to Clancy's right withdrew and then reappeared again between the panel table and the audience, taking center stage. "Friends!" he said. "Jesus tells us to love our enemies and pray for those who persecute us—Luke:14:9. Let's not give the devil what he desires—he wants us to meet him with our fears and wrath and not with loving-kindness. No, friends, what this poor sinner needs is the ministry of deliverance... Oh, don't you feel the Spirit moving in this place tonight, to cast out unclean spirits?!"

And once again the preacher Blattery raised his arms above his heart, palms out facing the audience, and he began speaking, but in a language thoroughly strange to Clancy, and impossible to make out. It sounded not a little like the gabble of human infants before the acquisition of their capacity for intelligible discourse. And then he cried, in plain English that his followers could easily comprehend, "Satan! In Jesus name, you are REBUKED! DEPART!" And he turned from the audience to gesture towards the Reverend with the second and third fingers of his right hand forked.

"Oh, for God's sake!" Clancy heard Reverend DeBassompierre mutter. "Give me a break. Fake glossolalia and now he's playing exorcist. I don't get paid enough for this. I'm done." And before Clancy knew what was happening, the bin he'd stowed away in was lifted onto the table and Clancy was effectively abandoned, left on the cold hardwood floor of the stage— a casualty of his curiosity.

Oh, Lord! he cried in his mind. *Oh, I knew it! I knew I shouldn't have come here, and once I got here, why didn't I just stay put! Oh, what am I going to do? How am I going to get back to the church! Oh, Lord, I wish Ottoline was here!*

Why the panicked rat wished for the presence of the pigeon, who herself would have no means by which to get him home safely, he could not have said. But that is who he wished for.

Meanwhile the Reverend, huffing with the weight of the bin half full of hardback books that he had clasped to his torso, made his way off the stage and up an aisle to the exit. As he passed through the crowd thus burdened they shouted at him, some craning their faces just inches from his, and when one large-bellied white man wearing a red baseball cap and a large firearm strapped across his own torso blocked his way with a sneer, the Reverend DeBassompierre seemed to freeze. Clancy had never witnessed such a confrontation between humans, and did not know what to think, until he heard, from the front row, Grace's son Tommy's distinctively young voice. "OMG, Mom, they're gonna kill him!"

Whether this was hyperbole or not Clancy had no way of knowing, so utterly unpredictable were the strange ways of human beings. All the rat knew was that he could, at the risk of exposure, and the likely sacrifice of his own skin, create at least a distraction. Without a second's hesitation that's what he did. Loping forward as fast as he could out from under the skirt across the front of the table, he scrambled up the dark denim-covered left leg of Pastor Blattery and sank his teeth into the soft protuberance of the preacher's left buttock.

"OW!" cried the preacher, reaching behind himself. The blade of his hand encountered Clancy, who grabbed the thumb with all four paws, bit it, then dropped to the floor. "What the FUCK!" the Preacher yelled. "Jesus CHRIST! GODDAMN!!!!"

That third epithet did the trick. With an audible collective gasp, the audience turned to the stage to regard their leader, who was sucking his thumb and massaging his rear end. Sensing a shift in the attention of the crowd, Reverend DeBassompierre himself turned to see what was happening and, upon witnessing the odd contortions of his opponent, his jaw dropped. And then, for the very first time in his life, Clancy heard his role model in ministry laugh out loud. In the front row Grace, Mercedes and Tommy stood looking toward the exit, and there Clancy saw his only chance. He dashed forward and into the dark depths of Grace's typically unzipped pocketbook, just before she reached down for its straps and slung it over her shoulder as she ran for her life with her son and her best friend and her employer. They ran out of the auditorium and into the parking lot. They gave a collective cry of relief when they were all crammed into the cramped sanctuary of Grace's Honda and the click of the automatic door lock assured them that they were safe.

❧

"OH, GOD..." The Reverend DeBassompierre picked up the thread of his panic as Grace started the car and maneuvered like a fly dodging a swatter out of the densely inhabited packed parking lot and onto the boulevard that led towards home. Clancy, hidden in Grace's capacious pocketbook on the floorboard of the passenger seat between Reverend DeBassompierre's familiar shoes, thought that his little heart was going to drum itself right out of his furry chest.

"That was pandemonium. And I knew it would be! Didn't I, Grace!? I tried to *warn* Marge. But she just doesn't listen......" The Reverend's voice suddenly became thick. "I just pray that all this won't jeopardize your job, Grace. I hope that, whatever they do to punish me, they'll take care not to produce collateral damage. I know I don't always give you the credit you deserve for all that you do to keep the place going....But believe me, I'll make sure Marge understands, that you're the *real* heart of St. Aloysius—I'm just the mind—and that you should not only stay on as admin, but she should consider you for a more official pastoral role....After all, you're only a few credits away from certification as a licensed pastoral counselor."

Clancy, inside Grace's pocketbook, picked up the thread of his own fear....Could the Reverend be right this time? Could he really lose his position on account of the debate? Could the church—and Clancy—find themselves without a priest?

"Oh, Silas," said Grace, "You know that if you go, I go, and that's all there is to it." The vehicle then changed direction in what felt to Clancy to be an abrupt fashion, and then he could hear the familiar but now very close sound of gravel crunching under tires as they pulled into the unpaved parking lot of the church.

And once again Clancy let himself being lifted up and out of the vehicle. This time, however, he had to steel himself against being jostled amongst loose change and a billfold and a sunglasses case. He could hear more crunching as another car entered the parking lot, and he could hear Tommy grunt under the weight of the plastic bin full of books he was carrying.

"Christ!" blasphemed Mercedes. "I never thought I'd be so glad to see this church! I'm still shaking! That was about to become a pogrom!"

"What's a pogrom?" said Tommy.

"A religiously sanctioned massacre," replied Mercedes. "You should *know* that. Didn't you learn any history in high school?!"

"I don't think so," said Tommy.

From within Grace's pocketbook, Clancy heard the key turning in the lock of the large red double doors of the church, then the cheery series of four beeps as Reverend DeBassompierre punched in the four digit PIN to disable the alarm system. "Where are you going?" asked Grace, and then, from the left, Clancy could hear Reverend DeBassompierre. "I'm going to the Sanctuary," he said, "and I'm going to say Mass. This may be, after all, my last chance."

"Oh, Christ," said Mercedes. "Here we go with the martyr act. If they try to fire you for how that disaster played out, you know good and well I'll represent you. They haven't got a leg to stand on. You were sold down the river. The bishop didn't even bother to show up to support you."

"She's on a leadership retreat!"

Mercedes snorted. "How ironic. Anyway, it wouldn't matter if she was at the Vatican. She could have sent a representative from the diocese. She set you up, and that's obvious. You didn't have a prayer, pardon the expression, there was no official support for you whatsoever, no effort was made to expose Blattery for what he is- a slick hatemonger and a rabble rouser ...not even by you, as we all know, but that's not the point...and even if there had been, given the religious demographics of this area, it wouldn't have made a difference. You're too much of a typical squeamish liberal not to play right into his hands by losing your cool and throwing a fit. If the bishop didn't realize that, she's incompetent. Now, spare me all the ceremony. This isn't going to be your last supper. And that reminds me, anyway. I'm starving. Let's get something to eat."

"Good idea," said Grace. "Where should we go? What's still open?"

"You go wherever you want," said the Reverend with a paradoxically sulky firmness. "I'm staying here. I need to be in the Presence."

"Oh, what bull—" Mercedes began, but Grace shushed her.

"Oh, Merce...let him be. I don't really feel like going anywhere anyway. Let's stay here and order a pizza or something."

Clancy's heart leaped and his mouth watered with the memory of crusts and dried cheese left behind in the wastebasket of the parish hall every Friday evening by a now long defunct youth group. With the possibility of pizza on the horizon, all thoughts of the Reverend losing his job were shoved aside by the awakening of his appetite. Clancy was a pizza rat.

"Whatever," agreed Mercedes. "Maybe you can turn our pizza into the Body of Christ."

Reverend DeBassompierre pointedly ignored that blasphemy from his former flame. Clancy, meanwhile, felt himself within Grace's pocketbook being settled upon some narrow surface at a slight elevation from the floor. He sensed that it was one of the pews—then, to his surprise, Grace stuck her hand inside her bag and began to stir through the jumbled contents. "Where the hell is my phone...."

Clancy curled into as tight a ball as he could manage and closed his eyes and praised God silently but fervently when Grace's probing fingers encountered her cell phone before they encountered his pelt. The vaulted ceilings of the sanctuary then echoed the syllables of her delivery order.

Thereupon followed a period of companionable silence, during which Mercedes and Grace trailed off to the ladies' room together, leaving Reverend DeBassompierre and Tommy Holbach to themselves. Tommy, Clancy gathered, was meandering around the sanctuary, a space with which he had, to Clancy's mind, shamefully small familiarity. Reverend DeBassompierre was sitting on a nearby pew, for Clancy could hear the soft steady sound of his respirations. "That *was* really fucked up," Tommy said after some time. "I really thought some of those people were going to go after you when you started talking about Satan being one of God's helpers. Were you scared?"

"Absolutely not," said Reverend DeBassompierre sincerely, his panic having receded into unconsciousness in the safety and familiarity of the St. Aloysius sanctuary. "People like that are all sound and fury. They never or hardly ever make any effort to put their convictions into practice. They don't have any real initiative. They only operate under the influence of some charismatic charlatan like Blattery, who knows how to push the buttons of their neuroses and prejudices, and I knew he wouldn't take it to the point of actual violence. He's no genius, but he's crafty, and he knows I'm smarter than him, and I do have connections beyond this little county, and I wouldn't hesitate to sue him."

"Still," said Tommy. "Some of those guys had guns. White guys can take guns anywhere we want these days." He lay down on one of the empty pews and spoke as if to the ceiling. "You know, when you were on stage, Mercedes said she never realized you had such balls."

Clancy felt warm inside Grace's pocketbook. Had he been able to see beyond it, he would have seen that the Reverend too was flushed with embarrassment.

"She shouldn't talk like that, especially in front of a minor," said the priest, but his scolding tone was not devoid of a hint of gratification. Clancy, who was sensitive about the size and prominence of his own large testicles, wished for the thousandth time that he, like the human reverend, could cover himself with vestments when celebrating the sacraments and proclaiming scripture. He was imagining how he would look in a cassock when a familiar sound from the entrance to the sanctuary interrupted—a brief, polite, yet commanding mew.

"Macrina!" cried the priest. "Did we wake you up?"

The cat padded toward them. The Reverend remarked to Tommy that she must be hungry, as it was far past their usual suppertime. "She's a smart cat. She probably heard us ordering pizza and wants her share."

Macrina, of course, knew more about what was going on than the priest could ever imagine. She made her way towards him, nudged his dark trousered leg in what might have been a welcome, and accepted the stroke of his finger along the hard space between her ears and down her backbone. Then, her not inconsiderable olfactory powers confirming the hunch that had led her to the sanctuary against her usual routine, she made her way to where Grace's pocketbook lay on the floor and sniffed the unzipped opening.

"LOL, she's gonna steal Mom's purse," said Tommy, using the acronymic shorthand that made Reverend DeBassompierre clench his teeth.

Clancy was, of course, overjoyed to see Macrina, even if it was just a glimpse of her pale wet nose, which withdrew from the pocketbook immediately. She rubbed once again against the clergyman's leg and then padded to the entrance, stopped, and mewed imperiously.

"Good Lord!" said the Reverend. "She's talkative tonight! She must be starving."

The cat mewed again, with increased volume.

"I think she wants you to follow her," said Tommy, who was lying on the pew with his eyes closed. Macrina, noting the languid quality of his voice, judged correctly that he was too inattentive to bother with and continued her appeal to the priest to follow her.

"Macrina!" cried the priest, shocked. "My God, she never acts like this. There must be something wrong!" And he followed his cat out of the sanctuary and down the hall and back to his office, where Macrina inexplicably then turned tail and led him back to the sanctuary.

"Praise the Lord!" Clancy enthused in the meantime as he scrambled out of the dark fragrant dusty interior of Grace's bag into the open air of God's Sanctuary. "And God bless Macrina, what in the world would I ever do without her!" In a flash Clancy concealed himself safely underneath the console of the Hammond Organ, his favorite sanctuary, so to speak, within the sanctuary. And there he remained throughout the evening. When Grace and Mercedes and the Reverend returned, following Macrina, who curled up for a snooze on top of the linen-draped altar, to Reverend DeBassompierre's slight but notable consternation, Clancy was able to observe them and overhear their conversation as clearly as anyone could please. And when the pizza arrived, filling the sanctuary with the aroma of hot cheese as if it were frankincense, the hungry rat ground his teeth happily in anticipation of the crusts that were sure to be left behind in the wastebasket for him. It seemed fitting, for him as well as for the human reverend, to end the ordeal of the day with a celebration. Macrina must have sensed, or simply reasoned, that the rat was eager to feed, for no sooner had the humans each finished their slices, and Grace had placed the remains in the wastebasket of the adjoining sacristy, than she rose from her snooze, hopped down from the altar, and mewing again with an unmistakable urgency, led them all out of the sacristy to the front door of the church.

"She's very vocal tonight, Silas!" said Grace. "It's almost like she's trying to tell us something."

"She is," said Mercedes. "It's been a wild night, and it's time to go home and get some rest. That's what she's trying to tell us. Let's get out of here."

AND THE HUMANS followed the cat out of the church and left Clancy to his solitary feast upon their refuse, after which he made his way heavily down to the basement and collapsed upon his pallet of discarded choir robes. It occurred to him that he'd been gone all night and that Ottoline, if not others, would wonder why he had not made his usual appearance at the composter in the evening, to catch up with the doings of his flock at the end of the day. He moaned and told himself that he should at least step outside to reassure them, but he was just too exhausted.

"I can't do it all," he said to himself as he fell asleep, realizing he had never sounded so much like his mentor.

INVIDIA (ENVY)

C LANCY WAS MISERABLE. And what made it worse was that he knew that as a Christian, he ought instead to be rejoicing. Certainly, he had never before known Reverend DeBassompierre to be so truly happy and excited. Reverend DeBassompierre, in fact, seemed to have become a different person. It had all begun the previous Wednesday while Clancy was, as usual, observing the young rector at his desk in his office. Grace had just brought in his morning coffee and his toasted bagel with Neufchatel cheese when the landline telephone rang.

"Oh, for God's sake, I guess I'll have to get this," said Reverend DeBassompierre. "You have your hands full." Grace was still holding the French press carafe. "St. Aloysius Episcopal Church Welcomes You, Reverend Doctor Silas DeBassompierre speaking..."

There followed, from the other end of the line, a crisp, businesslike buzzing. Soon Reverend DeBassompierre's eyes steadily widened, and his mouth fell slightly slack. At one point there was complete silence, then a rather sharp call out from the other end, recognizable even to Clancy as the words, "Are you still there?" At that Reverend DeBassompierre seemed to jump out of a spell. "Oh! Yes! I'm sorry...I'm just a little...this is so unexpected.... Yes, of course. Of course, I absolutely accept. Yes, yes, a thousand times yes! Thank you so much, Dr. Richards."

A pause.

"Of course," the Reverend said. "Kate. Yes, Kate. I'll check my email immediately, and I'll print it and sign it and have my administrative assistant scan it so I can send it back as a PDF. Thank you so much, I..." The Reverend's voice became very thick. "I'll talk to you then. Goodbye. God Bless You." And then, as if he was, like the Apostle Paul on the road to Damascus, struck suddenly blind, he covered his eyes with his hands, fell back in his swivel chair, and cried out loud.

"Silas! What is it!" said Grace.

"Oh my God!" said the stricken clergyman, still covering his face. "Oh my God. I'm going to Harvard." And then, as his voice broke on that final (and to Clancy unfamiliar) word, the priest's hands fell to his desk and he burst into tears.

۞

THE TEARS PASSED QUICKLY after Grace—not altogether jokingly—threatened to slap him if he didn't get himself together and tell her exactly what the hell was going on. Reverend DeBassompierre blew his roman nose and motioned for her to sit down in the visitor's chair on the other side of his desk.

"It's a miracle, Grace. An honest to God miracle. And just in the nick of time, after that disaster with Blattery. Oh, God, what have I done to deserve this?"

"Silas! Who *was* that?!"

"All right," said the Reverend. "You remember last summer, when I went up to Boston for George's wedding? Remember, I told you I decided while I was up there to see my old dissertation advisor, just to see if she had any leads for me—maybe a postdoc somewhere, anywhere? Well, she didn't, but she said she'd keep her eyes and ears open. Then a few months ago she did let me know about an assistant professorship position in Patristics, and of course I applied, and of course I didn't hear anything. But apparently, someone paid attention to my materials, because that was the Chair of the Byzantine Studies Department. They need an emergency replacement for a lecturer who just got fired for stalking one of their Graduate Assistants. They've seen my CV, they consulted with the hiring committee for the patristics position, and somehow or another someone pulled some strings, and—they're offering me the lectureship! It's not tenure track, of course, but it's full time...three and three...full benefits, including pension! And there's a possibility —a strong possibility, she said—that it'll be renewed for as long as there's steady enrollment. Oh, Grace! I'm finally getting *out* of here! I'm saved!"

Grace Holbach looked for a moment as if she might burst into tears herself.

"Oh, Silas," she sighed. "That's amazing." But she did not sound amazed. She sounded, in fact, rather resigned and sad.

The dazzled clergyman shook his head slowly from side to side. "I can't believe it. I just can't believe it. This sort of thing just doesn't happen, Grace! Not to me! I'm a loser!"

"You are not a loser, Silas."

The priest continued to shake his head in slow, wonderstruck negation. "It's too good to be true. I shouldn't accept it, should I, Grace? I'm jumping the gun, aren't I? I mean, there's no guarantee it'll last beyond a year, if that even, and as miserable as I am here, at least it's a steady income, at least as long as I don't end up killing somebody or myself..."

"Silas," said Grace. "As much as I hate to say it, you're going to accept. This is the chance of a lifetime. Who knows, maybe there is a God and your prayers have been answered. You'll never forgive yourself if you play it safe, Silas, and you know it."

"You're right, Grace. Of course, you're right. You're always right, aren't you . . ." Reverend DeBassompierre stood and turned... not away from Grace, but towards the window behind his desk that looked out over the grounds behind the church building, the graveyard, the playground, the community garden, and the woods beyond... the dimension, unknown to him but nevertheless real, of the church that was spiritual home to a number of animals. "I wish you could come with me," he said, ostensibly to Grace.

⊙⌘⊙

CLANCY SPENT the remainder of that day feeling as if he'd been skinned alive. Reverend DeBassompierre was leaving! Well, it wasn't as if the possibility had never been raised before; the malcontented priest was always imagining that he was about to get fired either by the bishop or the vestry for some reason or other. And Clancy, along with anyone else who observed the Reverend with any degree of attention, was aware that he was always applying for teaching positions, although he had very little faith in the possibility that he would ever really be seriously considered for one. "I'm a throwback," he would say. "Patristics is out of vogue. And I'm getting old, and I don't have the right connections anymore." But he'd never stopped trying.

And now, it seemed, his hopeless persistence had paid off. Behind the bookcase, Clancy couldn't avoid overhearing the jubilant telephone calls. "That's right, Mother! Harvard! Harvard! Oh, there really is a God! Finally, *finally*, my work on the Cappadocians is getting the attention it deserves.... Mother... are you still there? Well, anyway, Mother...maybe you shouldn't say anything to the family just yet. I haven't even spoken to the bishop yet.... What? Oh, all right. No, I understand. I forgot, it's Wednesday and you have your game. All right then. We'll talk soon. Goodbye, Mother. I love...."

The very next call, Clancy soon discerned, was to the bishop. "That's right, Marge. Harvard Divinity. A full-time lectureship. And to be perfectly frank..." A pause. "No. No, but the position has always been renewed in the past, it's just a matter of—"

Another pause, during which the Reverend DeBassompierre drummed his fingers on the surface of his desk. "I don't think so, Marge. I can't ask the vestry to consider that. I just...can't do it. It would be hedging my bets...." A very long pause. "I wish I could believe that but I can't. Marge, you know as well as I do, that you and I—and the vestry—have simply been tolerating one another. Let's just finally put our cards on the table. Now maybe we can all move on."

Another pause. "I appreciate that, Marge. I truly do. And while I'm sure you're already aware of this, I just have to say that without Grace, none of the positive changes over the past couple of years here would have happened. She deserves all the credit, and so...well, no matter what happens, I'd like to have your word, that she'll be recognized—and not let go...."

A final, brief pause. "Thank you. I knew you'd understand. God bless, Marge."

Thereupon followed a series of soft, snuffling noises, as if the Reverend had a cold.

When that passed, the next call was to—of all persons!—that alarming Mercedes Hernandez. "Mercedes! Listen...you and Grace and I are going out for lobster tonight. Tommy, too." A pause. "That's for me to know and you to find out. But I will say, be prepared to celebrate. Meet us at the Channel Marker. Seven o'clock." And without another word, the Reverend DeBassompierre hung up the phone with relish and began to hum Beethoven's "Ode to Joy."

☙❦❧

JUST AS HE had felt after the near massacre at the Community College, Clancy didn't feel like leaving the building that evening to share the remains of the day with the pillars of his own church. After Grace and the Reverend left to meet Mercedes and Tommy for their celebratory supper, Clancy took to his makeshift bed. But this unnaturally early retirement caused him to wake up in the middle of the night. He was suffering from vague and unsettling phantasmagoric dreams, in which he was trapped within the interstices of the Hammond Organ in the sanctuary, dodging gears and springs and other mechanistic impedimenta as the instrument played, as if of its own accord and at an excruciating decibel level, Beethoven's "Ode to Joy." The dream left a baleful psychic residue that seemed to permeate the atmosphere of the cellar. And he couldn't imagine that going upstairs to the sanctuary where the nightmare Hammond Organ sat would make him feel any better. There was nowhere to go but outdoors.

He immediately felt less disturbed once he was out in the open air under the starry sky. The night was still and silent, a relief after the haranguing music of the dream. From the composter beside him came the warm familiar stench of vegetable rot, off-putting but perfectly natural and necessary. Perhaps it was that which gave him the feeling that he should offer his emotional burden to the Lord. Gazing up at the summer stars, he raised his plaint to the inscrutable heavens. "Why do things have to change?"

Of course, there was no answer. Clancy's sense of the futility of arguing against necessity for the sake of personal convenience literally deflated him. He heaved a sigh that then caused him to cough. He decided that he might as well go back inside the cellar and try to get back to sleep so as not to start the day ahead exhausted. But the decision of his will seemed not to be shared by his flesh, which indeed had a will of its own—and that will was to stay put. It was consoling enough, at any rate, to linger leaning limply against the composter, observing a land-scape at once familiar and changed by the deep darkness of the night. But no sooner had he relaxed into a kind of melancholy peace, than out of the darkness, from around the corner of the fence that belonged to the convenience store on the adjoining lot, a low, lumpen shadow appeared and began to make its way toward him. Clancy tensed at first, but something in the slow

steady ambling progress of the figure conveyed familiarity.
When it got within a few feet of him he could see that it was
Ometa the Opossum, with her ever present offspring clinging to
her pelt.

"Hey there! Thought that was you!" she hissed with her characteristic heartiness. "What're you doing out here s'late?"

"Oh, hi, Ometa." Clancy said. Of all his regular parishioners,
Ometa was the one he felt least connected to; while he liked her
and appreciated her indomitably cheerful if caustic spirit. Ometa
made it no secret that she found Clancy's sermons and his ideas
regarding God and Jesus incomprehensible. So far she had
declined to have her numerous offspring baptized, and attended
services at St. Aloysius Jr. mainly, as she put it, for "something
to do."

"I just wanted to get out of the cellar for a little while. I
couldn't sleep. It's nice to see you. I'm so used to seeing you on
Sunday morning, I forgot, you're usually nocturnal."

"Oh, yeah," said the opossum breezily. "It's not always easy
for me to keep these kids awake through some of your sermons,
to tell you the truth, Reverend, but anyways I enjoy it, and like I
say, everyone's been real nice. How come you can't sleep?" It was
characteristic of Ometa, Clancy had noted before, to leap from
subject to subject with the alacrity of a flea. Still, it always caught
him off guard.

"Something wrong, Reverend?" the opossum pressed. "You
look like someone stepped on your tail."

Such was Clancy's feeling of forsakenness that he blurted out
something like truth. "I had a bad dream," he said.

"Oh! That means there's a big change coming," Ometa said
confidently. "That's what my mama always told me, and she was
right. Every time I have a bad dream myself, something big
changes."

Thinking critically despite himself, Clancy pondered Ometa's
mother's claim. He couldn't help but think that "something big
changing" was a category too vague to be correlated to a bad

dream with any significance. But still... he did feel that the dream was telling him something.

"I hope it's a good change," he said. "It was a really bad dream."

"Mama said the worse the dream, the bigger the change," said Ometa, and this, despite the tenuousness of its logic, held for Clancy a doleful ring of truth.

⚜

REVEREND DEBASSOMPIERRE, feeling generous and expansive like never before in his life, had brought what he called a "kitty bag" back from the restaurant that evening for Macrina. Though he called it a bag, it was actually a small pressboard carton that held the remains of a half-eaten lobster tail and some scallops. Macrina consumed the treat with her usual delicate relish. "Macrina!" crowed the Reverend, "I've got fantastic news. You and I are finally leaving this godforsaken swamp and moving to Boston. I'm going to teach at Harvard! What do you say to that?!"

While Macrina had no real sense of what or where Boston or Harvard were, she understood perfectly that her keeper was intending a permanent change, and that he was taking for granted her accompanying him. After all, she'd overheard, along with Clancy, the telephone conversations in the rector's office that morning. She'd had all day to consider her own position, but had not yet come to any decision. She liked the Reverend, enjoyed her quiet life with him, and did not wish for it to change in any way. Additionally, she liked spending her weekdays in the office, with someone to talk to who could talk back to her from time to time—namely, the Rat. Now the most amenable domestic situation she'd experienced throughout her far too peripatetic young life would have to end. Why were these humans never, ever satisfied?

Not for the first time in her life, Macrina decided she was

not going to give in without a fight.

GRACE HERSELF WAS NOT unaffected by the prospect of the Reverend's leaving. It felt like—to use the cliché that occurred to her—the end of an era, if not for the congregation, at least for herself. For she had never known St. Aloysius, nor any other church apart from the best forgotten Southern Baptist church she'd had to attend growing up, without Reverend DeBassompierre. Never having worked in a church before, never having had any interest in religion whatsoever, she'd come across the advertisement for her current position in a newsletter sent to her house but addressed to the previous owner. On a hunch, she had applied for it. Her divorce had just been finalized, Tommy was still in high school, and she needed full-time employment as soon as possible. She'd been pleased to accept the Reverend's rather off-the-cuff on-the-spot job offer because of the nearness of the location and the slight flexibility of the hours. She'd remained, even in the face of some serious early disagreements with Silas, because she enjoyed it. Silas was querulous and demanding, uptight yet unpretentious, and made no effort to be admirable—which, after her narcissist of an ex-husband, was refreshing in a man. Silas was perfectly willing to leave much of the work of running the church to her in order to concentrate on his sermons and scholarship, and that is how she came to realize that she had a knack for pastoral counseling. It was Silas who had recognized her interest, Silas who had encouraged her to pursue education and training in the field on the diocesan dime, and Silas who gave her the freedom to do as she pleased. The truth of it was that, if it hadn't been for Silas and his faults and virtues, she would not be as reasonably happy with her life as it was. He had given her, by being his troublesome self, a new lease on life. He assured her that her position, along with her understood role as the congregation's counselor, was secure and would very likely be enhanced officially, and she appreciated that. She knew it wasn't the end of the world, but it just wasn't going to be the same without Silas.

ॐॐ

EVENTUALLY, of course, Clancy found himself confiding in Ottoline. "I'm so depressed I don't know what to do. Reverend DeBassompierre is going away!"

"Going away!" Ottoline said. "For good?"

"Yes!" cried the rat. "He's going back to a place called Harvard. I guess he likes it better there, because I've never seen him so happy. I know I should be happy for him, but Ottoline, I just hate to see him go. He's such an inspiration to me. I don't think I would have had the nerve to accept God's call to me to become a minister if it wasn't for Reverend DeBassompierre to show me the way. And now he's leaving. What if they get someone who isn't nice?"

"Oh, I'm sure that won't happen," said Ottoline. "I'm sure Grace wouldn't allow anything like that."

Clancy wasn't so sure, but he didn't want to contradict Ottoline. At least not at the moment. "Well, I know I'm being selfish. But it just doesn't seem right." And in that last sentence, Clancy heard in his own voice the voice of his dear departed Aunt November, who had raised him in the faith. She herself, when old Reverend Bickel had died suddenly on the golf course and Reverend DeBassompierre had been hired to take over, was so unimpressed by the erudite sermons and what she considered to be the "fancy" liturgical innovations of the new priest—such as the use of thurifers and his affectation of chant when he pronounced the Eucharistic Prayer—that she'd seriously considered relocating to another parish. Taking Clancy along, of course. And had death not intervened, taking Aunt November herself to be with the Lord and presumably her own preferred rector, Reverend Bickel, Clancy might never have received a call to ministry that he could accept. It seemed to Clancy that his world was turning upside down.

Ottoline could tell that the Reverend was really distressed, for his tail was raw and scabby and it was his habit to gnaw on that appendage when he was stressed or distressed. She endeavored to soothe him. "I know you set great store by the Reverend DeBassompierre, and although of course I'm not as familiar with him as you are, I agree that he is a fine upstanding human being, and it certainly won't be the same without him here. But, as intelligent and thoughtful as he is, I'm sure he wouldn't do anything he didn't think was for the best for all concerned..."

"But he doesn't *know* that *we're* concerned..." lamented Clancy. "That's what's so awful. I wish there was some way to let him know what he means to us. Maybe then... he'd stay?"

Ottoline hesitated to respond. As much as she admired Reverend Clancy's warm heart and often surprisingly sharp pastoral instincts, as a mother many times over she realized that in many respects he was still very naïve. Most if not all attempts (of most if not all nonhuman animals) to communicate with humans, no matter how well intentioned, led at best to frustration and at worst to loss of life and/or habitat. And yet it was true that, at one time, when in a best forgotten series of events the composter holding Hertz and all his hundreds of progeny was knocked over, it had been Reverend DeBassompierre, summoned by none other than Steven tapping on the office window with his beak, who had come to the rescue and saved countless lives. Reverend DeBassompierre was human, yes, but he seemed to possess one of those rarest of human qualities; he was humane. But that didn't mean he would stay when he knew he would be happier somewhere else just for the sake of a rat's feelings.

"I'm not sure that would be a good idea," she said. "You know that you never can tell how they'll react..."

"You're right," said Clancy. "It's no use." He looked down at his tail, suddenly feeling the self-inflicted pain caused by his anxious gnawing. He dropped it and it landed with a soft sound on the hard concrete apron at the head of the community garden upon which the composter rested. "He'll never know what he means to me."

⸙

IN THE WEEKS THAT FOLLOWED, it was neither easy nor pleasant for Clancy to continue to observe Reverend DeBassompierre as he prepared for his departure. This preparation consisted mostly of gleeful telephone calls to former professors and mentors and acquaintances far and wide to inform them of his change in fortune. "I'm so happy," he told them all in effect. "I've never been so happy in my life. Not even when I was first ordained." It hurt Clancy's heart to hear that. His own calling to ministry, in which Reverend DeBassompierre played a role even though it was figurative, was the highest point of his own existence, and he couldn't imagine that his hero did not feel the same. Clancy also felt the uncomfortable stirrings of irritation towards the happy priest, especially at such moments when, while engaged in some mindless task such as packing up his books and papers, he would hum in a deep and carrying register Beethoven's "Ode to Joy."

He shared his misgivings with Macrina one afternoon while Reverend DeBassompierre and Grace were at lunch at their favorite diner, Cox's, down the boulevard. "I just hate that he's leaving," he said. "I'm so upset I don't know what to do."

"I'm not sure what to do myself," said Macrina. "Of course, he expects me to go along. I can't blame him for that. But I haven't made up my mind...."

It had somehow not yet occurred to Clancy that Macrina would be leaving too! This was another devastating blow for Clancy. The priest and the cat, both of whom inclined toward solitude, had been in spite of that inseparable ever since Macrina had come to the churchyard as a stray. "Oh, Macrina!" Clancy moaned. "Of *course* you have to go with Reverend DeBassompierre! I mean... it's not that I *want* you to! I don't want either one of you to go, really... I'll *miss* you....I'll miss you *both*!"

Macrina—to whom *missing someone* was a vague and unfamiliar, if not unappealing concept—yawned—not, as the act usually signified, out of boredom or fatigue, but rather out of a sudden and unsettling recognition of the dilemma facing her and the need to mull it over in a state of deep relaxation. No matter what she decided, in the end, due to circumstances beyond her control, she was going to end up in an altered situation, one that was not ideal."Maybe..." said Macrina, "I can get him to stay put."

"Oh, Lord! said Clancy. "How?"

"I don't know," said the cat. "But I bet I can figure something out."

"But he really wants to go to Harvard!" cried Clancy. "I've never seen him so happy!"

"But I'm not happy," said Macrina. "I don't like change."

"I don't either," said Clancy. "But...." He began, thinking of various situations he'd encountered in his early days in ministry, in which unforeseen and unwelcome changes had shattered the lives of his flock, "...If you try to stop things from changing, you might get hurt."

"I'm going to try," said Macrina. "It's my life."

"It's his, too," said Clancy. "Oh, this is so awful."

☙❧

CURLED up on the cushion of the prie-dieu, eyes almost completely shut, Macrina was not asleep, but strategizing, as the priest, humming merrily and intermittently, gazed at the screen of his laptop as if into the eyes of a lover. He was looking at apartment listings. Macrina knew this because every once in a while, he would interrupt her rest by calling her name and her attention to some image on the screen he knew full well she could not see. "Oh, look at this, Macrina," he would say. "2300 a month…that's not bad….Only 450 square feet, and a shared kitchen, but it's right in Central Square. I wouldn't even need to take the bus….Oh, damn it. No pets. Oh well." And, tapping and clicking, he'd navigate onto another listing, "One bedroom, full kitchen, full bath…2500 a month, plus wifi…Revere…ugh! That's too much of a hike…still, right on the water….Thousand-dollar pet deposit! Holy Mother of God!" And on and on. For all his frustration, the priest was still deliriously happy and undaunted. "Don't worry, Macrina," he said at one point. "I'd never leave you behind. I'll find us a place you'll like if it kills me!" And without so much as a glance in her direction, he was back to tapping and scrolling, as if that was the answer to everything.

⚜

ALTHOUGH SHE WAS PLEASED for Silas, Grace was apprehensive about his future. Unsuited as we was for parish ministry, indubitably committed to rigorous theological scholarship, did that necessarily mean he would be happy up at Harvard? She knew better than perhaps anyone else how easily he could sabotage himself, and she couldn't help but feel more protective of Silas than perhaps he deserved. It did seem sad that after several years in the current job, he hadn't managed to win over even a handful of the congregants to his austere, intellectual style of ministry. The more she thought about it, the more she wanted to be able to do something that could give him some sense that he'd had a positive impact. Attendance and offerings had declined steadily since the Reverend DeBassompierre's first disastrous year on the job on account of—so it was held—his lack of initiative and aloof pastoral manner. No, any "celebration" of him would be so suffused with a spirit of insincerity that Silas would smell it coming a mile away. But what else could she do?

Oh Silas, she addressed his image in her mind. *Why does everything with you have to be so difficult?!*

She sighed. Maybe she should just take him out to dinner.

But the thought of such an unimaginative gesture made her so depressed she actually felt tearful. Gritting her teeth against such unhelpful emotion, she stood up and make her way into the Rector's office. It was empty, as it was only 7:30 am, and Silas rarely made it to work before 8 on his best day.

She wasn't sure what led her to the bookcase, which was almost completely empty, its holdings packed into cardboard boxes stacked up on its right. Only the top shelf, which she knew contained Silas's most frequently consulted tomes, remained for quick access up to the end—his *Greek Septuagint*, his *Interpreter's Bible*, his *Eusebius,* and his *Ante-Nicene Fathers*. And his own book, his pride and joy: *Gender, Consciousness, Time, and Eschatology in Cappadocian Metaphysics*. "Gobbledygook to me," Grace muttered silently, but she opened it and turned to a page near the beginning. "Acknowledgements," she read. The acknowledgements in fact went on for a page and a half in small type, listing first his parents and brother, then his faculty advisors, a long list of advance readers, his best friend George in Waltham, Grace herself ("for keeping the wolves at bay and for her patience, kindness, understanding and sharp wit,") and finally, "and last but not least, to my Good Shepherd, Fr. Angelo Schiaparelli, who made a fellow shepherd out of a lost sheep."

Suddenly Grace herself acknowledged what led her to the bookshelf, and what she had to do.

She got back to her desk just in time as the Rector walked into the admin wing, humming, as was his habit lately, "Ode to Joy" out of tune.

⌘

SITTING at his own incongruously executive desk at the L'Arche Center, of which he served as director, Father Angelo Schiaparelli, OFM, hung up the desk phone absently, already miles away. *So!* he said to himself. *Silas has finally gotten his heart's desire.* The wiry abbot brought his palms together, as if to pray, interlaced

his fingers, and rested his sharp bearded chin upon his remarkably hairy knuckles. Never one to stay still for long, Father
Angelo then grabbed his cell phone, a pocket calendar, and a
pencil, and went outside to park himself on a bench in front of
the pond.

It wouldn't be easy. He'd have to cancel some appointments,
and inevitably he'd end up disappointing somebody... but having
been invited to share Silas's deliverance from a phase of life that
had brought him relatively equal measures of frustration and
growth, he wanted to be there. Silas DeBassompierre—maybe
because he'd been as arrogant and insecure as he was intelligent
and determined—had been a challenging postulant to say the
least. But in their eighteen months together, when Silas as a
young priest fresh out of seminary had sought to enter the Franciscan Order as a means by which to escape his many internal
conflicts, he had grown on the then young but crafty abbot. He'd
enjoyed the struggle to help the gifted young priest overcome
some of his more destructive allegiances, primary among them a
commitment to neo-scholastic theological method that was
proving to be intellectually—and otherwise—castrating. When
on the wings of that liberation came a flight from Roman
Catholicism, Father Angelo was not at all sorry. For some individuals the ideological tapestry of Roman Catholicism could
prove inspiring and at once liberating and humbling. For others
—particularly young Americans of a certain class background—it
led to insufferable smugness. Silas had been one of those young
Americans given over to a snarky and brittle certitude. And
while leaving the Church of Rome hadn't rid the freshly
ordained Episcopal Reverend DeBassompierre of all traces of
arrogance, Father Angelo felt that the young man's arrogance,
based as it was now upon intellectual integrity, was not without
virtue. Over the years they'd kept in close touch via email and so
he knew that Silas' tenure at St. Aloysius had been at times
incredibly rocky. Father Angelo had been sincerely moved to
have been included in the Acknowledgements for *Gender,*

Consciousness, Time, and Eschatology in Cappadocian Metaphysics. But it was clear from this Grace person that Silas had kept himself together with not a little help from her. And now he seemed to be offered a chance at vocational happiness. *You've worked another wonder in Silas*, Father Angelo informed the Almighty, *now help me figure out how I can get down to North Carolina to congratulate him without causing too many ruffled feathers. We don't have a whole lot of time.*

"It would mean a lot to him if you could be here," Grace had said. "To be really honest, Fr. Schiaparelli—"

"Please, call me Angelo."

"—Angelo, I don't know how much he's told you, but St. Aloysius is a pretty demanding congregation, apparently used to a certain kind of minister that doesn't really match his style, if you know what I mean. They expect a lot of...affirmation, and as you probably know, Silas is...reserved. It just hasn't been a great fit...."

Father Angelo wondered if Grace could hear him grinning, for she had begun to laugh herself. "Silas has always been unyielding."

"Yes," she agreed. "Anyway, if you can possibly make it, let me know, and please call back on this number—" She gave him her cell phone number. "I'd really like to surprise him, if it's okay."

"Of course. I'll see what I can do; I'll be in touch soon. Thanks for calling, Grace....and if I can ask one thing—has Silas had any...counseling throughout this time?"

"Just me," she sighed. "As far as I can tell."

⚜

MEANWHILE CLANCY HAD to struggle mightily against feeling bereft. Reverend DeBassompierre's happiness was like birdsong in the dead of night when one is desperate for sleep, or music from a party to which one has not been invited, innocent yet nevertheless injurious. Clancy dreaded the inevitable departure, but he was determined not to let his emotions interfere with his ministry. On the Sunday before the Reverend DeBassompierre—and presumably Macrina—were set to leave, Clancy preached what he considered to be one of the better sermons of his career. The Thursday before, the Reverend DeBassompierre had practiced his own sermon explicating John 20:17, pointing out that in order to truly worship, one must acknowledge and respect the essential difference between God and Creation. The intricacies of the human Reverend's exegesis had been hard for Clancy to follow, and so he'd been thrown back upon his own reflections regarding faith and loss.

"*Don't you touch me!*" Clancy began his sermon with what was for him an uncommon vehemence that struck curiosity, if not alarm, into the hearts of his familiar listeners. "That's what Jesus said to one of his very best friends on the very first Easter Day, the day He rose from the Dead. Isn't that a strange thing for the Lord, who loves us all so much, to say to someone so excited to see Him? I don't know about you, but if I was Miss Mary Magdalene, that would have really hurt my feelings. And we all know that Jesus wouldn't want to hurt someone's feelings unless He had to. Jesus was a gentleman. So I believe that there had to be a really good reason for Jesus to tell his friend to stay away and not come near Him."

Clancy paused, and from his slight elevation atop the composter, looked down at a congregation that was more than normally attentive. He couldn't help feeling proud. And it always gave him a nice, safe feeling to see all of those faces looking up at him, as if they would catch him if he fell.

"I think that every single one of us here knows how it feels to lose someone they care about. I think we'd probably all agree that it's just about the worst feeling in the world. It's like a part of us is missing! Sometimes we lose someone and it's our own fault! We might have done something or said something to hurt them or make them not want to be around us anymore. Other times we might lose someone we love because things just change!

And sometimes the ones we love get sick, or get hurt, and they die and they go to be with the Lord in heaven."

Clancy felt his ears becoming warm, for he was remembering, as he knew he would, his beloved Aunt November, who herself had not been tactile in her affections, and would have resonated with Christ's rebuke of the Magdalene.

"We just can't always be as close, or stay as close as we want, to the ones we love. Maybe Jesus could have said it a little nicer, but maybe she was coming towards Him so fast He just had to speak sharply. Just imagine, after all, what it must have been like! Jesus was dead, after all that awful being nailed up on a cross, and now He's alive again. If you were Miss Mary Magdalene you'd want to just hug Him and never let him go, wouldn't you! But when we hold on to something or someone too tight, or too long, why, what happens to them? They're caught by us! They can't move! Now, do you want to be the reason that someone you love can't move?

"Jesus told Miss Mary Magdalene that she shouldn't touch Him, because He hadn't yet ascended to the Father. Now, I'm not sure what that means, but it sounds to me like he needed his Daddy. Jesus wasn't dead, no, but that doesn't mean he hadn't been hurt bad by what happened, and when you've been hurt...." Clancy paused. "Sometimes it takes a while before you can trust anyone again, except maybe the one who took care of you when you were small. We all have to remember, don't we, that some-times the ones we love need their space. It's not easy.... But no one—not even Jesus—promised us a rose garden when we decided to follow Him...."

After pausing for effect, Clancy said "Amen." Then, as usual, he instructed his members to join him in reciting the creed.

⚜

"WHAT AN DELIGHTFUL CHURCHYARD," said Fr. Angelo Schiaparelli, OFM. "The garden, the playground, the cemetery....It's a little slice of life, from beginning to end, that you can see from your window...." He looked back over his shoulder at the window of Reverend DeBassompierre's soon-to-be empty office, for the two clergymen were standing outdoors following a tour of the church grounds, beside but upwind of the composter. "There's something about it. I feel the presence of God in a very unique and vital manner just standing here. It's hard to put my finger on why...."

Reverend DeBassompierre figured that his former abbot, mentor and friend was suffering a bit of jet lag and indulged him with a smile. "It is nice, I guess," the young priest said in an attempt at sincere agreement. While gazing out at the grounds and the forest beyond had from time to time provided him succor in troubled moments, he would nonetheless be glad to see the last of the community garden, a thorn in his flesh because it was yet another one of his initiatives that had received next to no support from the vestry.

Father Angelo could sense the Reverend's ambivalence. He grinned within his scruffy beard. "I know it hasn't been easy for you here, Silas," he said. "But I'm glad you had this time here, to experience the impossibilities and rewards of parish ministry. I think one day you'll look back on it with some gratitude and nostalgia." He glanced over at his friend. "And your secretary is a real treasure. I'm so glad she got in touch with me." The abbot took a deep breath of the warm coastal air, slightly tinged with compost.

"I still can't believe she got you here, Angelo," said Silas. "You're right, she is a treasure." His voice was as stiff as his clerical collar, in unconscious compensation for the complete loss of his composure when, the evening before, the abbot—habit and all—had strolled into Grace's living room behind Mercedes, who had picked him up from the airport. Silas was so surprised and moved that he burst into tears, to the total consternation of everyone gathered except for Father Angelo, who had seen it all before. "Mazel Tov, Silas!" the abbot had said. Then he had taken the much taller priest in his arms and lifted him for a moment off the floor. "Did you think I wouldn't move heaven and earth to celebrate your dream come true! God forbid!" And he set the priest down with a thump.

When he got himself together, Reverend DeBassompierre turned to Grace. "How did you know?" he asked. "How did you know this was just the man I needed to see?!"

"A little bird told me," said Grace.

"The Holy Spirit," said Father Angelo.

"Oh, bullshit!" said Mercedes.

WHEN THE SHOCK WORE OFF, the gathering in Grace's home had become appropriately festive. The dining room was decorated with balloons and banners, and Tommy brought out a cake in the form and image of a Holy Bible, presenting it to Reverend DeBassompierre with a diffident manner that hid his eagerness. "It's red velvet," said the young man, "Mom said you'd like that."

It seemed to Father Angelo that the feeling towards Silas among the others gathered was one of sincere though not uncritical affection. He thought the young woman named Mercedes was particularly interesting in this regard. She struck him very powerfully, as a matter of fact, as a female version of Silas himself....Silas in drag, as it were. Together they shared striking Mediterranean handsomeness and coloring; both were quick to leap to their own defense, and they also seemed at once devoted to and covertly possessive of Grace. But Mercedes radiated a self-assurance completely lacking in Silas, that Father Angelo could well imagine Silas would experience as competition. There was also between them a peculiarly wary sexual tension, like one might perceive existing between a couple of scorpions. He knew now why Silas's emails to him over the past year or so had been so vague. Silas hated to discuss the subject of his highly conflicted attitude towards persons attractive to him.

It was clear that Grace was in every respect the backbone of the group, and this made the abbot feel relieved, for with that being the case this little group would stay in reasonable touch despite Silas' crippling diffidence. For, no matter how much better Harvard might be suited to his gifts, he would still need his old friends. This, Father Angelo recognized, was the healthiest family system Silas had ever experienced.

"So, what was Silas like as a monk?" Grace asked the abbot at one point. "I really can't imagine it."

"Franciscans aren't monks. Technically, we're Friars. But in a certain sense it amounts to the same thing: we live in community. Of course, Silas never made a full profession, he wasn't with us long before he—we—realized that he would best serve the charism outside of the order. Pursuing his theological study with integrity within the Order, and by extension within the Roman system, would have led to conflicts and tensions that wouldn't have done anyone any good. So it was a bittersweet experience— like his time with you all, I imagine...." He couldn't resist a quick glance at Mercedes, whose expression was arch.

But Grace was looking at the Abbot approvingly. "Yes," she said. "It has been. We've had some hard times, but we've also had a lot of fun. I really dread having to work with another priest, to tell you the truth. Silas knows it's always best for everybody involved to let me handle everything."

Gentle laughter followed this quip, but Father Angelo wasn't fooled. A very comfortable dynamic for both Grace and Silas was at an end, and they were both grieving, whether they realized it or not. The Abbot thought of his oldest sister, Rosemarie, and the abandonment he'd felt—unexpectedly—as a nine-year-old boy when she'd left their childhood home to get married. Grace, he realized, had become Silas's sister. And her little brother was growing up and leaving the nest.

"He learned his lesson well in the abbey," said Father Angelo. "Let me tell you, he was quite a handful for an untried novice master like myself... "

Throughout the abbot's judiciously teasing recounting of Silas's stormy postulancy, in which he hadn't been able to avoid confronting his issues with authority all the way up to the papacy, Silas sat at the dining room table self-conscious yet amenable, the guest of honor, smiling and blushing and enjoying his slice of the ersatz bible that Tommy baked for him.

❦

"For God's sake, Grace, where is she?!" The Reverend DeBassompierre was frantic, as it was time to go, and go for good. "She's got to be in here somewhere!" He raked his hair with both hands, mussing it so that he began to look as disheveled as any representation of John the Baptist. He'd been growing his hair out ever since the call from Harvard, as if to externalize his sense of liberation from constraint.

Macrina was all of a sudden nowhere to be seen. Just a few minutes before, Silas had at first attempted to wheedle her into a carrier. When that achieved nothing, he had lifted her off the cushion of the prie-dieu so that he could place it into the packing case to give to Tommy to put in the U-Haul. "It's all right, Macrina," he'd said. "Just a day or two and we'll be home in Cambridge, and you'll have your bed back."

Macrina had not resisted being lifted, but she did wriggle herself free in an instant, hit the hardwood floor front paws first with a pointed thud, then stalked away. But she hadn't left the office....Had she?

"Grace!" he called again. He went to the doorway. Grace was at her desk, looking into the screen of her desktop computer and applying lip balm. "Grace! Did Macrina come through here when I was out at the truck?"

"No...."

"Are you sure!?"

"As sure as I can be." Grace put her balm in her desk drawer and looked around. "She isn't in your office?"

"If she was would I be asking you where she is?! " He raked his scalp again. He could hear the strangled quality in his own voice that always signaled hysteria. "Grace, what if she got outside!"

"Calm down, Silas," said Grace, but she made an effort not to sound too sharp. This was it. This was goodbye. Of course he was going to be an impossible wreck! She counted silently to ten. "I'm sure she didn't get out. Why would she? She hates being outdoors, you know that. She's probably just looking around. I think she knows she's leaving...." She touched her now former employer's shoulder and bent to look under the desk.

"I just *looked* there!" said Silas petulantly, but he then followed Grace's motion, and followed her out into the administrative suite, looked under her desk, under the old vinyl upholstered chair where parishioners who were waiting for an appointment sat, and even in the waste basket. But Macrina was not in any of these places, nor would she ever have been. It didn't occur to either Reverend DeBassompierre or Grace to look in the very narrow space behind the now empty bookshelves. Why would a cat with an entire church at her disposal squeeze herself back there?

"All right," said Grace, with forced calmness. "Let's check the sanctuary."

And as the two sets of footsteps faded away toward the front of the building, Macrina emerged from behind the bookcase and stretched and flicked her ears and addressed an unseen being. "It stinks back there," she said. "How can you stand it!"

"I guess I'm used to it," said Clancy, not a bit offended. "I guess I should have cleaned up, but I didn't know I'd have company!"

Macrina's ears stiffened. "Shhh...." she said. "They're coming back." And, taking a breath of relatively fresh air, she wriggled back behind the heavy bookcase.

"Oh *God*!" the priest was moaning. "Where *is* she!"

"Silas, she's in here somewhere, she's got to be. Now look.

Stop catastrophizing. No pun intended. We'll look until we find her, that's all. I know you want to get on the road, but if you're a little late turning the U-Haul in, it's not like they're going to put you in prison. Tell you what. I'll call them now and let them know you're delayed."

"Oh, God."

"Now, don't start! Silas, this is nothing. It's not the end of the world, it's not a bad omen....It's a nervous cat, doing what cats do when they're nervous. All we have to do is be patient and maybe give her a little incentive. Tell you what. I'll pop down to the Burger Quik and pick up a fish filet. That'll bring her out no matter where she's hiding. You know how much she loves that nasty fake fish."

The Reverend nodded, but when he spoke, it was as if he had heard only his own foreboding. "I can't leave without her, Grace," he said. "I can't. She'll think I've abandoned her...."

Grace, who was on her way to finishing her intensive training in pastoral counseling theory and methodology through a program at the local hospital, thought this comment a breathtakingly transparent example of neurotic projection. But of course she kept that to herself. "All right," she said, as gently as she could manage. And she left to fetch a temptation for Macrina.

When Grace was out of the building, Reverend DeBassompierre lowered himself, not without some unsteadiness, to a cross-legged seating position on the floor in the middle of the empty office. "Oh, Macrina...." he said, lifting his face to look out the window at the blue sky over the garden and graveyard. His voice was a husky whisper, even though for all he knew he was alone. "Macrina, please come back. God, if you can hear me, please let her be all right, and make her come back from wherever she is, so I'll know I'm not making a big mistake...." The clergyman now bent his head, hung it, really, so that it was exactly parallel with the floor.

After a moment he stood up, walked over to the window, and

looked out. "Macrina," he said in a less tortured voice. "Are you scared? Are you scared to leave? Is that it? Are you scared to go so far away? Well, believe it or not, I am too....I mean, I know this is what I've always wanted, but still....Oh, Macrina, I still think it might all just blow up in my face. I mean, it seems like everything else I've done so far has turned out to be a disaster, or almost one....What makes me think this is going to be any different?" he sighed.

"It's not my scholarship I'm worried about. I've proven myself there. I'll put myself up against anyone at Harvard when it comes to the Cappadocians....But the thing is...I'm still going to have to *teach*. I'm still going to have to deal with people. The classroom isn't a congregation, thank God, but it can still be a real battlefield. I'm just not a people person, Macrina, I never have been. What if the students hate me, Macrina, what if I just can't get them to realize the importance of this material? Oh, Macrina! Maybe we *should* just stay the hell here." And so saying, Reverend DeBassompierre, like an agitated inmate in an insane asylum, began beating against the window with the heel of his hands, with gradually increasing frequency and force. Behind the bookcase, Clancy could sense that his beloved mentor was about to lose control of himself. This wasn't the first time he'd observed the Reverend accelerating from nervous gesture to self-harm. And there was nothing that Clancy could do to stop it. But, he realized, not without a sharp and bitter sense of the basic injustice of life on Earth for a lowly rat, Macrina could.

Squeezed in with Clancy behind the bookcase, Macrina felt herself becoming unexpectedly uneasy. Her tactic was having the desired effect, and if she kept her cool, she would have her way. The human reverend would stay put, she would stay put, and everything would stay put, the way it was supposed to. But as the beating against the glass continued, and the glass in fact began to rattle in its pane, even she couldn't help getting nervous. The most likely scenario unfolded before her cat's mind's eye in vivid detail. The clergyman, already beside himself, would continue his compulsive pounding in an attempt to discharge an increasingly violent inner tension, and eventually the glass would break. This would set off in the clergyman a full-scale panic attack, complete with hysterical screaming, and then Grace would walk in on it, and find her employer in no shape to leave...or even to stay. She would inevitably call for professional help. It wasn't inconceivable that he could lose everything if he didn't get ahold of himself. But surely, she would be taken care of no matter what.

"Oh, Lord..." Macrina heard Clancy say under the sound of a pounding fist and rattling glass. "Macrina, he's going to hurt himself!" And Clancy prodded his friend's tense haunch with his blunt damp snout.

Macrina knew she had no real choice but to give in. It really wasn't fair. With something between a purr and a growl, she slithered out from behind the bookcase, padded over to stand beside the Reverend and announced her presence by rubbing against his trouser leg.

WHEN THE RED double doors that were the main entrance to the church were locked and the alarm was set and the coast was clear, Clancy still remained hidden behind the bookcase, now all by himself. Never again, he reflected, would he ever lay eyes upon the austerely handsome human form of Reverend DeBassompierre. Never again would he hear the matter-of-fact vocalizations of his dear newest friend Macrina. Now they were gone, out of his life as completely as if they had gone to be with the Lord just like Aunt November had done when she'd died. But, he found himself thinking, this was even worse than if the priest and the cat had died, because it seemed to him that they were all the more inaccessible to him alive. Had they died, then he would still be able to address them in prayer, in the Spirit, and feel certain that in the Presence of God they would have some consciousness of Clancy's prayers for them. But they were not gone to be with the Lord, they were gone to Harvard. They were now as far away from poor Clancy as if they had gone to Hell— or as if Clancy had. Oh, Lord, he thought to himself, why can't we all be together in one place for all our lives and our deaths?

As if to get away from a too-close-for-comfort proximity with his own existential alienation, Clancy came out from behind the bookcase, into a rector's office that was emptier and more soundless than ever in his experience, even in the dead of night. Out he crept into the administration suite, and down the long hallway, past the Sunday school classrooms and the door to the stairway that led to his own basement, past the utility closet and the food pantry and the two restrooms and he came to the threshold of the sanctuary. There he paused, as if in dread that, should he enter this Holy tabernacle, he would find it, like the rest of the church, empty as well, now that the Reverend and Macrina were gone away. For the Sanctuary *was* empty, at least of any sentient life that he could see, if one did not count the wilting bouquets left to decorate the altar. Dust motes drifted in the multicolored streams of sunlight that the stained-glass windows admitted. Coming from the adjoining sacristy Clancy could just barely hear the uneven gurgle and hum of the vital organs of a refrigerator on its last legs. Above the altar was suspended the old familiar crucifix, and the tormented bronze-work Christ affixed to it had His anguished eyes gazing up to the ceiling, as if trying hopelessly to see through the woodwork to some deliverance beyond it. Following the gaze of the Crucified, Clancy felt even more abandoned.

"Oh, Lord," Clancy said to himself. "Why couldn't I be Macrina instead of me?"

Beyond the windows and walls and roof of the church the members of Clancy's own congregation were busy going about their day, and in the ornamental belfry just above, Ottoline was working out her interpretation of the hymn she planned to suggest for the next Sunday service, but in his current dejected state Clancy couldn't hear a note.

AVARITIA (GREED)

TO MOST ANIMAL EARS the sound was like the sound made by a plague of cicadas, underscored with the rumble of distant thunder, but Bertram, with his ability to see from on high, knew the cacophony for what it was —the clearing of acreage. "Oh, huzzah!" he said to himself. "There's going to be plenty of grub for me and Sudie Mae!" Of course, as a good Christian buzzard, poor Bertram couldn't help but feel some guilt about his unearned good fortune. And so as always, whenever his conscience smote him, he decided he had better go see the Reverend, whom he knew could be found, at this dusky time of day, hanging around the composter, chatting with Ottoline and sometimes Steven and Hertz as well.

Descending in his usual devolving spiral into the little gathering on the ground, Bertram greeted his fellow church members. "Hey ya'll," he said. "Mighty hot, ain't it!" For it was unseasonably warm that evening, and Bertram himself was more than usually pungent on account of the temperature.

"Yes, it certainly is!" warbled Ottoline agreeably. "Why, I was just saying to the Reverend, that I can't recall such a stretch of warm and humid weather, with so little rain to show for it, in a long, long time. It does seem to me that there is a decided warming trend these days no matter what the season."

"Lord, yes," Clancy added. "I swear, if it gets much hotter around here, I don't know what I'll do!" As if for fear of offending the Almighty, whom after all Clancy considered to be the master of the elements, he quickly added, however, "...but I'm sure it'll cool down soon. It always does, doesn't it?" Again, as if to remove from his beloved Almighty any hint of culpability in the discomfort of His creatures, Clancy turned the subject to the constant noise from the near northwest. "Anyway, I'll take the heat any day over all the racket that's been coming from down the boulevard. What in the world is going on down there?"

Bertram's heart leaped, so validated did he feel by the rat reverend's intuiting precisely the reason for his own visit. "As a matter of fact, Reverend, I wanted to let y'all know....I was down the boulevard, you know, looking for something to take home for supper, and I saw what they're doing. They're building a freeway extension, looks like, through that part of the woods that butts up on the marsh."

"Oh!" Ottoline exclaimed. "But that's where Magnus and his family live! I hope they're not impacted...." Magnus was a noble and thoughtful buck deer who with his family consisting of a mate and three offspring sometimes attended Clancy's Sunday services.

"Lord!" cried Clancy. "As loud as all that grinding is, I don't know how they can stand it! Why in the world do the humans want to build a road way out there?"

It was a question, of course, for which there was no answer, for there was of course nothing that could be done. The ways of human beings were as inexorable as they were inexplicable. As every nonhuman creature who lived in any degree of proximity to them sooner or later became aware, what the humans wanted, they got, one way or another, no matter whom it hurt. It was also the case that to some degree every member of the church had at some point been forced to accommodate their own way of life to some incursion of human activity. It was a terrible but accepted fact of life. Still, Ottoline endeavored to be optimistic. "I'm sure Magnus will find another spot for them if he has to."

"I know," said Clancy. "But I hope he doesn't have to go too far away! He's part of the St. Aloysius Jr. family!"

"There's still plenty of woods round here, Reverend," said Bertram, aiming to reassure his pastor and his friend. But having seen, just in the relatively short time that he'd been living and scavenging in the area, the rate at which the forests and the marshes were dwindling, he knew that it wouldn't be long before even he and Sudie Mae might have to find less spoiled—if not happier—hunting grounds.

❧

CLANCY WAS RELIEVED, of course, when Magnus and his family showed up for services as usual on Sunday. In spite of their troubles, the deer looked healthy, and the young ones were growing fast. Indeed, the size and robustness of the deer family did cause Clancy a twinge of anxiety, as they were growing more and more conspicuous. Clancy had always arranged for his services to take place at the same time as those of the "mother" church so as to minimize the chances of his gatherings being noticed by the humans, but he had to wonder if having five nearly full-grown deer in attendance was pushing their luck. Still, for the time being there had been no sign that they were causing alarm. With Reverend DeBassompierre gone, and a different supply priest conducting services every week until a replacement was called, attendance at St. Aloysius Sr. was at an all-time low.

But despite Clancy's lingering grief over the departure of the priest and the cat, his own church rolled on as smoothly as ever, the choir was spirited, and while this Sunday's sermon was uninformed by Reverend DeBassompierre's exegesis, it was still heartfelt. Thinking of his own loss, Clancy preached fervently of his own perennial hope that in "the sweet bye and bye," as his

Aunt November had often referred to the afterlife, humans and nonhumans would be able to live together not merely in peace, but as equals, and communicate and share resources accordingly. Adapting Isaiah's lion and lamb imagery to his particular situation, Clancy wove a bright and vivid verbal tapestry of a happy land overflowing with milk and honey and pizza, where the human would lie down with the rat. The congregation listened with fond indulgence, and Clancy was gratified by the compliments he received during fellowship time.

He was eager to check in with Magnus, of course. He made his way as soon as he could to where that noble figure stood at the edge of the community garden with his lovely wife and three offspring. "Magnus! Bertram told us that they're paving a road through y'all's part of the woods!"

"I'm afraid that's right, Reverend," said the buck. "They're chopping down all the old pines."

"Oh, Lord!" cried Clancy. "That's awful! What are you going to do?"

Here Magnus' middle offspring, a young buck named Hans, ducked his head. His mossy antlers were almost as impressive as his father's, and he walked a bit away from the gathering to stand at the other end of the community garden, where he came to a standstill and looked to the east. Magnus regarded his son with evident concern in his soulful brown eyes. "We're still looking for a spot where we can settle," he said to Clancy. "It's been hard on Hans, specially. He was just starting to make friends around the marsh, but now, you know, everyone's scattered."

"Oh, shoot," said Clancy. "It's just a shame, isn't it? Well, at least he has friends here at St. Aloysius." Clancy, having been raised in relative isolation from his own kind, had never had friends of his own species or age, and so had no real sense of how the companionship of beings of similar age and outlook and experience could be particularly consoling. "Do you think it would help if I had a talk with him?" he asked Magnus.

Magnus, knowing his middle child's lofty temperament,

doubted that the reverend rat, as winsome as he certainly was, would get anywhere with Hans, but he figured a few kind words wouldn't hurt. "I think that might be all right...." he said.

"Oh, good," said Clancy. "Tell him if he wants to, to come see me this afternoon, after the church is clear."

◈◈◈

It was well past sundown, and approaching Clancy's usual bedtime, when Hans finally appeared at the edge of the woods, first as two gleaming eyes, then as a slim, graceful, silent shadow, then as a three dimensional figure of flesh, making his way along the east perimeter of the community garden to stand before the rat, his head held high and his ears alert, as if he was prepared, at the slightest hint of trouble, to fight or fly.

"Hey, Hans!" said Clancy. "I'm so glad you decided to come see me! Your daddy told me that you're pretty sad about that new highway extension, and having to move and all."

"I'm not sad," said young Hans, and his deep brown eyes blazed rather ominously in the dying twilight. "I'm mad. I hate them."

Clancy put a paw to his snout. The last thing he'd expected was to hear such an ugly sentiment from a creature so young and beautiful. *Oh, Lord,* Clancy thought to himself, *don't listen to him. He didn't mean that!* Clancy knew from his own experience that it was sometimes difficult to distinguish his dislike of something or somebody from his fear of it or them. And yet it seemed clear from the cold, firm intensity of Hans' statement that, at least in the usual sense of being somehow overpowered, he was afraid of nothing. Clancy, barely the size of the tail of the young yet imperious creature standing before him, felt rather overpowered himself.

Remembering, however, that he was obliged to be pastoral, Clancy told himself that Hans had reason to be upset, and that his feelings should be respected, but that he must not be encouraged to hate. "Oh, Hans, I think it's terrible, that you all have had to go through this. It must be awful, to have to start all over like that, but..."

"It's not just awful," said the young deer quietly, but without a hint of tenderness. "It's wrong. And I don't care what my dad or anyone else says—the humans should have to pay for what they've done to us. They ruin everything for everybody, and they always have." And Hans, very likely without realizing it, lowered his head with its velveteen horns as if to challenge some approaching adversary.

Clancy backed up a few steps, hoping he didn't appear too obviously rattled. "Well, you know, Hans...I don't think they really realize what they're doing when they do these things. You know, they really don't seem to understand we have to have some place to live, too...."

In that Clancy himself lived among the humans, albeit without their knowledge, he felt a bit obligated to defend them. After all they weren't always the ones trespassing, were they! "But I know that your dad will find you all a place just as nice as the old one, and maybe even nicer! You know, I hate it myself when things change, but sometimes they have to change, and we have to remember that God is in charge, and knows what's best for everybody...even the humans...."

Hans, having lifted his head, gazed over and past Clancy at the blank stone wall of the church building and the large window that looked into the now empty rector's office. Then he shifted his head with a slight twist of his long slim neck and looked eastward towards the city of men. "I don't think anyone's' in control. The trees are dead and gone. And some of the birds. And some of the squirrels and snakes and possums. And some of my friends."

Once again Clancy felt a strong urge to defend the human race, but deep down he knew that, with a few exceptions, their unfathomable and self-serving behavior was impossible to defend.

"Is there anything I can do to help, Hans?" was all he could think to say, and he said it with more evident timidity that he would have wanted.

"No," said Hans, opening his eyes. "It's too late."

"Well..." said Clancy, not sure what to make of that. "I'll just keep you in my prayers."

At that the young deer stepped back, then took off into the night.

❧

HANS WAS LEARNING. He was learning effortlessly, as if there was something in the air that imparted to him a kind of sinister wisdom regarding the humans, something that helped him understand what they knew, and what they did not know, and what they needed, and what they feared. Compulsively, he surveilled them. The more he observed of them, the more he understood about them, and the angrier and more contemptuous he became. But this was a cool, clean, steady, almost elegant anger, befitting the robust delicacy of his form. Since his family's displacement, Hans had taken to venturing ever so carefully into the human world under the cloak of night. He discovered, by moving along the edge of the treeline, that some distance down the boulevard a network of narrower roads branched off, penetrating into a once densely and now haphazardly wooded area. Here numberless humans had built their ugly, squarish, impenetrable dwellings. Hans felt drawn closer and closer to these bleak, artificial structures. Those that were not enclosed within fence work he was sometimes able to approach and peer into, for they were usually punctuated with transparent panels. He was very often disgusted by what he saw; his disgust had the same steady, adamantine and subtle quality of his anger. For the most part these strange, denuded upright creatures spent their evenings immobile in front of flat moving images which cavorted and contorted in mad displays on rectangular planes of various sizes, but from time-to-time Hans observed them consuming food that they pierced with extensions from their limbs and placed in their mouths. On a few vile occasions he observed them mating. And on one reconnaissance, he witnessed a scene in which a large male human subdued and overcame and injured what was apparently one of his own offspring. It was this last nightmarish scenario, as a matter of fact, that sealed Hans' conviction that the humans were beyond redemption. His father, and the reverend, and the other creatures of the church who seemed content to accept the world that the humans were making just did not know—because they did not want to know —how evil their oppressors could be.

⚜

IT BEING a major holiday weekend for the humans, traffic was heavy on the highway leading into the coastal town, and so the boulevard and the secondary roads were a veritable buffet for Bertram. Snakes and raccoons and squirrels and opossums and deer galore, and Bertram was glad he had Sudie Mae and his remaining family with whom to share the bounty. It was just a shame that he was still having trouble finding a mate to give him a clutch of fledglings, for certainly there was enough to feed a whole flock of buzzards! Oh, well, he consoled himself as he circled the main arteries, I'm still young. And if I say so myself, not too hard on the eyes. This positive estimation of his own appearance was bolstered by the fact that his daddy, a parent almost wholly critical of him, had nevertheless always held that Bertram, like himself, was a fine male specimen.

Such were the desultory musings of the young buzzard, as he spiraled down towards a stretch of shoulder along the highway from which tantalizing fumes were invisibly rising. The lower he got, the more clearly he could discern that a woodchuck, or at least the splayed remains of that type of creature, lay fresh and juicy on the asphalt. Oh, he loved woodchuck! Such rich, fatty meat! Bertram felt so blessed that he took a moment to close his eyes and thank Clancy's Lord for providing such a tasty treat. It was at that point that he sensed he was not alone with the corpse, and his eyes flew open. He glanced around and saw, at the edge of the forest, just a few yards away, a not unfamiliar young buck.

"Hey!" he cried, startled. Then recognition dawned. "Hey, aren't you one of Magnus' kids?"

Hans stepped forth and regarded the buzzard with his beautiful and unyielding brown eyes. "Yes."

"Well, I thought so!" Bertram said. The freshly killed woodchuck lay between them, plump and steaming in the heat, and Bertram's stomach grumbled with anticipation. Oh, it was going to be so yummy! But it would be impolite, if not offensive, wouldn't it, to just start gorging. He wanted to be companionable to a fellow member of the church, but boy, he sure wished that the deer would go away so he could chow down! He figured a subtle hint wouldn't hurt. He indicated the dead animal with a nod. "Poor thing," he said. "I always feel bad for fresh meat like this, even though, you know, it's how I feed my family...."

"It's not *your* fault he's dead," Hans said. His quiet voice was flat. He looked past the buzzard, and Bertram turned to follow the deer's gaze, and he got the point. Automobiles guided internally by humans sped past them one after the other, heading into town, too many to count, and though some drivers and passengers glanced at the curious, grotesque spectacle of a dead woodchuck lying between a buzzard and a deer, they just kept on going at their inexorable, unnatural rate of speed.

"Oh, I know it's not my doing, but still—I just don't know...." Bertram fumbled to express himself. He hated talking about his diet to non-buzzards. He wasn't sure why he'd even brought it up, apart from the fact that something about this young deer made him a little nervous.

"They should be stopped," Hans said after a moment, his

voice at once soft and steely. "All of them. Or at least the ones around here."

Bertram was taken aback. He was accustomed to hearing the human race disparaged....His own daddy had hated them with a passion, but of course his daddy hated most creatures that were not exactly the same as himself, inside and out. Still, Bertram had never heard anyone suggest that the entire species should be wiped out. It seemed extreme. At the same time, he found that he couldn't help but wonder what a freshly deceased human might taste like.

The young deer regarded Bertram, and what he said next came so uncannily close to what Bertram had been thinking that it chilled the buzzard to the bone. "It would mean more meat to go around for you and your kind. Meat that *deserves* to be eaten...."

Bertram swallowed hard, and not just because the fumes still wafting from the corpse between them were so tantalizing. What was the young buck saying? Could he really be suggesting that he, Bertram, be a party to...violence?

"Have you lost your mind?" gawped Bertram instinctively. "I think something must have bit you and gave you rabies. You're not making any sense. You can't kill humans! They'll kill you right back! And besides, it isn't right. Just ask the Reverend. Thou shalt not kill. That's what Jesus said. The Reverend'll tell you."

For Hans, to encounter a show of spunk from any creature involved in the St Aloysius Jr. community was novel. He regarded the buzzard before him with the beginnings of respect. "Maybe you're right."

Bertram blinked. Having come from a contentious family, it never failed to throw him when someone accepted his opinion without argument. "Well," he said. "I don't really think you have rabies. But you can't just talk about killing like it's nothing. That's not right."

"Maybe not," said the young buck. "But I don't understand..."

Hans could not prevent a kind of fervor—something that his cool lofty air normally kept at bay—from affecting his vocalizations. "...why we all just sit by and watch them take over and ruin everything. No one takes a stand. No one tries to stop them."

Bertram thought about it. He had to admit: the young buck had a point. It was universally felt, if not often discussed among secular urban wildlife, that the way the humans conducted themselves was on the whole selfish and destructive. But no one ever did anything about it. "I guess we're all just too busy," he said.

Hans' ear twitched. "What's the point of living?" he wondered, and he seemed to be speaking primarily to himself, "If we can't make a difference."

Bertram could think of innumerable reasons for simply getting on with life in spite of the uncertainties and injustices of animal existence. There was good, rotten meat, beautiful vultures, his friends at St. Aloysius Jr...but he sensed correctly that Hans was not asking him for an answer.

"My father thinks the best thing to do is to stay out of their way," Hans went on. "But what good does that do? They just take more and more. They aren't going to stop. Until somebody..." Here he paused and flicked a glance at Bertram. "...or somebodies with some spine stops them. Or at least takes a stand that they can't ignore."

The young deer lifted his noble head, with its sturdy thick neck, its sensitive broad nose, its beautiful brown eyes, and the formidable branching antlers, their clear bone color breaking through patches of dun velvet. The ears twitched, then lay back, as if hearing and accepting, in the silence following his subtle appeal for comradeship, that he would act alone. "Enjoy your meal," he said again, and he turned and bounded off into the forest.

Bertram devoured the succulent flesh of the dead groundhog, but without any of his usual relish and pleasure. He now wished he hadn't even smelt it in the first place. The encounter with

Hans left him feeling a rare despair. There was no way this was going to end well for anybody.

ॐ

IT WAS the Reverend Jean Grey's policy to begin each day with a visualization drawn from Scripture following the preparation and prior to the consumption of her breakfast and coffee. On the day she was to interview with the vestry for the position of interim rector at St. Aloysius, she rose at 6:30am, washed her face—pale and seamed with the passage of years into what she acknowledged to be the phase of the Crone—poached an egg and toasted a slice of rye, then sat down in her usual place at the kitchen table where she took her meals and which, on account of its placement before the broad window overlooking the eastern and thus normally sunny grounds of her townhouse development, also served as her preferred place to study, journal, and contemplate. She folded her slim hands upon her soft, low-slung bosom and closed her eyes. Her inward eye, which was the bliss of her solitude, presented her instantly with the unexpected and evocative image of a lily, solitary in a vast green meadow, pale and fresh with morning dew, gradually opening its petals to imbibe the sunshine. The image was not wholly random, she thought; it brought to mind, as a matter of fact, one of her favorite passages from Scripture: the admonition of Christ to his followers to "consider the lilies of the field; they do not toil or spin." It was an image and a passage that communicated utter and divinely ordained serenity. "Blessed be..." she murmured aloud to the sunlit kitchen, then opened her eyes, genuflected loosely, and smiled. She lifted her still steaming mug of coffee to her narrow lips. The image of the lily in the valley remained alive before her mind's eye; this was somewhat unusual following a morning visualization, though not unheard of. At the same time, she felt fully present in the warm bright familiarity of her townhouse kitchenette, as the imagined scene admitted, as if from the periphery of her internal vision, first a shadow, and then the form—majestic, noble, and exuding an air of vigor—of a young buck deer. This beautiful and imagined creature approached the lily, turned its head briefly toward her as she observed, as if to observe its observer. Then it presented its downy yet formidable antlers, bowed, and began to pull up the lily by the roots and eat it. At her kitchen table, with the *New York Times* and her breakfast and coffee before her, Jean Grey gasped. "My Word!" she cried aloud.

Putting down the coffee that had not even met her lips, she once again closed her eyes in a vain attempt to reexperience the vision. But it was gone, its clarity and mysteriously unbidden quality now a mere memory. She knew, from former experience, that there was nothing to do now but set aside the craving for more and consciously appreciate the experience, whatever it might signify. "So mote it be," she said to herself. "Thank you, Spirit." She pressed together her palms, separated them, and began to eat and drink and read. Whatever the showing signified, its significance would reveal itself in time. Or not.

That settled, she broke her fast, brushed her teeth, showered, dressed in her clerical twinset, accessorized with her favorite art deco print silk scarf and pyramid earrings, took a few moments in front of the mirror to try to fluff some life into her limp chlorine colored short haircut, misted her houseplants lovingly, and made her way in her dusty navy-blue Volvo to St. Aloysius Episcopal Church on the other side of town.

There was no rush. She was in the habit of giving herself plenty of time and the interview was, after all, merely a formality, as the diocesan buzz held that St. Aloysius was in fact a moribund parish, and no one in their right mind, so she'd come to understand, would volunteer to clean up the mess left by the feckless, self-serving and allegedly alcoholic Reverend Silas DeBassompierre. Luckily, she said to herself silently as she drove, her countenance arranging itself into a pursed yet mirthful expression, I'm an old ESTJ, the Guardian, solidly in my *left* brain, and I love to arrange chaos into order. Her late-in-life call to ministry had proceeded, not from the typical sense of something missing in life, but from her innate sense of her own competence, her delight in problem-solving, and her willingness —rare in women of her capabilities—to suffer fools. She was at heart a successful businesswoman, and the church was, in a certain sense, an organization like any other. And while St. Aloysius might well have come, like all systems will, to the end of its viability, there was some spiritual virtue in making the best of such things. Jean Grey was excited about this opportunity, short-lived as it might be. At 62, she too had no guarantees. And from her preliminary interview with the Senior Warden, which had taken place two weeks previously, she'd left with the impression that, dysfunctional and failing as the church may be, there were some indications of wholeness and holiness. The building itself was well maintained, the grounds neatly if not meticulously kept, and she'd been pleased to see that there was a community garden. And she'd taken an immediate, instinctual liking to the parish administrator, a fortyish young woman named Grace Holbach, whose general attitude towards her work was one of wry affectionate exasperation, as toward an eccentric, difficult yet winsome toddler. "Attendance is low...pledges are low..." Grace had said to her, "...and it's not all because of Silas. This isn't a church for just anyone. But it's still a good church."

As it should be, the Reverend Jean Grey reflected as the GPS alerted her to the fact that in half a mile she should turn left, having arrived at her destination. No one thing is for all, that is the beauty of particularity. How boring, if we all were content with the same things. For her own part, Jean Grey maintained that she would be more than willing to forego Heaven itself if it was nothing more than like-mindedness. So struck was she by this self-realization that she could not be sure, afterwards, that she had been paying attention to the road when she nearly struck the deer.

Looking back upon the near disaster, it really was as if the creature had appeared on the boulevard out of nowhere. But of course that was impossible. Still, there was something deeply uncanny about how one moment the coast was clear, and the next moment she was within inches and seconds of a terrible collision. Providentially, despite her age, her reflexes were as swift and sure as those of any younger driver, and just in time she slammed on the brakes hard enough for the shoulder strap of her seat belt to sting against her collarbone. And there, gazing at her accusingly through the windshield, stood a deer, identical, it seemed to her, to the one in her morning visualization, but close up and in the flesh—and from its extraordinary stillness in the face of its near destruction, formidable. As their eyes seemed to meet through the dusty Volvo windshield, Jean Gray became aware that she had soiled herself. There was no way now that she could go through with the second interview.

Jean Grey did not consider herself to be a prophet, but neither was she a fool. This was no coincidence or random encounter; there was more to this deer, like Balaam's ass, than met the eye. The deer turned and made its leaping way into the woods beyond the church, and Jean Grey made a U-turn and drove herself home. She drew a bath, and only after she felt restored to herself did she telephone that nice Grace Holbach at St. Aloysius to explain that she had suddenly become stricken gastrointestinally, and that that was why she failed to appear. She felt that to bring up the deer would be to invite speculation as to her mental and emotional stability—and that, she knew, was the last thing a newly ordained woman of more than middle age needed. And now that the danger was past, it seemed to her that the deer itself had not been to blame.

"We thought it might be something like that," said Grace. "Well, these things happen. I'll let the Vestry know you had an emergency, and I'll be back in touch soon to reschedule."

"Don't bother, dear," said Jean Grey. "My mind-body connection suggests to me that it is for the best not to proceed forward at this time. And I always listen to the mind-body connection. I'll be in touch as soon as possible. That's a promise."

At her desk in the administrative suite at St. Aloysius, Grace found herself at once relieved and disappointed. She'd happened to like the blowsy, rather lofty, yet genial old woman priest when she'd come for her first interview. But she wasn't sure she was ready to hand over the reins of the church, having held them since long before old Silas left for Harvard.

OTTOLINE COULDN'T BELIEVE she'd been the only one to hear the unfortunately not unfamiliar sound of screeching brakes right in front of the Church that morning. When she'd hopped up onto the small cross of the ornamental belfry she saw a dark blue sedan, which, if she'd been human, she would have recognized as a late model Volvo. It come within inches of colliding with the deer, whom she did recognize as Magnus' young buck Hans.

"Oh, Reverend, it came so *close!*" she moaned to Clancy that afternoon when he emerged from the church for his usual visit at the end of the day. "It makes me sick to think about it! If that car hadn't screeched to a stop, I'm afraid we'd be planning poor Hans' funeral! I don't understand it! He knows better than to cross the street that time of day! And he's normally off somewhere deep in the woods anyway! What in the world possessed him?!"

"That was Hans?!" cried Clancy. As a matter of fact, he had heard the screech of tires and the crunch of gravel himself. The noise had awakened him from yet another uneasy dream. For, since the Reverend DeBassompierre and Macrina's departure, he'd found it was sometimes difficult to find a reason to get up at a reasonable hour in the morning, since there was no reverend to observe and no conversation with Macrina to look forward to.

"Yes, it was..." Ottoline shuddered. "It *was* Hans, and like I said, I don't know what he was even doing there. It was so strange, Reverend—he just stepped in front of that moving car as if it were nothing more than the wind. And when the car finally came to a stop, he just turned and looked right inside it at the human driving it, and then he ran off. Reverend, I could see that human inside the car, and she was shaking like a leaf! Reverend, it was almost as if he was trying to scare her to death!"

Clancy took this all in and shuddered, for the whole scenario as Ottoline so vividly described it had the quality of a bad omen. Hans' behavior lately was getting more and more inexplicable and alarming. "Oh, Ottoline!" he wailed. "What am I going to do?! Do you think Hans is trying to hurt himself? He's always been so nice, just like Magnus, but ever since the new highway started going through...well, he's not normal! Even Magnus says so! I tried to talk to him, you know, but I'm not sure he even listened to me, it's almost like he wants to be mad, and stay mad, and get even madder!"

What the Reverend was saying rang true to Ottoline, as from what she'd witnessed that morning, the young deer had gone beyond the pale of survival-based behavior. It was almost as if he had become in some hidden sense human: invasive, destructive, restless, tormented to frenzy by some implacable inner chaos.

"I just don't understand..." Clancy said, unconsciously twisting and kneading his tail. "Doesn't he realize he's worrying his father to death?"

⊛

AS DEEP AS he could be in the dwindling woods behind the churchyard of St. Aloysius, Magnus and his spouse and their offspring grazed in a tiny sunlit clearing. Magnus was preoccupied with his middle buck's strange behavior of late; Hans grazed as far away from the rest of the family as possible, as if he did not want to be any more associated with them than he had to be.

As a matter of fact, Magnus had never been as worried about

anything as he was lately about Hans. Never outgoing but always thoughtful, Hans seemed so altered by the recent upheaval that Magnus felt as if he no longer knew his own kid. Though the other youngsters had become somewhat obstreperous, they had been amenable to correction. But Hans, without being openly defiant, was not listening to his father. He was, for example, disappearing for hours at a time in the middle of the night, which worried the entire family and was particularly frightening for his mother. "Hans." Magnus had upbraided him sternly after the most recent disappearance. "You know better than this. You know what kind of danger you're putting yourself in, and you know what it's doing to the rest of us. Anything could happen. I know you're not happy about having to leave the marsh. None of us are. But we've got to be considerate of each other if we're going to get through all this."

Hans had ducked his head, averting it slightly to the east to clearly signal that this presentation of his budding antlery was not meant as a gesture of aggression, but of deference, howsoever grudging. "I'm sorry, Father," he'd muttered.

Magnus's nostrils flared. His son's apology sounded sincere enough, and yet there was still a subtle note of sad insolence, as if he really believed that simply mouthing an empty apology would satisfy his father.

"Son," said Magnus. "Hans. Maybe all this has been harder on you than the rest of us. You're at that age, I know, when you want to feel in charge. But son, you have to realize, there's only so much that we can do when it comes to what happens to us. Being a deer, son, doesn't get any easier even when you sprout a rack, or even when you get to be my age. The world is so wild, and there's so much to watch out for, and it's easy to get so focused on one danger that you lose sight of all the others. Son, that's why you can't just hold onto what the humans have taken away. There's nothing we can do about it. And son, no matter what, no matter how hard you fight, things can't stay the same forever, because if they did, it would be worse than if they didn't.

Trust me, you have to remember that, son. You've got your whole life ahead of you."

Hans kept his head respectfully lowered, but deep inside, he seethed without ceasing. Why didn't his father understand what to Hans was so clearly evident? It wasn't just about their old habitat, that was just the beginning....The humans were only getting worse. Getting out of their way was getting them nowhere. Hans knew his father was only trying to survive, but that meant playing it safe. Hans didn't feel he had anything to lose. But he wasn't yet so bold that he could say this to his father, so he said nothing.

※

PROFESSOR SILAS DEBASSOMPIERRE, MDiv, ThD, Lecturer in Patristic Theology and Koine Greek at Harvard Divinity School, looked down upon the human menagerie of Harvard Square from where he sat alone at a small concrete table, the surface of which was designed to function as a checker or chessboard should the person or persons seated before it have a companion and the desire and the implements with which to play. Silas DeBassompierre had neither checkers nor chessmen nor anyone to play with; he did have a cup of hot coffee, however, with which he was, for the moment, more than content. It was Thursday afternoon, bright, sunny, and warm, but not so warm that he was uncomfortable in his dark slacks, white oxford shirt and grey tweed blazer, and he had just taught the last class of his third week as a faculty member of Harvard Divinity School. He was living his dream, and it was finally beginning to sink in that it was not a mere dream, but the reality he was born for. Just looking out at the Square, which in his happiness he fancied was not unlike some holy shrine that summoned to itself pilgrims from all walks of life, of every complexion, costume, and habit. Such was the intensity of purpose, and thus of life, that Harvard Square could boast. With his height, his generally striking appearance, and the contrast of his coloring, the Reverend tended to stand out in a crowd. But not here, where everyone, it seemed, had something interesting and intense about them. It was refreshing, he reflected, to blend in while still retaining his individuality. He mused that perhaps the beatific vision was analogous.

He raised his cup of coffee, he sipped and swallowed, and his eyebrow arched. The beverage had not exactly grown cool, but it was becoming lukewarm. He sipped again. It was still refreshing, and if he wanted to badly enough, he could simply go back into what used to be the Au Bon Pain and order a fresh cup. But for now, he was perfectly content with his lot.

And yet...he had to chuckle to himself. As at home as he felt now, and as much as he had despised his former situation at times, he couldn't deny...he was a little bit homesick. He missed St. Aloysius! He shook his head in wry wonder at his own emotional complexity. Of course, he did not miss the vestry, he did not miss 90% of the congregation, he did not miss the backwater town, he did not miss the disrespect and willful ignorance of much of the populace, and the drudgery of second-rate tourist trap city life. But he did miss Grace, and he did miss Tommy, and even Mercedes, for though they had not shared his misery, neither had they contributed to it. They had made it, in fact, bearable. He didn't want to go back to them. But he wished they were here!

He supposed it wasn't surprising. He'd been in Boston for over three weeks now, and it was about time, he supposed, that he found himself somewhat at loose ends. It was Thursday afternoon, after all, and his working week was at an end, and the unscheduled three-day weekend flaunted itself before him like a saucy harlot. Of course, there was worship on Sunday morning in the opulent chapel of the Anglican Benedictine monastery overlooking the river, where he sometimes met with his spiritual director Brother John, but apart from that...nothing but free time.

He peered into the small sipping slot of the plastic lid of his coffee cup, as if trying to discern the level of liquid within. Free time—the phrase struck him as being at once anodyne and an indictment. The past two weekends he'd spent at least partly with his best friend George, George's pleasant wife Phillipa, and their toddler. He felt sure that he'd be welcome at their home this weekend as well, for at least a meal or two. But he had not been invited and didn't want to presume. No, he was on his own until Sunday, whether he heard from George and Phillipa or not. He must not overdepend upon them. It would not be respectful. And part of his bargain with God, when the manna of this opportunity had fallen from heaven into his lap, was that he would make an effort, insomuch as it was possible, to come out of his shell. Of course, when he'd made that deal, he thought it would be easy. He had not reckoned upon the fact that he was now pushing uncomfortably close to his forties, and more set in his ersatz monastic ways than he'd realized. He was contented— too contented, he thought—with the silent steady company of Macrina.

This new life, this new heaven, and this new earth, was not the absolute deliverance from himself that he'd anticipated. He might have known. For there was, in his personal eschatology, no real place for perfection. Perfection, he maintained, was a peculiarly consumerist, capitalist modern concept completely foreign to the antiquity out of which the heart of his religion emerged. What would being be, after all, without some creative friction, the tension of unmet desire?

He sucked from the tiny hole in the beverage lid the last barely warm dregs of his afternoon coffee. He stood and stretched to his full height, then, still looking down upon the teeming city square, like Nebuchadnezzar emerging from the wilderness, he squared his shoulders and descended into the underground.

❧

AFTER HIS CONFRONTATION with the human in the vehicle, which he considered to be his declaration of war, Hans leaped and bounded, penetrating the woods in a haphazard but graceful path—he felt it necessary to keep moving, to get as far away physically as he could from the encounter, for it had left him feeling, in the end, more alone in his mission than ever. Earlier he'd hoped that he might have found in Bertram a fellow traveler, someone who might understand that if there were ever to be any peace, there would have to be a show of strength and fearlessness. But of course, the death eater was as complacent in the face of growing catastrophe as the rest of those bamboozled creatures whom his father had cast his lot with. He should have known. But it would have been so nice—wouldn't it?—to have someone alongside him when battle began. I guess, Hans said to himself with noble resignation, I'm the only one around here who's had enough.

He kept to himself for the rest of the afternoon and into the night, savoring without enjoying his own company and reflecting that it was doing his mood some small good to remain this far removed from the domains of the humans, his glimpses into which always left him feeling tainted as well as enraged. And though he felt a stubborn sentimental longing to say goodbye to his family, especially his well-meaning but uncomprehending father, he figured that, when all was said and done, the less said the better it would be for all of them. For as soon as the female human who opened up the church building every morning arrived and unlocked those red double doors, he was going to charge in. He was going to storm the building and do as much damage as he could, until, inevitably, someone put an end to him. But not before they got at least a little taste of what it was like to have your habitat invaded.

Coming to a small clearing, Hans gazed up at the stars. He hadn't asked for any of this—the loneliness, the anger, the creeping dread of an inevitably violent, if meaningful end. He could not help but wonder, why him? Why did it infuriate him, more so than the rest of his family, even his strong-minded, sensitive father, that their old home place had been overrun and obliterated? The deer weren't alone in being displaced; he wasn't alone in being upset, and yet he was alone in his conviction that something had to be done immediately or the encroachment would accelerate. Why? Why couldn't he be complacent like everyone else? Like the rest of the animal kingdom, why didn't he just try to make the best of a situation beyond his power to change? He tossed his head, as if to ward off these questions. From the heavens above the newly full moon cast a pale silvery sheen upon his pelt and velveteen antlers, and he imagined that to human eyes he would, at that moment at least, appear formidable. Among his siblings, he knew without any undue pride or false humility that he was the strongest, the smartest, the most endowed with natural gifts and a striking presence. This was simply the way things were. It was these advantages, he felt, that made him uniquely responsible for the well-being of the others. To whom much is given, much is required; he seemed to remember the rat having said that recently during one of the long, often banal monologues that he referred to as sermons. Every once in a while, the rat made some remark worth pondering. Lowering his head, Hans munched meditatively on a fallen leaf. Maybe the rat, given his devotion to that peculiar human named Jesus, who had apparently died a painful death in order to save the other humans from their sins, could be made to understand. At least, Hans told himself, it was a way of saying goodbye.

HERTZ VASTLY PREFERRED sleep to waking consciousness, so he was more than a little annoyed when in the middle of the night, for Ground's sake, he was awakened by the sound of someone or something tramping past the composter. But his annoyance flared into indignation when he heard a soft, low, yet nonetheless inconsiderate voice calling out for the "Reverend."

Hertz did not immediately react, but when, after several of these increasingly unquiet summonses, there seemed to be no response from the cellar, and the stupid creature who was summoning the rat did not just take the hint and go away, Hertz uncoiled, tunneled to the nearest ventilation slot, and thrust himself halfway out of the forest-green plastic casing into the balmy night air. "Shut up!" he hissed, just as loud as he possibly could. "Some of us around here work for a living!"

Hans, his snout at the crawlspace door, started and reared back, then assumed a defensive posture, for while Hertz' voice was barely audible to him, it was decidedly confrontational, and seemed to have come out of the darkness. After a moment of absolute silence (apart from the cicadas in the distance), Hans gauged that the rude words had proceeded from the general direction of the composter. He turned in that direction and lowered his horns.

"Freeze!!" Hertz exclaimed. "Don't move one inch! If you knock over this composter, I promise you one thing, it'll be the last thing you ever knock over!" Well aware of the emptiness of this threat, Hertz nonetheless meant it, and extended himself as far as he could out of the ventilation hole as if he were himself a tusk or horn.

Hans, perceiving that the slim protrusion from the side of the composter was addressing him, experienced, for the first time since his earliest fawnhood, wonder. Of course, throughout one's life, one came across earthworms from time to time, usually following a rainstorm, but in that he never considered that he and that type of creature had much in common, he'd never really spoken to one. This was, he had to admit, one interesting thing about his father's new and inexplicable attachment to this "church." It had had a cosmopolitanizing effect, bringing him into contact with all types of creatures that before he'd never really noticed. "I wasn't about to knock over anything," he said. "I let things alone if they leave me alone. I'm no human."

Hertz could have gone limp with relief. But he held himself firm, just in case. "Well, that's a low bar," he said drily. "Neither am I, thank Ground! Now, do you mind? I've got a whole colony here to run, and we want peace and quiet. Come back tomorrow and talk to the rat if you have to."

"I won't be around tomorrow," said the young deer in a morosely apocalyptic tone. "It doesn't matter. Just tell him...tell him to tell my father I'm sorry. Tell him to let everyone else know that they should lay low for a while. It's too late for me to back down now, and I don't want anyone to get hurt except for me...and *them*."

Despite himself, the worm was alarmed. "Sorry for what? What the Ground are you up to?"

Hans averted his face; his nostrils flared in the cool of the evening. "I'm going to let them know I'm not scared of them, even if everyone else is."

"Who?" said Hertz, though he knew.

"The humans," said Hans. "They ruin everything."

Hertz's sympathy, in spite of his better judgment, gravitated toward the young deer, for after all, the kid was clearly not naïve to what far too few of the creatures he knew were aware of, and that was the real and dangerous and virtually unstoppable lunacy of the majority of the human race—if not the animal kingdom as a whole. "That's true, kid," he said, with more tenderness than he knew he was capable of. "But don't think for a minute that anything you or I could do will make any real difference. You can't stop stupid. All you can do is hope to Ground that it gets so stupid it just ends up destroying itself somehow without taking too many of the rest of us with it. That's it." And so saying, the worm extended himself even further out of the slot in the composter casing, and with a slight waving motion seemed to beckon. "C'mere," he said. "I want to show you something."

Hans blinked. Being told what to do, and that by such a lowly creature as a worm, chafed against his sense of self-possession. Still, the worm rather surprisingly and gratifyingly shared his contempt for humanity, so perhaps he was worth paying some attention to. The young deer stepped closer, and Hertz coiled himself around the topmost prong of the deer's right antler. "Head to the office park," he said. "You know what I'm talking about?"

Hans didn't dignify that with an answer. He knew where everything was in this section of the city. He lifted his rack with a haughty motion, but Hertz had a firm, moist grip and was not one bit dislodged.

With terse directional commands, Hertz guided the young buck some distance into town along the edge of the woods, until they reached a grassy spot near the far edge of a sprawling office complex near the hospital. Hertz told Hans to slow down and bend his head so that Hertz could get orientated, and after the deer wandered a bit Hertz told him to stop.

"Here!" exclaimed the worm. "Right here." And the deer came to a halt with his head bent over a patch of grass that was indistinguishable from the turf surrounding it. "This..." declared the worm, "...this is where it all began for me. I'd know it anywhere."

Hans, with the instinctive, unthinking move of a much younger deer, prodded at the patch of ground with one forehoof, before remembering himself and resuming a dignified stillness.

"Go ahead," said Hertz. "I don't care. Stomp on it all you want."

The realization that he was behaving in a thoughtlessly destructive manner caught Hans up short. He reared back a step or two and lowered his head and rack as if in silent apology to the patch of earth.

"It doesn't matter," said Hertz. "They're all dead and gone now. Flooded out a long time ago in one of those big storms that come through here every summer. I'd be dead and gone along with them if they hadn't tried to trick me. Suckers. Now I'm in a situation where not even one of those storms can drown me and my colony out. And all because they thought they were being cute. I hope they suffered. I hope they suffered a lot."

Hans' ears pricked, hearing in the words of the worm a deep and abiding sense of injustice and a longing for vengeance that possibly matched his own. He remained still, as if awaiting further orders.

"You mammals have it easy," Hertz said after a while. His usually gravelly voice was now slick with resentment. "Born right out of your mothers, too weak and stupid to survive on your own, or to be expected to, always got someone looking after you your whole life practically. Well, it's not like that for the rest of us. Ground forbid you should know what it's like not to belong to anybody, to just be one of Ground knows how many eggs so that your mother doesn't even bother to keep track of them all...." Hertz paused. Suddenly he wanted to be far away from this unremarkable spot, even though, truth be told, it was a spot of no real significance; he had no idea where exactly in the park his native colony was located, as he'd been carried away from it by a robin who'd intended to eat him, but who had lost her grip on him as she flew over the graveyard of St. Aloysius, which is how he'd eventually ended up clinging to Rev. DeBassompierre's shoe and tracked into the sanctuary, where he'd been rescued by Clancy and nursed back to health in the soil of the potted fern that hung over Grace's desk. But this spot of grass was as good as any. For what he was trying to convey to the angry deer was a truth not dependent upon geographical accuracy.

"I stood out." Hertz conjured from his memory a younger self far more confident and complimentary to his current self-perception than had actually been the case. The reality of the insecure young Hertz who would have done anything to be accepted by his more robust peers and the charismatic leaders of the colony remained unacknowledged. "And if you stand out, you get noticed; if you get noticed, you better watch out. The ones on top will think you're a threat. The big shots told me I was one of them, the elite. But what they really wanted from me was for me to do the dirty work for them. They had this idea that to keep the colony going strong, every once in a while someone has to be offered to the birds. They took me in and fattened me up and then I was thrown out like a piece of meat. And I guess they figured that was the end of me. Well, it didn't quite turn out that way. I put up a fight and I made it, and where are they now? Who knows and who cares. And I'll tell you another thing: I swore I'd never trick anyone the way they tricked me! And you can ask any of the worms in my colony—no one thinks they're any better than anyone else, not even me. You may think that only humans are the selfish and crazy ones, but you've got a lot to learn. Every single creature on this earth—or in it—has evil in its heart, even if it doesn't have a heart. And that means you, too. You really think you can make some big stink to be a hero and it won't backfire on the rest of us? You're as stupid as any human I've ever seen. And a coward, too, if you just take the easy way and go after the ones that run the church— and I know that's what you're up to. And Ground only knows what that crazy rat'll do, probably lose his mind even more than he already has. He really believes the ones in that church—or their God, at least—give a damn about the rest of us. But he's right about one thing. They aren't the ones in charge. Their God isn't either, no matter what they say, or wouldn't He stop this madness? Now get me home. This place makes me sick...."

Almost as if he were one of those horses trained by humans to obey his rider's command, Hans turned about-face, feeling rather as if he were under a spell. At the same time, he was—and knew he was—completely in command of his own behavior. He did not have to do what the worm wrapped around his antler ordered. He was perfectly free, in fact, to fling the creature into the air and onto the ground with a brisk enough toss of his head. But the fact was that the worm, his bitter authoritativeness belying his apparent physical insignificance, had elicited in Hans an unfamiliar attitude—one of admiration. This worm, he understood, had no illusions. This worm was acquainted with exile and darkness of heart. This worm knew the truth, and obviously understood the way Hans was feeling, understood more readily and thoroughly than Hans' own kind, than the reverend rat, than perhaps even Hans himself. Hans knew he would be foolish to dismiss this worm's wisdom. He began to move, stealthily and carefully along the city streets as the worm on his antler directed him unnecessarily back to the backside of St. Aloysius Episcopal Church.

"Let me get back in," said Hertz. "Bow down." And, as if he were making an act of obeisance before the smelly plastic compost bin, Hans lowered his horns. Hertz unwound himself and inserted himself back into his domain, shivering with relief at the fetid warm moisture. Once in, he turned and extended his tip to regard the young deer once more.

"Relax," he said. "Take a load off for a second. No one's around."

Still under his willing obedience, Hans lowered himself onto his haunches.

"Listen," Hertz said again. "You're a smart kid like I was. I can see that. Smarter than most mammals. You aren't all warm and fuzzy like a lot of them. And I think you can hear what I'm saying to you. Don't do anything I wouldn't do, kid. It won't make any difference; it'll only be more of the same. I get it. Those humans are the worst things in the world. But let me tell you something I wish I'd known when I was your age and all fired up to get revenge. If there's one thing that's true about every living thing under that stupid broiling sun—human, worm, or whatever—if it cares about anything besides itself, that means it doesn't have any control. The world belongs to the ones who look out for Number One. And you can't get back at them no matter what you do. You can't touch them. And if you think there's any of that type around here, you're out of your mind. The humans around here are nobodies. Going after them is like going after the rat. What I'm saying is, you make trouble around here, and you're making trouble for the ones who really aren't responsible.... They just can't change anything. At least not anything that you want to see changed. But—" Hertz suddenly felt limp, and paused. Reluctance to admit something positive was always enervating. "But you know what? If it wasn't for them, I wouldn't have made it. You think I put this composter here? And put myself in it? No.... I hate to break it to you, but it was that human reverend and his secretary and that crazy rat that saved me. So cool it. If a real demon shows up, I'll let you know. I can spot them a mile away. Trust me."

Hans lowered his horns...not in obeisance, but in acceptance. And, he had to admit, he felt relief, the relief that comes to a reasonable creature heading for trouble upon being firmly checked. The beautiful young buck, knowing that no more needed to be said, rose and sprang into the woods to find his family and set his father's mind at ease.

❦ 5 ❦

SUPERBIA (PRIDE)

"**I** DON'T KNOW ABOUT THIS ONE, Reverend," said Bertram after the St. Aloysius' Choir's fourth attempt at Ave Maria. "This is a tough one. Lots of high notes and lots of long ones, I'm not sure any of us got those kind of pipes. Maybe we ought to sing something we already know a little better...."

"Oh, durn," said Clancy. "It's just the right song to go along with my sermon idea. But if ya'll aren't comfortable with it, well, I guess I can try to figure something else out. I wish I could sing, I'd sing it myself if I could, I just think it's so beautiful...." And, allowing himself to be swept away, as was his wont at times, by his own enthusiasm, the Reverend Rat lifted his lofty if rather weak falsetto, and squeaked the first couple of lines, then succumbed to a fit of breathlessness before gasping and beginning again. And so it happened that for a moment Clancy thought that a miracle had taken place, and that God had transformed his meager little voice into that of an angel from heaven. Because, unbeknownst to him, from seemingly out of the blue, a voice so melodious, supple, and sweet— and, what's more, in tune — accompanied him. Clancy was so amazed that he fell silent almost immediately, but the other voice warbled on, rounding out the first chorus of the Ave Maria. And then, as if out of the dusky sky itself, a small dark form took shape, and came to perch upon the rim of the birdbath, beneath which the choir held their practice. "I don't mean to be rude," he said. "But I was just going to pop in to freshen up in your bath here—hope you don't mind—and I couldn't help overhearing. That's a gorgeous piece, but you really need to work on your technique. You don't have any breath control at all."

The Rat Reverend—and the members of the choir of St. Aloysius Jr.—regarded this visitor with varied degrees of surprise and consternation. Sudie Mae, for her part, was at once suspicious of the sleek little bird with its apparent lack of inhibition. It was a pretty little thing to be sure, with feathers that at a glance appeared as black as the Reverend's eyes, but which were on closer inspection a rich purple, almost mesmerizing in their dazzling yet deep darkness. And its voice, even as it chirped conversationally, possessed that same bright yet august quality. But where had it come from—and with what nerve?—to suggest that the Reverend's singing wasn't good enough!

"Praise the Lord! Welcome! Welcome!" Clancy stood himself up to get a good look at the stranger, who was perched on the rim of the birdbath looking down at them. "And I appreciate your honesty! I know I'm not much of a singer, so don't feel bad. In fact I praise God for your good advice, because you know, sometimes I do lose my breath when I'm preaching. If you know some exercises for that, I'd sure enough do them! But I was just telling my choir here that this is one of my favorite hymns. It's called Ave Maria. You know, it's the actual words of the Angel Gabriel to the Blessed Virgin Mary when he told her that she was going to have the baby Jesus, the Savior of the World. He's saying *Hi, Mary, you are truly blessed and so is the baby you're going to have....*"

"Who's this Mary? You?" said the bright, dark little bird with his narrow beak and lilting voice, regarding Ottoline.

"Oh, my, no!" Ottoline chuckled. "No, my name is Ottoline.

This is my mate, Stephen. This is Bertram, and this is Sudie Mae, and of course, the Reverend has introduced himself. And you are?"

"Christopher," the bird said promptly. "Christopher P. Martin. I'm a Martin, maybe you've heard of us? We're pretty well known for our voices. The humans love us."

"Oh!" exclaimed Ottoline noncommittally. For the fact was, she'd heard of martins—who hasn't?—but she had not heard anything of their voices, though it was certainly the case that this martin had a very distinctive one. "And what brings you here, Christopher, if I can call you that?"

"Oh, I've just been taking a little time to myself, self-care, you know," the smaller bird said with a whiff of evasiveness. "Sometimes you just need to get away, especially when you're under pressure. Anyway, who *is* Mary? And who is this baby? And what's an angel? And who in the world is Aloysius?"

Ottoline demurred to the Reverend Clancy, who explained, in his idiosyncratic and yet somehow intelligible way, that he was afraid he didn't know as much about Aloysius as he should, apart from the fact that St. Aloysius was the name of the Church. He also related that Aloysius himself had been a particularly helpful specimen of human being known by some as *saints*, which were persons (usually if not always deceased humans), who could be petitioned to advocate for one before God, and in honor of whom churches were sometimes named. He explained that Jesus was a human being who lived long ago. He had been (and in some sense continues to be) a manifestation of God, said God being the kind and generous Creator of everything, to whom every creature should feel gratitude. Angels, such as the afore-mentioned Gabriel, were messengers made entirely of light who could assume various forms. Church was one way for creatures to show gratitude—banding together for mutual support and companionship even across the lines of species. "We'd love for you to join us!" said Clancy, "and with your voice, maybe you'd be interested in joining the choir!"

"Okay," said Christopher P. Martin. He never turned down the opportunity to use his considerable talents. And his ear for melody being so refined that he practically had the hymn by heart after hearing it just that once, he launched into song, and his rendition of the Ave was so exquisite that even Sudie Mae, who couldn't say she welcomed this stranger, was moved.

🐀

IT GOES without saying that Clancy was thrilled to death. He related it all to Hertz with as much excitement as if the Lord Himself had deigned to join the choir. Hertz, however, as was his way, remained ill-disposed toward the newcomer whom he'd yet to meet.

"For Ground's sake!" cried Hertz. "Aren't there *enough* damn birds around here all the time?! This is why I have to keep my offspring inside, you know. No matter what you say, this church isn't safe for everyone...and you know it."

Knowing the worm as he did, the Rat Reverend Clancy was prepared for this outburst, but he was no less exasperated by it. "Oh, Hertz..." said the rodent. "You know you're being silly. I've told you a zillion times, I'm never going to let anybody eat anybody else in this congregation. It's never happened before, and it never will. And you know I haven't ever invited any robins to church because I promised you I wouldn't take that chance, and that used to make me feel like I wasn't giving *them* the chance to know their Savior, but then I realized that even if they never come to church and never hear of the Lord, I can still pray that the Lord touches their hearts, and I do pray for that, every single day. And Hertz, I know you don't really mean it, but I would love it if you wouldn't talk about birds that way. Ottoline and Steven are birds, after all, and so are Bertram and Sudie Mae, and no matter what you say, I know you love them very much, and they love you and I know they would never dream of hurting you or any of your offspring, any more than old Macrina would ever dream of hurting me, even though you know as well as I do that I was real scared of her in the beginning. Anyway, Hertz, Christopher isn't a robin. Why, he doesn't look anything like a robin, he's that pretty purply color, and every robin I've ever seen is brown and red. He's a...I believe he said he's a Purple Martin, and he promised me on his heart that he has never eaten a worm in his life, he just eats seeds and sometimes a mosquito or two when he needs energy, and of course I feel bad for the mosquitos, they're God's creatures after all too, but they can be real aggravating, and...."

Thus chattered on the Rat Reverend, his dismay at his oldest friend's characteristic yet unhealthy xenophobia yielding before his delight at having won a fresh soul for the Lord just the evening previous. It had been God's will, Clancy was certain, for it had all been so providential. What were the chances, after all, that Clancy should have attended the weekly Thursday evening practice of the St. Aloysius Jr. choir, when he hadn't attended choir practice in weeks, so busy was he lately with the demands of coming up with sermons without Reverend DeBassompierre's practice sessions to guide and inspire him. It had only been on a whim that he'd scampered over to the birdbath to see if a little musical interlude might help him think.

"He's going to be trouble," grumbled Hertz balefully. "You just mark my words. I feel it in my bones."

"Oh, Hertz...." Clancy said. "You know you don't have any bones. I think you're just being silly. I promise you, Christopher is going to be a good Christian, and you don't have to worry. And you won't believe how nice he sings!"

Hertz, whose ear for music was nearly nonexistent, simply withdrew, leaving Clancy to his absurd happiness.

❀

CHRISTOPHER P. Martin, to be sure, was also happy, if not to say relieved, at having been recruited for the choir. It could not have come about at a better time, for somehow, through means he was not quite ready yet to examine closely, he had found himself, for the first time in his short but full life, separated from his kindred, his flock. He was all alone and on his own. He wasn't sure what on earth had happened. It seemed like one moment he had been flying along in formation with the others on the way to Brazil for their annual stay in that lush and congenial climate, and the next he was on the ground, as the others had suddenly broken formation and turned on him so that he was forced to descend in a hurry. This sort of hostility had erupted before, but never before had they taken off and left him behind like this. The leader of the flock, his own cousin, even threatened him with real violence if he uttered another peep. And all Christopher P. Martin had done was suggest, to all who cared to listen, that there must be a more scenic route than along all this boring coastline.

Oh well. Christopher P. Martin was no stranger to his suggestions being resented even when they were accepted. It was the price one paid, he supposed, for more than ordinary natural endowments. He was, after all, even according to his detractors among the flock, a standout in several ways. The youngest hatchling of a prominent family, attractive in form and address, and even among similarly gifted vocalists an amazing talent, he was often called upon to convey significant messages to the group. He was possessed as well of a growing sense of himself as a potential leader, and he was ever ready with ideas as to how the day-to-day proceedings of the flock could be made more efficient and pleasant. He wasn't sure why lately everything he suggested seemed to ruffle feathers. It just goes to show you, Christopher Martin told himself after taking leave of the strange and friendly rat and tucking himself in for the night into the interior of a decorative gourd on the front porch of a gift boutique in the strip mall across the boulevard from St. Aloysius, no good bird goes unpunished. He couldn't help but agree with the rat, that some sort of guiding force had led him to a new situation where he might be better appreciated.

❧

"FRIENDS!" Clancy proclaimed from his perch atop the composter the following Sunday morning. "I want to introduce our newest member: Christopher P. Martin. Let's all give him a great big old St. Aloysius welcome! We're so happy to have you with us, Christopher!"

Gathered together in His name, the small but growing and certainly dedicated congregation of St. Aloysius Jr. Episcopal Church greeted the stranger with a warm, brief cacophony of coos, snorts, snuffling, hisses, growls, squeaks, and brays, each of which expressed, in its own way, a sincere welcome. Standing to the side of the composter/lectern/altar with the four original members of the choir, Christopher P. Martin accepted the welcome of the congregation without the slightest awkwardness or bashfulness. He simply lowered his beak in acknowledgment.

"Christopher has agreed to join our choir, and I know that we're all happy about that. He's a wonderful singer; he has a really unusual and strong voice, and he's going to be a real addition. As a matter of fact, he offered to start off our worship this Sunday with a solo that he's been practicing ever since he decided to join us earlier this week. So, let's all be real quiet and give him our full attention while he sings one of the sweetest songs I've ever heard. It's called *Ave Maria.*"

With that, Clancy sank on his haunches, gazed down upon the choir, and swayed his snout gently along to the haunting and slow melody as the young purple Martin lifted his supple voice in the first few lengthy and rising notes of that ancient and modern salutation to the Mother of God, while the original members of the choir remained still and silently attentive.

It was, it must be noted, a truly stirring performance. Even Hertz, that least musical, least bird-friendly, and most cynical of all the members of the church, had to admit that the little purple-black bird had some serious pipes and mad skills. The bird could hold a note like a grudge. He could break down a melody with all the deftness and precision and effortlessness of a snowflake descending and disintegrating upon a warm surface. By the time the Martin trilled off the final note, the entire congregation, including the original members of the choir, was quite spellbound. It took everyone a moment to come back to themselves. The first public acknowledgement of the effect of the performance, which also served to break its spell, came from the ever-irrepressible opossum Ometa, who whistled like a kettle through her snaggle teeth. "Dang!" she remarked. "I didn't understand a word of all that, but it sure sounded pretty."

Clancy, rising almost dreamily to his hind paws, so lulled into a state of adoration had he been, took a moment to collect himself. "Well," he said. "Thank you so much, Christopher, for that beautiful solo. I think everyone here can agree with Ometa that we sure don't need to understand the words to know that the Lord was speaking to us through that song. And that, I guess, is as good a place as any for me to just go ahead and preach this Sunday's sermon, which is taken from today's reading from the Gospel According to Mark: "...And they took offense, and Jesus said unto them: 'A prophet is not without honor, save in his own country...'Because, you know, sometimes the most important things in life, and the most precious, too—like our Lord and Savior Jesus Christ Himself— are the hardest to understand, especially if we take them for granted, or just think we understand them. And that can be real frustrating sometimes, when the things we think we have all figured out turn out to be a lot more complicated. It means that sometimes it's more important and smarter to admit we just don't know and we don't have all the answers—even though as Christians we think we should—and that when we ourselves feel like no one understands us, it doesn't mean that someone's in the wrong.... Sometimes we just have to leave it to the Lord to tell us what He's got in mind...when He's ready."

It was, Clancy thought when he wrapped it up, not one of his better homilies, but it had some truth to it. Still, he hoped it had touched his flock in some way, or at least planted a seed. He was going to have work harder now on his preaching, he could see that! Christopher P. Martin was a tough act to follow!

⌘

IT IS by no means always the case that word travels fast among nonhuman animals. There are, after all, innumerable deep and ancient and indeed quite understandable enmities at work that necessarily make interspecies communication spotty. At the same time, however, there is often an undercurrent of shared awareness about anything in the immediate locale that is either suspicious or remarkable, and the strange regular interspecies gatherings behind one of the human buildings was considered to be both. Thus, many creatures who had either avoided or ignored Clancy's invitations to join the church nevertheless kept their eye on what was happening. So when Christopher P. Martin made his triumphant debut as a soloist, it did not go unnoticed by even the most disinterested observers. Sure, everyone knew that some birds had pretty voices, and there was no creature with any degree of sentience that had not at some point been uplifted or at least moved somehow by hearing a snatch of particularly melodious birdsong. But no creature around had ever heard anything like Christopher P. Martin's rendition of *Ave Maria*. Hence, tongues were wagging.

And so, over the course of a very few Sunday services, the attendance numbers of St. Aloysius Jr. grew steadily. Clancy regularly declared himself thrilled to death. Birds of every feather, squirrels by the dozens, frogs and skinks and snakes and various winged insects, and even a pack of coyotes had been observed enjoying the soloist's performances, though none of these unaffiliated animals ever stuck around for the entire service. Still, it was gratifying to know that in some way the Word was reaching the unchurched. From his Aunt November's teaching Clancy knew that old Satan had a stronghold among most members of the Animal Kingdom, and he knew from his own experience that the propagation of the Gospel was often one step forward and several steps back. When someone took to the skies or to the woods as he approached to welcome them and introduce himself, Clancy managed not to take it personally. He just reminded himself that the Lord was moving in ever mysterious ways to glorify His Name.

As for Christopher P. Martin, why, he couldn't be more pleased. Now, this was the sort of respect he deserved. Sometimes even he was astonished by the impact his singing could have. He'd always known, of course, that he was gifted, but it clearly wasn't until he found himself in the choir singing these strange, often plaintive, sometimes haunting, sometimes jaunty compositions called hymns and spirituals that his voice really came into its own. He wasn't sure what it was about them that gave his delivery that certain spark, but in the end he supposed it didn't really matter. He was being listened to, and that was what life was all about, wasn't it?

The other members of the choir each had mixed feelings about the fresh popularity of their performances. Of course, it was exciting to be a part of something so increasingly popular; something so impressive and powerful. But even easygoing Steven chafed at the idea that there was only one voice now that mattered. Ottoline told herself that she was being petty. Bertram had no illusions about the quality of his own very limited and gargly singing voice. But in singing, as in most things, he was full of enthusiasm, so he could relate to Christopher P. Martin's reveling in the acclaim, even as he was determined not to take second place to him. Sudie Mae was flat-out pissed-off. Who did this little squirt think he was, showing off like that? Sure, he had a good voice, but goodness wasn't everything. No one had the right to take over all the Reverend's attention.

❦

"OH, HERTZ!" Clancy, to Hertz' profound exasperation, had of late taken to the habit of visiting the composter multiple times a day to enthuse about the latest developments in the life of the church. "It's a miracle, Hertz!" he cried, oblivious to the worm's elaborate pantomime of lifelessness as he dangled limply from one of the ventilation slots in the composter casing, his usual signal that the rodent's conversation was proving tiresome. "Ometa just told me that even a whole crowd of seagulls down at the dump have heard about Christopher's singing, and they're planning to visit us this coming Sunday! She said she thinks maybe a hundred might show up! Oh, the Lord really is at work, isn't He? He's using Christopher to spread the Gospel just as sure as I'm a Christian and a rat! Just imagine, Hertz! A hundred seagulls, all accepting Jesus Christ as their personal Lord and Savior! Think of what it could mean for the Church!"

"I don't have to think of what it means," Hertz sneered. "I know what it means. It means noise and stink and trouble! Some blessing. Don't you have any sense? Even *you* have to realize that if this keeps up, if a bunch of nasty loud creatures keep showing up every Sunday, you're going to have more than you can handle. Take it from me. I know you, rat. You don't have any idea what it takes to manage a big organization. I'll hand it to you—and don't give me any of your lip about my not having hands—I never thought any of this church stuff would last this long. You have managed not to screw it all up yet, but you're right on the edge of it, if you keep letting a bunch of riffraff that doesn't give two poops about your Jesus show up just to watch that pipsqueak sing his head off. What do you think is going to happen if a hundred seagulls show up? Those humans will see them and hear them and freak out! You think you can keep a hundred seagulls quiet? You're out of your gourd!"

"Now, Hertz..." Clancy tried to respond, even as Hertz, having come to the end of his temper, withdrew back into the composter. "It's going to be all right, Hertz. God is in control."

But even as he said so, he knew, with a familiar uneasiness, that the worm was more than likely right. He, Clancy, had a hard enough time keeping the current congregation cognizant of the need to fly beneath the human radar. A hundred seagulls were sure to attract unwanted attention. But surely God would provide!

"Lord..." he said to himself. "All I can do is leave this in Your paws. Your Kingdom come, Your Will be done. Amen!"

◈◈◈

Sudie Mae—who was, of course, the latest to join the choir until Christopher P. Martin came along—was nonetheless very invested in being a part of it. It was a point of pride for her, after having spent such a great deal of her short life intimidated by her father, and suppressing her own authority, to find herself before the congregation, using her voice. The next practice came along, and when Christopher P. Martin started right in complaining about the hymn that they had decided to work on weeks before he ever knew the church existed, Sudie Mae decided she had had enough. The little bird was just getting too big for his feathers.

"What do you mean, it's too simple!" she screeched. "It's SUPPOSED to be simple! That's what it MEANS!"

Christopher P. Martin was not a little surprised by the vehemence with which the hard-favored female buzzard was reacting! All he'd said was that he was sure they could find something a little less simple and a little more challenging to sing. He was, after all, a professional.

Ottoline, as ever, endeavored to be diplomatic. "Yes, this one is rather singsong," she said. "But, Christopher, don't you think Sudie Mae is right?—the simplicity is intentional, and really, it's part of the charm of the piece. I think we should give it a chance. I think that the church will find it an interesting departure from the baroque style we've adopted lately."

Christopher P. Martin didn't mean to give offense, but he was dubious. "Okay, but it's so short! Just four lines, no chorus, no coda? It'll be over in a heartbeat!"

"It is terse," Ottoline granted. "But let me explain, dear, apparently it's a type of song that the humans call a 'round'— that means we each sing the lines in a staggered succession and end by harmonizing. The effect is supposed to be very nice. And the simplicity, while it may constrain your range, Christopher, lends itself well to the range of all our voices. Let's give it another try, all right?"

Christopher P. Martin still had misgivings, but he felt he could afford to be gracious. "Fine with me," he said. "I can be as simple as the next bird if I have to be. Let's go, then..." And he filled his breast with the balmy evening air of the season, opened his beak, and sang. "'Tis a gift to be simple, 'tis a gift to be free, 'tis a gift to come down where we ought to be..."

There was some confusion about who was to follow, as Bertram and Sudie Mae were both eager to hear how they sounded, and so the next few moments were taken up by the four original choir members proposing one order, then another. This caused Christopher P. Martin to become impatient, and he couldn't hide it. "Listen, for something simple, this is getting too complicated. Let's do something else. What about that nice *Ode to Joy*?"

Ottoline, who liked *Ode to Joy*, and who was almost as weary as Christopher P. Martin of the whole issue, was inclined to agree. But Sudie Mae was adamant. "Why don't you calm down!" she snapped at the new bird. "We just got a little mixed up! That's why we have PRACTICE, for Pete's sake! Don't be such a brat!"

Christopher Martin looked at her with fire in his bright little black eyes. Who was this nasty, insistent creature, to call *him* a brat! Along with the indignation, he felt a bright sliver of unease, and even an uncanny familiarity: he was experiencing *déjà vu*. It was as if he'd been the object of her exasperation in some dim and inaccessible place in his memory, but of course that was not possible. As he glared at her, however, this unsettling sense of familiarity faded into a far more comfortable, if deeply unfamiliar, feeling of pity, if not compassion. He found himself feeling sorry for Sudie Mae, poor thing, so ungainly and unattractive to him, just like her brother in appearance and bearing, but of course it was all the more unfortunate in a female. He let her rudeness to him pass, congratulating himself for his forbearance.

"All right," he conceded. "Let's just start over. How about this: Bertram starts, then you Ottoline, then you, Steve, then you, Sudie Mae, then me, and then we'll all finish."

When the round was done and the last note faded on the wind, the members of the choir each, as if in unconscious consensus, avoided looking at one another. The juxtaposition of Christopher Martin's supple melodiousness with the spirited but harsh vocalizations of the buzzards, plus the rich but limited warbling of the pigeons, produced an unmistakably awkward if not ludicrous effect. It was anticlimactic, at best. Christopher Martin felt increasingly indignant. Oh, this was a big mistake! It was going to be embarrassing, not just for him, but for everybody. Couldn't they see that—or better yet, hear that?

Sudie Mae, however, felt jubilant. "That was real pretty!" she crowed. "See?!"

Christopher P. Martin held his tongue. The choir went through the arrangement a few more times, and afterwards Christopher P. Martin took off across the boulevard and sang *Ode of Joy* to himself as if to cleanse the palate of his ears.

As BIRDS swiftly converging from near and far peppered the Sunday morning sky and a larger and denser crowd of ground-dwelling creatures than he had ever before preached to populated the area around the composter, Clancy felt such an amalgamation of excitement and dread that it was all he could do not to burst. Lord, he thought, this is too much! It really is! He hadn't meant to think that, but that is what he thought. He hated to admit it, but Hertz' baleful view of things was more than likely right. Things could very easily get out of control.

"But God is in control!" Clancy reminded himself as he nervously gnawed at the tip of his tail. But the cold heavy sensation deep in his bowels that reached his testicles remained and grew all the more uncomfortable. And, as hard as he tried to perish the thought, he could not help but admit the awareness that none of these strangers were coming to hear him preach the Word of the Lord.

Well, then, he would just have to make sure he did his very best. Luckily, or providentially as the case may be, the text for the day had been particularly inspiring. He always loved to preach on odd and inexplicable incidents in the life of Christ, and this Sunday brought one of his favorites: the pericope from Luke in which Jesus invites himself to sup at the house of a little person who had climbed a tree to behold him above the crowd. Clancy had a great deal to say about Christ's affirmation of this determined, disadvantaged individual.

God is in control, he reiterated to himself. "Praise the Lord!" he announced to the gathering, lifting his forepaws in a gesture meant to command silence and attention. "Welcome to all our visitors this morning here at St. Aloysius Jr. Episcopal Church! (An open and affirming Christian community.) I am Reverend Clancy, and in just a minute, we are going to begin our regular Sunday service, where we worship the Lord through Scripture, Song, Sermon and Sacrament. So, if I could just get everybody's attention, please. I know we have a real big congregation today, and so it's important that we all try to be real mindful of one another and of the fact that our human friends are worshiping right now inside the church building, and we don't want to disturb them by making too much noise or mess. So, if everybody could just be still, and if we could all just have a moment of silence." Here Clancy paused and waited for the din to cease, which it did not do, though he decided to imagine that it abated somewhat. He took a deep breath and began the liturgy. "The Lord be with you..."

From among the tumult of unsettled forms and the cacophony of their restless vocalizations, there could nevertheless be heard, from the old and faithful members of the church, the proper response: "And also with you." Clancy paused again in the vain hope that the crowd would arrive at some degree of composure, but there was no appreciable change. There was nothing for it but to press on and hope for the best.

"Friends..." Clancy raised his voice as high as it would go. "... And our welcome visitors. Today our text is from the Gospel According to St. Luke. If we could please have everyone's attention while Ottoline recites it. This is a very important part of our service, and I would hate for anyone to miss hearing the Word because someone else is making too much noise.... Ottoline?"

Dutifully, with her characteristic aplomb, Ottoline hopped up to the top of the composter and warbled out the verses of the Gospel, ending her recitation with the usual formula: "The Word of the Lord...," after which a few straggling voices pronounced the expected response: "Thanks be to God." It seemed to Clancy that Ottoline's authoritative delivery served to mitigate or at least counterbalance the congregation's restlessness, so he figured it was a good time to make a final call for silence.

"Folks...." He raised himself to his full height and remonstrated at the top of his lungs, having to stop for breath every few sentences on that account. "Before I get started, I want to remind you that we are not alone in this world or in this Church. We share this moment with one another and with our human friends inside, so it's important that we be considerate. I think we all know that humans are real nervous, and they don't like it when they feel outnumbered. So if we could all just keep the noise down...and that way everyone who wants to hear can hear the little sermon I've prepared about the story from Scripture that Ottoline just recited, and I just hope that it touches your heart in some way...."

The slight diminution of chatter amongst the congregation that had ensued upon Ottoline's recitation did remain long enough for Clancy to hear one seagull say, "What's that rat going on about? I thought we were going to hear some good singing?!"

Clancy hated to generalize about other species, or perpetuate harmful stereotypes, but he couldn't help but remember all the unflattering remarks his Aunt November sometimes let pass about the trashy conduct of shorebirds. *Lord*, he said to himself, *strengthen me*. He relaxed his jaws with a real effort of will and began to preach, but not before casting a quick and nervous glance at the window overlooking the back of the churchyard, which was the window of the currently uninhabited rector's office. He was half certain he would see a human face there with an expression of horror. But thank God, he was just imagining things. He lifted his forepaws for attention and fancied that the noise died down a little. "Thank you," he began, "and thank you all for coming this morning, our visitors and our regular members. It is good to be together, isn't that the truth? And you know, our Scripture for the day is just perfect, because it tells us —doesn't it?—all about how important it is to be kind and considerate, especially when you are a guest in someone else's habitat. Jesus knew, didn't he, that he was welcome to have supper in the little man Zaccheus' house, but he was careful to let Zaccheus know that He was coming over, because it's always easier for us to be good neighbors if we have some time to prepare for company. You know, it's these little things—and I don't mean just little Zaccheus—that make all the difference in the world when you really think about it. Maybe it doesn't seem as important as raising the dead or healing the sick or feeding the hungry, but Jesus knew that little Zaccheus deserved every bit as much love and respect as a sick person or a hungry person or a dead person, and He made sure that he treated Zaccheus with respect. Jesus knew what mattered, and He knew that it's the little things...and the little creatures...who can get overlooked sometimes. And you know, He was so right! How many times, friends, do we let ourselves get all excited and upset over some great big problem that we could never fix, while there are just a whole lot of little messes we can clean up if we just try? And sometimes it's these little problems that add up to big problems that we can fix if we just take them one step at a time. And how many times do we let the things around us take up all our time and all our energies, and get between ourselves and Jesus, to where we don't even remember or honor Jesus anymore? I believe little ole Zaccheus must have understood that, because he was always getting ignored because he was so little and so easy to overlook, don't you think? He was smaller than everyone else around Jesus that day and couldn't get close enough to see Him or talk to Him because of that big crowd of folks that just weren't paying attention, and it would have been easy for him to just give up and grumble and feel sorry for himself. But Zaccheus wanted to see Jesus more than he wanted to give up, and so he found a way to get what he deserved, he found a way to lift himself up above the crowd by climbing up that old sycamore tree. He didn't let feeling 'less than' stop him! No, he did not! And Jesus appreciated that! Jesus loves it when we do something unexpected to rise above all the problems that keep us from being with Him! Friends, when we stand up for ourselves, it sure makes Jesus happy! It sure makes Jesus proud! Why, I believe it makes Jesus want to do all that He can to show us that He appreciates us just being ourselves! Oh, friends...when you think about the story of Zaccheus, just remember that you shouldn't ever think that you're too small, or too big, or too anything, for Jesus to love you. No, Jesus loves the least of these, He says so just as clear as He can in Scripture. He loves the little as much as the big, the living as much as the dead, and the simple as much as the complicated. No matter what we have to offer, it's enough for our Lord Jesus, and it's never too much for Him. And now, I'd love for us all to join wings or paws if we have them, and pass the Lord's Peace to one another, while the St. Aloysius Jr. singers treat us to a special hymn chosen for today's scripture, an old Shaker hymn, called *Simple Gifts....*"

And Clancy made a gesture towards the choir assembled beside the composter, and the attention of the congregation shifted. While there had been some diminution of the noise while Clancy preached, it was nothing compared to the breathless silence that descended when the song commenced. This struck Clancy like a jab on the nose. He could not help but wish that the visitors had had enough consideration to at least pretend to listen carefully to the sermon he'd worked so hard on and which he considered to be one of his best. Oh, well, he told himself, he could always preach it again another time.

As planned, Bertram took the first line, croaking and hissing the tune in his energetic, if jarring manner. Then Ottoline warbled out the initial set of notes unaccompanied, in her pleasant alto. At this, however, a not-so-subtle wave of impatience swept across the largely seagull crowd; they had not come all the way from the dump and the beach to hear a plain old pigeon coo. Then, to exacerbate their dissatisfaction, Steven took up the round, his style very much like Ottoline's, though with undertones of masculine gravel that added warmth to the performance for those with ears to hear. Then Sudie Mae joined in, her delivery consisting of a tuneless but forceful belted screech. And then Christopher Martin stepped forward.

He told himself afterward that it wasn't as if he had not intended to restrain himself. It had been his suggestion, after all, that he go last, as to allow the less polished voices to set the tone, so that he would be forced to follow rather than lead. And he stuck to that arrangement...at first. As a choir they sang the round thrice, as planned. And at the end of the third repetition Christopher Martin held the final note for several beats before releasing it to fade upon the silence. The performance having come to its foregone conclusion, the choir members all lowered their beaks. Another ripple of consternation circulated among the gulls. "Is that what all the fuss is about?" a female seagull, itself hardly melodious, piped up indignantly. "Big deal."

Atop the composter, Clancy grew uneasy. The crowd of strange, pale, unruly birds before him appeared as sheer distractions, as if in relief against the more familiar members of his regular flock. They were not here to share in the joys and sorrows of Christian fellowship. They were just sensation seekers. His sermon—not to mention the Scripture that inspired it and the message of the very song they had come to hear—had gone over their featherbrained heads like drifting clouds. As individuals, maybe they would be receptive, but *en masse* they were more trouble than they were worth. He drew a deep breath, so he could perform the previously unthinkable (to him) pastoral task of excommunication.

At the same time, Christopher P. Martin was struggling with his conscience. The hymn would have been better received, he knew, if he had sung solo. As it was, it felt like a cheat. Three repetitions of the same old lines in five voices, only one of them competent, what was the point in that? A song, any piece of music should have more texture to it, more structure; there should be some rising and falling action, a climax, something for the listener to remember. Something distinctive. He felt like he'd been arrested in mid-flight, exactly as if he'd crashed into a window. Maybe the rat and the others were satisfied with mediocrity, but Christopher P. Martin just couldn't stand it. And he suspected that the seagulls, unless they got what they came for, might make trouble. The rat'll thank me later, he told himself, and if he doesn't, who cares. He made up his mind, filled his breast, and opened his beak.

So did Ottoline. "I think I need to remind our welcome visitors that we gather together for worship, not for entertainment. If you are unhappy with the performance of the choir, we hope that you would hold your criticisms until a more opportune time to offer them, perhaps following the service...." Ottoline was determined to give the unruly seagulls a piece of her mind. But as it happened, not even she could hear her own reprimand, for it was at that very moment that Christopher P. Martin piped up.

The tune was recognizable, of course, as *Simple Gifts.* And yet, rendered now in Christopher P. Martin's powerful, supple, and disciplined voice, it was, in a sense, a new creation, utterly transfigured, a humble tree made glorious by extravagant ornamentation, which paradoxically and thus miraculously enhanced its humility. The little bird's voice dipped and soared, trilled and moaned, whispered and shouted. It captivated even Hertz's rudimentary organs of hearing with its capacity for nuance without straying from the basic melody. It was magnificent, a tour de force, and Christopher P. Martin himself was quite carried away. He'd lost himself in song before, to be sure, but never had he transcended himself so thoroughly. It was as if the song itself was he himself, and his own ego the shell out of which a deeper self was emerging. As the song had its way with him, as his awareness of the sheer providence of his voice came clear to his subjectivity, he felt a profound disorientation, which he would have recognized, had he any previous experience of the phenomenon, as gratitude. And with that, his interpretation of the hymn drew to its conclusion. With a series of consecutively minor notes, he fell silent, and the silence that followed upon that was significant. Even the most restless of the gulls hardly twitched a tail feather. Even Sudie Mae was disarmed for the moment by the beauty of the performance.

"That was a very nice encore, Christopher," said Clancy when he could speak . "I think we all appreciated that. But right now, it's time for us to take up the offering. Ometa?"

Well accustomed to the part she played at this point in the service, Ometa the Opossum dutifully circulated among the members of the congregation, not omitting the seagulls, who had no idea what she was up to, collecting in her marsupial pouch the bits of foodstuffs that the various species, with their various dietary restrictions, brought to Mass each week for the Rat Reverend to consecrate for Holy Communion.

Afterwards, during fellowship hour, Christopher P. Martin, feeling unusually self-conscious, held himself aloof, remaining at the composter while the congregation at large pursued their usual chit-chat. In an oblique sense he was aware that he may have rendered himself obnoxious to the rest of the choir, and yet he knew he'd done the right thing at the time. But at what cost? Was resentment—and the ensuing loneliness—the inevitable price of discipline and excellence? For all of its incoherencies, contradictions and minor melodramas, he liked being a part of the choir, a part of the church. He liked these other creatures, even—and maybe especially—that poor, hopelessly unattractive, yet fascinating oddly compelling female buzzard Sudie Mae, who, he could not now help but notice, was glowering at him with quite open and renewed indignation from where she stood a few feet away with the pigeon named Ottoline.

Christopher P. Martin stepped out of the funky shadows of the composter and approached the two female birds, both of whom regarded his advance with something akin to curiosity. "I'm sorry..." he heard himself saying, and he sounded like a stranger to himself—albeit a relatively unobjectionable stranger, unguarded and thus unthreatening. "I just want you to know, I wasn't trying to show off....I just couldn't help myself."

Ottoline, ever quick to forgive and empathize, hastened to reassure the little songbird, but Sudie Mae was ready with the truth. "You're not sorry," she said. "You just don't want us to be mad and kick you out."

"Sudie Mae!" cried Ottoline.

"You're right. I don't," said Christopher P. Martin looking up at Sudie Mae with determination. "We need each other, whether you like it or not."

LUXURIA (LUST)

GRACE KNEW IT WAS silly—though she also knew that it was not—that she talked to the potted plants in the administrative wing of the church office whenever she watered or otherwise tended to them. "I'll be back in a week," she said to the potted Boston fern that hung above her desktop computer. She plucked off a few browning fronds and dropped them in her wastebasket. "I'm off to your hometown, Fern, for a long overdue vacation. Although... how much R & R I'll get, dealing with Silas, remains to be seen. But...if nothing else, it'll be a change of scene. Right?"

As if she was a little wary of an answer to this speculative and rhetorical question, Grace hurried down from off the stepstool upon which she stood, set her watering can on the windowsill, lifted her sweater from the back of her chair, shrugged it on, shouldered her pocketbook and walked out of her office and out of the church. She couldn't help but feel as if she were abandoning some devoted and dependent and sentient creature that was going to feel her absence.

BUT IN FACT, it wasn't until Grace had been on her vacation for a couple of days that it dawned on Clancy that he was running out of food. With Grace away for such an unprecedented extended period of time, his stores were bound to run low. He said as much that evening to Ottoline and Bertram when they joined him at the composter to chat.

"I've just always been able to get by on what Grace doesn't finish," he explained. "She always leaves me some crust from her tomato sandwiches, or some apple core or some pasta salad or French fries or whatever she brings in. There's always something. And when Reverend DeBassompierre was here, Lord, he never finished anything! Of course, I can always get in the food pantry, where they keep the good stuff for the homeless people, but if I take too much Grace'll figure out quick that they have a rat, and then I'm in big trouble."

"Oh, dear!" Ottoline cried. "Reverend! What are you going to do!? I admit, I have never thought about how you manage to provide for yourself! I guess we're always learning something new about one another. Well, at any rate, we'll have to come up with some way to help you, at least until Grace returns. Where has she gone, anyway?"

"She's gone to Boston to visit Reverend DeBassompierre," said Clancy, making no attempt to disguise his wistfulness. How unfair it was! But at least she would come back with some news of the human Reverend, which he would overhear when she discussed it on one of her on-the-clock phone calls with Mercedes. "And to spend a week with him at some place called Provincetown. She's so lucky."

"Your time will come, Reverend," said Ottoline obscurely. "But in the meantime, what will we do about your meals! Of course, Steven and I have plenty of seeds, and we are more than willing to share, but I don't think that would be enough variety for you."

"And I know you don't want *me* sharing with you," said

Bertram. "But I might can find something you like when I'm out hunting for myself and Sudie Mae...."

Clancy held back a shudder at the thought of what provisions Bertram might think suitable to offer him. "That's all right, ya'll.... I guess it won't hurt me to reduce some more anyway. I'm back to having to squeeze in and out of the crawlspace door."

Ottoline was about to caution the Reverend against becoming overly weight-conscious when a moving cruciform shadow coursed over the little gathering from above. All three creatures looked up. "Here comes Sudie Mae," said Bertram, for it was in fact his sister's shadow which had enlarged, before being displaced by her very self as she descended in a devolving spiral to perch on the ground alongside them. "Thought I might find you here!" she said to her brother. "Whatchall doing?"

"We're having an emergency meeting," said Bertram importantly. "The Reverend's out of food!"

"Do what?" said Sudie Mae, with rather outsized alarm, as if Bertram had suggested that the Rat was on the very brink of death. She inclined towards Clancy, who glanced at his own stumpy shadow on the concrete. Sudie Mae had lately taken to gazing up at him during his sermons as if hanging on his every word. It was at once gratifying and unnerving. He wasn't sure why.

"But you've got to have food, Reverend!" Sudie Mae sounded as horrified as if the rodent were perishing of inanition as they spoke. "You can't just starve!"

"That's what we're discussing, dear," said Ottoline patiently. "It's just a temporary issue; don't worry. Grace has gone on vacation, and since she's our Reverend's primary supply of scraps, we've just got to figure out how to keep him going in the meantime."

"Durn that Grace!" cried Sudie Mae. "Leaving the Reverend without anything to eat! Who does she think she is!"

Clancy, who had said as much to himself, nonetheless felt obliged to defend the secretary. "It's not Grace's fault," he said placatingly. "It's just the way things are. I was brought up to live on what the humans leave behind. But Ottoline's right. I've just got to figure out how I can get by until Grace comes back."

"I can bring you something, Reverend!" said Sudie Mae. "What do you like?"

Clancy felt reluctant to go over his diet again. "I just eat what they bring to the church, Sudie Mae," he said. "I can't really be picky. I appreciate your help, but I don't think you're going to be able to find that type of thing on one of your scavenges."

Sudie Mae responded with a chastened little nod, at once dainty and grotesque.

"If nothing else, Reverend," said Ottoline, "we can all keep an eye out for any chance leavings we might come across in the course of our own day. I know that my cousin Frieda, who lives on the roof of one of the hotels on the island, finds a lot of human food left behind on the beaches, and sometimes she treats herself to it. Of course, that's mostly during the summer."

"Oh, I wouldn't want you to go all that way," said Clancy. "And it's so crowded with humans in the summer, anyway."

"I don't understand why the humans don't finish their food," fumed Sudie Mae. "Seems to me they just waste, waste, waste. I always make sure to eat every bit of what Bertram hunts so hard to bring me. You never know what tomorrow's gonna look like. You know, every single morning I see some man or other come out the back of that store right next door and throw a whole bunch of food into that big green box behind there. You'd think, as many people as there are around, they'd find someone to finish what they have before just getting rid of it."

"Sudie Mae!" Ottoline's wings spread with excitement. "That's it! Reverend, Sudie Mae is absolutely right. I don't know why I didn't think of it. Your problem is solved! Bless you, Sudie Mae! What would we do without you!"

The already ruddy color of Sudie Mae's featherless head and neck deepened. She nipped at a spot on her left wing.

The other animals all looked to the right at the plastic lidded

green metal dumpster, visible through the diamond-shaped interstices of the shabby fence that separated—with a number of easy
transgressed bows and gaps in the latticework—the churchyard
of St. Aloysius from the lot of the neighboring convenience
store. Clancy regarded it with a frisson of unease, for Aunt
November had always made it clear that dumpsters were
dangerous habitations of unsavory characters. And not long after
her death, as his ministry was just getting started, Clancy had
encountered, for the first time in his life, a male of his own
species, who apparently made his home in that dumpster. But
when Clancy had screwed up the courage to make a pastoral call,
the other rat had not responded, with the result that Clancy over
time came to forget he might have a neighbor who was a rat like
himself.

"But you know," Ottoline was saying, "now that I think about
it, I've never seen Ometa or any of the squirrels or raccoons take
advantage of such a bounty so nearby. There must be some
reason they've avoided it. I think, before we go too far, we'd
better figure out why. Let's ask Ometa what she knows."

"I'll go get her right now," cried Sudie Mae. And with that
she was airborne, unwilling for Clancy to go without a guaran-
teed food source for one second longer than he had to.

⚜

"Oh, THAT DUMPSTER THERE," said Ometa breezily. "I've always
left that one alone. There's one of you that likes to stay in there,
you know, Reverend. A big one of you. Sometimes more'n one.
Thought you knew that! Guess not." And so saying, Ometa
flicked a bland glance at the heavy metal structure on the back
of the lot next door.

Clancy was silent. Lord knew, it was important for him to be
transparent with his parishioners, but he couldn't bring himself
to discuss that dramatic first encounter he'd had with Macrina,
before she came to be adopted by Reverend DeBassompierre.

Clancy had approached her, and then, when she'd advanced upon him in what seemed to be an attack, she'd been repulsed by the sudden appearance, out of the blue, of a large rat who'd knocked her sideways and who had then darted off to disappear into that convenience store dumpster. Clancy, once he'd recovered from his shock, had then approached the dumpster to thank what seemed at the time to be his defender, but when no answer or acknowledgement was forthcoming, and with Hertz insisting that he'd seen the whole thing and that the only rat involved had been Clancy himself, Clancy figured that his mind was playing tricks on him, so he just got on with the business of establishing the Church.

"He's a big fella," Ometa went on. "'Bout as big as you, I'd say, Reverend. Anyway, I hear he can be fractious. Me, I don't like trouble, so I just work the other side of the street. Plenty of places around to find good human grub."

"But crossing the boulevard can be so dangerous. Remember what happened to poor Timmy the squirrel! Please be careful, Ometa."

"Oh, I'm an old pro at crossing, Miss Ottoline," Ometa said. "And a gal's gotta eat! Right, Rev?" And Ometa nudged Clancy chummily.

Clancy forbore with Ometa's jocular overfamiliarity with his usual patience. He was still processing the fact that the rat he'd seen so long ago was not just wishful thinking, as Hertz had claimed. A rat! And right next door! Clancy knew, he just knew, that the Lord was leading him to make another attempt at evangelizing his own scorned species.

"Well, that settles that!" said Bertram. "Let's go over there and get that other rat to give the Reverend something good to eat!"

"Wait a moment, Bertram," said Ottoline. "Ometa said this other individual might be...how did you put it, Ometa? You always put things so colorfully...."

"Fractious," said Ometa. "Stingy. Might not take kindly to

just anyone coming around his territory. Critters who claim dumpsters tend to be like that. They know they've got a sure thing, and they don't want to lose it. They get spoiled, if you ask me. A lot like the humans, if you want to know the truth. Anyway...if ya'll do get in there, be real careful. And listen, Rev, if it doesn't work out, just hang in there. I'm used to having a lot of mouths to feed, you know that, and I can always scrounge up something for you. Matter of fact, tonight I'm going down to the Bojangles after they go home. There's always lots stuffed in their outdoor wastebaskets. You want some chicken?"

"Thank you, Ometa," said Ottoline. "That's kind of you to offer. Well, then, Reverend? That covers your breakfast tomorrow, at least. Maybe once we've all had a good night's rest, we'll be able to see a way forward. I'm fairly bushed, myself, and so I'm a little fuzzy-headed. It's been a long day for me. Good night, all!"

"'Night, Ottoline," Clancy murmured, still dazed at the revelation that he had not merely imagined his savior's existence.

"Well, I'm off to the shops," said Ometa. "See you in the Morning, Reverend. I bet I'll find a great big biscuit for you."

Clancy nodded, only half aware of what the opossum was saying.

"Guess I'll head on back to the perch, too," said Bertram. "Come on, Sudie Mac."

"Coming," she replied, but in fact she remained still, facing the Reverend. To her he seemed obscurely troubled. Bertram took off, but Sudie Mae couldn't bring herself to follow; she followed instead the Reverend's abstracted gaze as he turned and looked through the chain-link fence at the dumpster next door.

"He's really real!" she heard the rat mutter. "It *wasn't* me who chased Macrina away that time!"

"Reverend?" said Sudie Mae, after a long moment had passed during which Clancy's tail whipped back and forth against the hard concrete as if it was trying to detach itself. "Everything okay?"

Clancy's response was prompt but slowly articulated, as if it took great effort for him to wrench enough attention from whatever thoughts were in his head to Sudie Mae's question. "I'm fine...." he began. "I'm just...remembering...."

Sudie Mae adopted a respectful silence.

"He's been here all this time!" Clancy mused, whether to himself or to her, Sudie May could not be sure. "All this time, on the other side of the fence.... But why hasn't he visited the church?"

"He's fractious, that's what Ometa said," Sudie Mae endeavored to reassure her Reverend. "If he doesn't want to come to church, Reverend, well, then that's his problem. He doesn't know what he's missing!" Sudie Mae's gargly voice rose with assurance.

As if a spell had been broken—or perhaps had been spoken—Clancy's wringing paws were released from one another, and Clancy turned to Sudie Mae. "I didn't believe my own eyes.... Oh, me of little faith...."

He stood up on his hind paws, to his full height, as if to peer over some obstacle. "I'm gonna go invite him to church right now."

"Me too," said Sudie Mae.

⚜

CLANCY WOULD HAVE PREFERRED to approach the new (or rather, newly rediscovered) neighbor without Sudie Mae's company, but he didn't know how to dissuade her without hurting her feelings or discouraging her burgeoning confidence and her own sense of belonging. He scampered over to the length of chain link fence that feebly separated the church lot from the lot of the neighboring convenience store, then he squeezed himself through a gap while Sudie Mae took a flapping leap to the top of the fence and then hopped down with a loud and odiferous flap to stand beside him.

Despite the cool of the evening, the dumpster exuded a hot, sickly sweet metallic aroma that was akin to, but markedly more unpleasant and less organic, than that of Sudie Mae or the composter. Looking up at the partially open sliding door set towards the top of the dumpster, Clancy imagined that he could hear some faint indication of life within, but now that he was here, he wasn't sure how to proceed. Sudie Mae's presence made him feel awkward. Oh, why hadn't she gone home with Bertram? She was a sweet thing, and he loved her to death, but she could certainly be a little clueless sometimes....

Clancy's reflections were dispersed into thin air when, just as he was about to suggest to Sudie Mae that having the both of them there might make their potential neighbor nervous, there appeared, in the dark opening in the green metal structure before them, the form—more than life size, it seemed to Clancy —of a rat standing on its hind legs with one forepaw held for balance against the edge of the opening. "Looking for something?" the big rat said.

Clancy forgot all about Sudie Mae's presence in the queerness he felt at seeing, in the flesh, a creature so much like himself. Never in his life, not even when Aunt November had been alive, had he ever been so aware of his own maleness and ratness. Standing above and before him was a being with whiskers like his whiskers, fur of roughly the same color and pattern as his own fur; having never seen his own eyes except in those of other creatures, he assumed that the glittering black eyes of the dumpster rat were mirrors of his own. The dumpster rat looked down at him with those familiar eyes now; the soft moonlight made visible his pale furry abdomen and testicles of obscene prominence. Clancy felt warm, remembering now that they were in mixed company. He glanced over at the young buzzard, but she seemed to find nothing unseemly or remarkable in the dumpster rat's shameless upright appearance.

"Cat got your tongue?" said the rat from above, and, as if to demonstrate that his own tongue was fully in his possession, he exposed it.

This obscurely challenging gesture made Clancy feel disrespected. What kind of a way was that to introduce oneself to visitors? And one of them a young female, at that! Aunt November had always told Clancy that most rats of his generation had been left to run wild and develop crude ways. Apparently she'd been right. Clancy was so offended for Sudie Mae's sake that he had half a mind to turn and leave without another word, but, remembering that apparently this rat had once saved him from what had appeared to them both to be the ultimate predator, he took a deep breath and let it pass.

"I...we don't mean to bother you. But I...we were wondering...would you mind if we...I borrowed some food...if you have any to spare? I hate to ask, but I live next door, at the church, and, well, I'm used to one of the humans there leaving a few things behind for me most days. But she's gone away for a while, so I'm not sure how I'm going to manage. I can pay you back, of course, when she comes home, but for now...I was just thinking that, since you helped me before that other time I was in trouble, with the cat...." Clancy trailed off.

The rat in the window of the dumpster leaned forward, still holding onto the edge of the dumpster opening with one paw. He peered down at Clancy. "I helped you before?"

"Oh, yes!" said Clancy. "I mean, I *think* it was you.... It was a long time ago, and I was outside here one morning, and there was a cat sitting over in the playground, and I wanted to invite it to join our church, and it came running at me so fast I thought for sure it was going to get me, and then you...or someone just like you...well, you knocked that cat away...." Clancy paused and studied the other rat's countenance for any hint that it shared the memory, but the other rat's expression remained inscrutably amused.

"But if you don't have enough food in there to share, please don't worry.... I'll find something to get by. I do have a good support system, after all. And, as a matter of fact...now that we've met, I'd love to let you know, if you haven't noticed, that I pastor a little community of creatures next door. We have our own church that meets every Sunday morning, and we all look after one another, and to be real honest with you, this whole time, ever since you helped me with the cat situation, I've wanted to invite you to worship with us. I should have a long time ago, but I've just been so busy what with one thing or another, and some of us were talking and we figured that it wouldn't hurt to see if you might have some extra to share, and that would be a good way for us to get to know you and whether you have any extra food to share or not, it's high time we let you know that we'd be happy for you to join us...." Clancy knew he was talking in circles again, so he stopped. "Sorry again for bothering you."

The dumpster rat shifted his probing gaze from Clancy to Sudie Mae. "And what brings you here, hon? You hungry, too? 'Doubt there's anything here you'd enjoy, at least right now...cuz I ain't dead...yet...."

Clancy felt mortified on Sudie Mae's account, knowing how sensitive she and Bertram could be sometimes about their eating habits. "Sudie Mae," Clancy muttered, "maybe you should go on home. I don't want Bertram to get worried about you."

The dumpster rat's little black eyes glittered. "You're welcome to come in and look around, sweetheart," he said to Sudie Mae. "But, like I said, not much here for a gal with your tastes." He turned his gaze back to Clancy. "But I think I can help you out, buddy. Come on up...."

Despite having invited them inside, however, the dumpster rat continued to stand in the narrow opening, as if to suggest that his visitors would be obliged to squeeze past him, making very close contact inevitable. Clancy swallowed hard and addressed Sudie Mae. "It's alright, Sudie Mae," he said. "I think Mr.—our new neighbor is going to be nice enough to share with me. Thanks for coming along with me, and tell Bertram not to worry, hear?"

Sudie Mae wanted to snatch the Reverend up in her beak and fly off with him to the roost she shared with her big brother, where she could keep an eye on him and he would be safe from this...riff-raff. Sudie Mae did not like this other rat one bit, she decided. Between this dumpster diver and the Reverend there was only the shallowest resemblance, as far as she was concerned, and that in overall form and basic coloration. The dumpster rat was dirty, beady-eyed, rough, oversized in every respect, and altogether nasty. Whereas the Reverend Clancy was just as sweet as he could be. Food or no food, church or no church, Sudie Mae did not think that the Reverend should have anything more to do with this rodent. She glowered up at the rat in the dumpster opening, and the ruddy mottled skin of her head and neck deepened.

The dumpster rat apparently sensed Sudie Mae's suspicion. "Don't worry, hon," he said, "I won't bite." And so saying, he bared his bright orange incisors as if to belie his own words. "Unless you want me to...."

Sudie Mae made a deep, guttural, gargling noise, which, Clancy knew from his experiences with Bertram and their father, signaled serious displeasure and the possibility of offensive action. "Sudie Mae," Clancy said, *sotto voce*, "it's all right. He doesn't know any better. Don't worry. I'll be fine. Go on now, so Bertram doesn't get worried about *you*...."

Sudie Mae was far from mollified, but she couldn't bring herself to undermine the authority of the Reverend, who, after all, was the apple of her eye and the smartest creature she knew. "All right, Reverend," she said. "I'll go on home. But if you need anything, just holler." She looked up at the rat in the dumpster opening. "I got real sharp ears—and eyes.... And a real sharp beak, too." And so saying, she opened and closed this formidable appendage with a pointed snap. "See you tomorrow, Reverend," she said, and then with a leap and much flapping, her tail feathers coming within a contemptuous inch of the dumpster rat's snout, she took off into the woods.

Clancy on the ground, the dumpster rat in the dumpster window: two rats regarded one another with real interest and curiosity. "Nice chick," said the dumpster rat, ostensibly of Sudie Mae. "I bet she *does* keep her eye on you."

Clancy was at a total loss for words. The dumpster rat seemed to be suggesting something that Clancy would rather not think about.

"Well, come on in," the Dumpster Rat said. "I told you, I got all you can eat."

⁂

THE DUMPSTER WAS, to Clancy's mild surprise, almost completely empty; nevertheless, inside all was dark and hot and the stench was—not quite, but almost—overpowering, redolent of sunbaked but rapidly cooling metal and perishing food and the extremely recognizable tinct of rodent droppings and urine. Having scrambled up and in through the narrow opening of the sliding window, after the other rat, with a wink, had hopped down inside and out of the way, Clancy did not feel as out of place as he thought he might. In fact, there was something about being at the bottom of a dumpster, with all its grime and hardness and stench, that was hauntingly familiar.

"Home sweet home," remarked the dumpster rat easily. "It's not fancy, but it suits me just fine. Have to make myself scarce, though, when the trucks come and turn the place upside down. But that's life." He settled himself on the metal floor before Clancy, so close that Clancy could smell him over the rest of the odors within the container: that grainy odor that indicated a healthy young rat was strong with him. Clancy scootched back into himself, and hoped the other rat didn't notice, or if he did, wouldn't take offense. And indeed, he didn't seem to either notice or mind.

"Well. So....You need a good meal? I know how that is. Look behind you. Still a box of Twinkies over in that corner, I ain't even opened it. Help yourself."

"Thank you," said Clancy with as much sincerity as he could muster through his disorientation. He wasn't sure why or how, but ever since he'd landed on the floor of the dumpster, he felt as if he'd somehow left a part of himself behind, and that this part was now observing him from above. He saw himself scootching into himself when the dumpster rat came too close, he saw himself skittering over to the corner where the box of packaged pastries lay. He saw himself gnaw around the edges of the box, he saw himself squeeze out a cellophane wrapped pastry, he saw himself chewing through the cellophane and finally getting to the sweet. All the while he was watching himself, he was feeling horribly self-conscious, which was only natural in that the dumpster rat continued to regard him with a discomfiting steadiness. Because of this, Clancy found that after a few mouthfuls he felt not sated, but uncomfortably stuffed.

"That's all you want?" said the other rat with exaggerated incredulity. "That couldn't hold me up for too long. But to each his own, I guess." He assumed a very languorous posture, his snout pointed directly at Clancy, the tiny nostrils occasionally flaring with what seemed like delectation, and his shiny black eyes gleaming as if he were sizing up his guest for some outrageous purpose.

"I've had a gracious plenty," said Clancy primly. "Thank you." He could hear that his own voice was uncharacteristically breathless as he spoke, as if something inside of him did not really want to be heard clearly.

The dumpster rat continued to regard him boldly, and his impressively thick and scaly tail moved several times from side to side, making a rough noise against the rusty, dry dumpster floor.

"I've got a big appetite, myself," said the dumpster rat. "But take what you want. I've got plenty and they're always bringing more. If you're done, why don't you come back over here so we can get acquainted? I told you—I don't bite...." And he bared his prognathic orange incisors.

Clancy crept forward almost imperceptively. The familiarity of the other rat's appearance and scent—and even its voice— were, alongside the overfamiliarity of its manner, deeply discon- certing and not a little alarming. This rat was, after all, a stranger, and in a more dangerous sense than the other creatures he now knew and loved had been strangers at one time. This was the kind of creature that Aunt November had always warned him of, the only kind she ever could have imagined he might be in danger of becoming. This rat was a wharf rat. She had told Clancy many many stories of the wild ways and tragic ends of this type of irresponsible rodent.

He moved a little closer.

"I don't think I know your name?" Clancy tried speak up.

The other rat's ears flattened against its head, and the gleam in his eyes narrowed to a focused glare. "Percy," he said through those orange teeth. And that thick tail swept the floor again as if with a menacing mind of its own.

Clancy thought that this name, apart from sounding slightly similar to his own, was basically unremarkable, so his response was an open silence meant to indicate that he'd heard and under- stood. The rat named Percy, however, seemed to take Clancy's silence askance. He advanced a few lengths toward Clancy, that thick ropy tail sweeping from side to side, then he stopped, and a tension all along his body eased, as if, upon getting a closer look at Clancy's expression, he found that whatever unwelcome reaction to his name he'd expected was not there. The two rodents were now almost snout to snout.

"Well, thank you again for the snack, Percy," said Clancy. "And I'm glad we've finally had a chance to talk. I really have been meaning to invite you to our church. I wasn't just saying that to get food."

"Wouldn't matter if you were," said the rat named Percy. "We all have our hustle." He relaxed and crept even closer to Clancy. "Tell me more about this church business," he said.

Clancy resisted the urge to shrink further. "Well..." he said, "the church itself—the building, I mean—belongs to the humans, and they're usually there only during the day. I was born down on the waterfront, you know, but my Aunt November brought me to the church when I was just a little thing, so I don't remember being down there at all. Aunt November's gone to be with the Lord, so it's just me now, but I started a church for all of us nonhumans behind the church near the garden, and that keeps me busy. We come together to worship and have fellowship on Sunday mornings, just like the humans do, and the rest of the time, why, we just try to look out for each other and help each other any way we can, and the ministry just keeps growing and growing. There isn't really anything special you have to do to be a part of the church, as long as you promise to try to be a good neighbor, and even though when I preach on Sundays I preach the Good News of Jesus Christ, that's because that's what I believe the Lord has called me to do. I try to explain what it means to follow Jesus and be saved, and I offer the sacraments, which means that if you want to be closer to Jesus, then you can do those things he's asked us to do to remember Him, like be Baptized and Confirmed and share in his Last Supper. Oh, it's a lot of different things, but don't worry if you don't understand it all. I don't understand it all myself! I just know that the Lord has called me to be a pastor. Anyway, we'd love to have you join us next Sunday. And you don't have to wait until Sunday. Anytime you want to talk, or have some fellowship, you can just come see me. Like I said, I'm just over there, next door, in the cellar."

Throughout Clancy's increasingly effervescent exposition, Percy had simply listened with a growing intrigue, for the prim timidity that Clancy had previously displayed seemed to fade like a mist as soon as he began to speak about his "church." What a funny, crazy little fellow! So, endeavoring to demonstrate an irrepressible admiration the only way he knew how, he hopped on top of Clancy and circled his thick, scaly, ropy, and coarse-haired tail around Clancy's stunned form, nuzzling his snout along the crease of Clancy's right ear. And, as if the floor of the dumpster, as well as the flesh of his neighbor, had turned as red hot as the flames of hell, Clancy scrambled out from underneath Percy and up the rusty wall of the container, leaped through the narrow opening of the dumpster window and catapulted himself out into the dark cool of the night.

☙❧

ALONE AT THE bottom of the empty dumpster, the rat named Percy ground his teeth with amusement, which eventually, however, dissipated into a vague sense of discontent. Percy hadn't meant to upset the funny little rat, nor make him feel uncomfortable.... Well, not really. He liked to come on strong with these nervous types. He thought it was good for them. Oh, well.

He considered—briefly—climbing out of the dumpster himself and going after Clancy to offer reassurance, if not an apology.

But what for?

He did rouse himself from his place on the floor to climb up to the window opening of the dumpster. He looked out through the ramshackle chain link fence and over the garden of the church next door. And of course, there was no sign of any other rat. Percy did see, perched in the highest boughs of one of the pines near the edge of the woods, a hunched dark figure—that young female buzzard. She'd probably been lurking there the whole time, and surely would have seen the rat leaping out of the dumpster like his tail was on fire. "Well, buster," Percy said to himself, "way to go."

He dropped himself back down onto the still warm rusty metal floor of the dumpster. Before doing so, he'd considered taking advantage of the cool quiet evening by taking himself down to the waterfront to look for someone to spend the night with. But the sight of Sudie Mae glowering in the woods, no doubt with an eye out for the rat who had so upset her reverend, squelched any half-hearted desire he might have for company or diversion. He might as well just call it a night.

He crawled over to the cellophane-wrapped pastry that Clancy had only nibbled. Despite his overall feeling of having caused distress, Percy took some satisfaction in having at least fed the crazy rat. He, Percy, didn't think he was all that bad, even if he was a bit of a scamp. Maybe he did like to play rough and assert his advantage, and maybe he wasn't too considerate of other creatures' hang-ups, but he never meant any harm. He just liked to have a good time! He always had! And who didn't? Didn't everybody, deep down, want to have fun? He sure thought so. He took a bite of snack cake but found that it was too sweet, and he wasn't all that hungry all of a sudden.

Rats. He was now suddenly in one of those moods, rare enough for him but still familiar, in which he was unable to shake the sense that there was something he was getting wrong. He was young, he was strong, he was good at getting what he wanted.... So what could possibly be missing? It was a puzzle.

Snap out of it! he told himself. *Get your tail out of this dumpster and get yourself down to the waterfront and find yourself a good time. That's what life's all about, and always has been.* But for the first time in as long as he could remember, the idea of fun felt exhausting. He was all of a sudden too pooped, it seemed, to even swallow the food in his mouth. He spat it onto the metal floor and closed his eyes, but that brought only restlessness, not relief. Rats! Now he couldn't even sleep!

Feeling mysteriously thwarted, his mood sank, becoming heavy, as if swelling with some inexplicable emotional edema. At least, he thought to himself, in an attempt to lighten up, if he'd freaked out the rat next door, he didn't need anyone that uptight around him anyway. Percy's long thick tail twitched, and his breathing became slow and meditative as he began to review his relationships. His mother had been poisoned by rat bait, his father could be any rat, and Percy and the rest of his litter were orphaned to the docks and the alleyways of the waterfront dining district. His siblings, except for one sister who was herself soon done in by a marauding alley cat, left him to fend for himself, and for a while he managed to survive against all odds by hiding in the very narrow and shallow space underneath a dumpster set on an apron of cracked and uneven concrete behind the McDonald's. His existence was detected soon enough by the sharp hearing of an elderly and outcast rat by the name of Bart, who had lost both of his eyes long before in a nasty fight over a female. Bart, seeing (figuratively) the chance to make his own life a bit easier, had allowed Percy to share the hideaway, and even though on account of his blindness and loneliness the old rat was demanding and even unreasonable, he did what he could to teach young Percy how to survive and thrive within a cutthroat (if not hostile) environment. By the time old blind Bart succumbed to a stroke brought on by sheer cantankerousness, Percy had grown large, and strong, and more than a little streetwise, and under Bart's demanding but not wholly self-serving and sincere mentoring, he'd gained a sense of himself as valuable and accomplished. He could hold his own in the concrete jungle of the waterfront. What's more, his self-possession and high spirits had brought not a little comfort and joy to the declining days of an old and forgotten and disabled elder. It was incredible, he found, how easy it was to have a good time, when one is young and strong and refuses to let life get one down. Because life would, if you let it, as old blind Bart had taught him all too well.

Rats! The way he felt tonight, though, the last thing he wanted to think about was poor, helpless old Bart. Bart had, towards the end, become a real pawful; he needed everything done for him, even to the point of having his food pre-chewed. But Percy would just as soon as have chewed his own tail off as abandon the miserable old rat who had taken him in and taught him how to hustle. Bart had shown him how a smart rat, even without eyes, could get respect. Percy, even as he was growing strong enough to be more than a match for even the scrappiest of his age mates, was constantly being taunted for his name. Having mentioned at one point to Bart that he was going to start calling himself by something that he thought sounded tougher, Old Bart had fairly bristled with contempt. "If you can't stand up for your own damn name!" he'd croaked, "you can't stand up for nothing or nobody. Percy's got class! I don't give a shit what any of those young punks say."

Percy had never liked his name, even before he perceived that his age mates considered it to be effete, but he was not so antipathetic regarding it that he could not hear the challenge in the blind old rat's outburst. The next time one of his peers said Percy's name with an exaggerated and affected lisp, they lost an eye as a result. And from then on Percy's reputation among the young rats of the waterfront was that of a formidable fighter.

And talk about fun! Even though he came to be known as someone not to be disrespected, Percy didn't enjoy fighting. He never again allowed a situation to get to the point where he would be obliged to bite another eye out. The experience had been sickening: he never ever wanted to again experience the sensation of his teeth piercing into the gelatinous interior of another creature's organ. No, he'd rather have the respect of his mates without having to fight for it, he wanted them to like as well as respect him, and to join him in what was after all the whole point of living—having a good time. He liked to eat heavily, play heartily, and above all copulate copiously, for pleasure was his middle name. Copulation, it did not take him long to discover, was his favorite pastime, and because he was big and strong and had a bold and winning approach, he was rarely without a willing partner. And it made him feel, more than any fight ever could, victorious. When a female rat, or even every now and then one of those pretty, pink-eyed males who were always so encouraging, could be charmed into favoring him with their acquiescence, he felt absolutely invincible and on top of the world. Of course, there were often complications in the aftermath. He had more offspring than he could keep track of, and the pickings along the waterfront were getting slimmer as his reputation for being promiscuous and irresponsible grew. This was why he sometimes liked to steal away to this out-of-the-way dumpster, just to have some time away from all the wagging tongues. Sometimes a little peace and quiet was worth a ton of fun. He would never understand why his "friends" got so uptight. He just wanted everyone to have a good time!

Rats! Thinking about all the fun he usually had had the effect of making him want to have some more fun, but it was as if the spark wouldn't catch tonight. He just couldn't bring himself to climb out of the dumpster and down the boulevard to try to find someone who hadn't heard all about him yet. The spirit was willing, but the flesh was weak. Rats!

🐀

CLANCY KNEW that he had blown it. Badly. *Oh Lord*, he said to himself, *what is the matter with me?* The dumpster rat...in his discombobulation Clancy couldn't remember the creature's name...was only trying to be friendly, after all. It wasn't as if he'd done anything wrong....Had he?

Back in the cellar of the church, in the damp familiar darkness of his fusty lair, Clancy composed himself by sucking the tip of his tail, as he recalled the incident and the feelings that had arisen within himself. The seemingly anodyne physical contact.... Certainly there had been nothing hostile about it.... It had felt, reasonably or not, aggressive and...yes, disrespectful to Clancy. It had about it the whiff of presumption. Clancy knew he had no experience of the ways of rats apart from himself and Aunt November, but from Aunt November he had gathered that strong values and a sense of decency had gone by the wayside when it came to most members of his species. The rats beyond the walls of the church, from whom he'd been delivered, including his own mother, were all hell-bent on being wastrels, according to Aunt November, and the males in particular were without restraint. "Nothing but foul language, precious angel, and fussing and fighting. I didn't want you getting mixed up with them. You could have been hurt!"

Wrapped up snug and tight in the cocoon of discarded choir robes that he used for his bedding, Clancy told himself that he was grateful to Aunt November for keeping him out of a lifestyle that would not likely have led to the knowledge of God. And yet he'd come to learn, since Aunt November went to be with the Lord, that there was more to him than he ever could have known. Since he'd been called to ministry, he'd especially learned that it did not serve the Gospel to be too careful. In his short time as a pastor Clancy had faced worse trials than an overly friendly fellow rat. Wrapped up snug and safe and tight in his choir robes, Clancy resolved to go back to the dumpster and apologize for running off without explanation. But that could wait until tomorrow.

❦

DEEP IN THE FOREST, high in the treetops, Sudie Mae snoozed restlessly in the roost she shared with her devoted big brother. Her dreams were uncommonly troubled; they all featured the Reverend in various situations of peril, from which she was help-less to rescue him. He was on fire, he was drowning, he was cornered by a shadowy predator; in one dream from which she woke up squawking and with her wings outspread he was falling from the edge of a precipice into an infinite depth. And in every scenario, the closer she came to him, somehow, paradoxically, the further away he went. And the subtle but obvious subtext of the dreams was that he did not want to be saved. He preferred to perish rather than be rescued by Sudie Mae, who only wanted to preserve him in safety.

Wide-awake, she raised her head and gazed out over the woods and across the city to the dark ocean beyond. Even with Bertram peacefully asleep above her she felt terribly alone. Of course, she being one type of creature and the Reverend being another, she knew that the tenderness she felt towards him was likely one-sided. But her dreams stirred up a sharper awareness, that as much as she cared for the Reverend, she did not really know who or what he was. And that made her feel like she had felt back when her dismissive, domineering daddy was still among the living—that there was nothing in life that she could really count on to make her feel important. She didn't think it was fair that a total stranger, just because he was the same species, should be equipped to support the reverend, and not herself, who only wanted what was best.

⚜

"Well, look who's coming to dinner," Percy said. "I was just on my way out.... The way you took off last night, I figured you decided you didn't like what I had to offer." He looked down from his perch in the dumpster window at a visibly abashed Clancy. "Come on in. You know I've got plenty." And his bright orange incisors shone in the dusk.

Clancy scrunched into himself. He couldn't help it. No matter what this other rat said to him, it made him feel as if he was the butt of some private joke. But he had promised himself he would make amends. "Oh, no! No, I'm not hungry today. I had a late lunch. No, I wanted to apologize for leaving the way I did last night. I was just...." He had to pause, because while he didn't want to lie, the unvarnished truth might hurt. "I don't mean to be rude. Your dumpster is nice, but it does get kind of hot in there, and I'm not used to the heat. I stay in the cellar of the church, you know, and it's always really cool. But I should have at least said thank you...."

"No big deal." The rat looking down from the dumpster at

him now sounded relatively straightforward, the usual teasing note was absent from his voice. Clancy felt something relax within.

"Well, thank you anyway, for understanding. And I wanted to let you know that I really meant it when I said that we'd love to have you visit the church or even become a member, and also that you're welcome any time to come over and see me if you even just want to talk. You know, I was brought up here all by myself, except for Aunt November, and I know how it is to be the only rat around. It can be real lonesome, until you get to know the other kinds of creatures around here. It took the Lord calling me to ministry before I had the confidence to put myself out here, and even then, it wasn't easy..."

Percy was only half listening. He'd slept away most of the day, had recovered his characteristic spirit, and had been gearing up for a trip to his usual waterfront haunts, when the little preaching rat had come along and called his name. Percy had decided to mind his own business...but now what? Tell him to scram, a part of him said. Why should you waste time with someone who doesn't know how to have fun? Plenty around who do. And yet, for some reason, the prospect of getting to know this strange yet similar creature was inexplicably appealing.

"...but, you know, we're not meant to be alone," Clancy continued. "That's what the Bible says...somewhere. I think right at the beginning. The Bible, you know, is a book that the humans wrote, that tells us all about God, and Jesus, and a whole lot of other things, and that's what we study in church...." Clancy's little voice rose with his usual enthusiasm for the Gospel.

Percy's thick tail swept to and fro as he balanced on the edge of the opening of the dumpster. The crazy little rat down there was dying for the company of his own kind. He was just having a hard time coming right out and saying so. Percy looked down at the uncertain but undaunted little rodent crouching on the concrete in the moonlight. He reminded Percy of someone, but Percy couldn't put his paw on who....

"I'd love to go to your place," he said cheekily. Then, sensing Clancy's renewed discomfiture, and rather enjoying it, he hopped down from the dumpster access opening and would have landed right on top of Clancy had Clancy not stepped aside. "Lead the way," he said.

"It's not really my place, you know," said Clancy stalwartly. "It's the Lord's."

৩৬৩

ALL AROUND THE churchyard and even beyond, certain animals found their attention drawn to the space between the church and the convenience store, observing that the Reverend was being accompanied to the crawlspace where he spent his nights by another, similar, but notably larger rat. Deep within his composter empire, even Hertz was stirred from a deep nap to consciousness by something novel in the atmosphere. He unwound and made his way to the casing of the composter and poked his tip from the ventilation slot. "Well I'll be damned," he grumbled to himself. "When the cat's away....!"

From the ornamental belfry atop the church building, her mate Steven fast asleep beside her, Ottoline sensed movement across the fence where the dumpster stood and trotted to the gutter spout at the roof's edge to get a closer look. She watched as the two rodents loped side by side from the fence to the side of the church building, and she could hear the Reverend say, as they squeezed through the old gnawed-out gap in the corner of the crawlspace door, "I should have invited you over a long time ago."

"Better late than never," came the reply from the dumpster rat, followed by two muffled thumps as the two rodents landed on the basement floor. Ottoline trotted back up to the belfry to mind her own business.

৩৬৩

DEEP IN THE WOODS, high in the treetops, Bertram and Sudie Mae, at rest after a heavy meal of snake and chipmunk, caught a glimpse, through their sharp eyes, of two rats slipping into the basement of the church. "Well how about that, Sudie Mae!" crowed Bertram. "The reverend and that other fellow have made friends. Ain't that nice!"

Sudie Mae closed her eyes and did not answer.

۞

"WOW!" Percy made himself right at home, scampering and nosing into every nook and cranny of the cellar. "You got all this to yourself?"

Clancy felt an obscure pride. "Well, if you mean the cellar, yes. I've been here alone since Aunt November passed away. The humans never come down here unless there's something wrong with the furnace. But, Percy, this isn't the important part. Let me show you...." And Clancy made his way to the foot of the wooden stairs that led up to the main level of the church building.

"Is this your bedding?" Percy, with the instinct of a born hedonist, had approached, sniffed, and stretched himself out languorously upon Clancy's pallet of discarded choir robes. "Very nice," he said. "Soft as a pelt. I sure wish I had a place like this." And he snuggled himself deep into the pile, while Clancy looked on, discomfited yet again by his new neighbor's forward manner. Clancy thanked the Lord that Aunt November wasn't around to see this. Or was she?

"It's a lot nicer upstairs," Clancy prodded.

To his relief, after a moment of performative lounging, Percy crawled out of Clancy's bedding, yawned, stretched, scratched, and scampered over to join Clancy at the foot of the stairs. "Now what?"

Clancy hopped and loped up the staircase and squeezed underneath the door with the usual breathless difficulty. He was worried for a moment that his guest, who after all was larger, might get stuck. But Percy for all his bulk was remarkably limber. He wriggled into the main corridor of St. Aloysius Church with a noisily grunting struggle that he seemed to enjoy. "Let me show you where I learned all about the Lord," said Clancy, "And then we'll go to the Sanctuary."

Percy, having never been inside a human dwelling before, was impressed by the scale of the space, the height and consistent lines of the walls and ceiling, and the cool blandness of the conditioned air. For most of his life he'd never had occasion or inclination to pay much attention to the human race, apart from acknowledging their peculiar ways, their disconnection from the rest of the natural world, and the addictive, artificial savoriness of their processed foods. He couldn't help but stop and stand up on his hind legs and look all around, whiskers and nostrils twitching. It was like being in another and totally unimaginable world, and he was overawed. But this passed, and he soon followed Clancy down the hallway to what the church rat called the administrative suite.

"That's Grace's desk," said Clancy, indicating a structure beneath a potted fern that dangled from the ceiling. "She's in charge until they hire a new Rector. They're having a hard time finding one that everyone can agree on. Some say it's time for a woman priest, some say it's time for a real man. I'm not sure what that means, because Reverend DeBassompierre *was* a man, but.... I'm sure they'll find someone, but I doubt that they'll find anyone as smart as Reverend DeBassompierre..."

Percy didn't understand much of what Clancy was saying, but he certainly could sense that Clancy had his own strong feelings about this DeBassompierre creature. His voice was high, and breathless with wistfulness. Percy looked around again. What a bizarre, forbidding, overwhelming environment this was! And yet this unassuming little rat seemed to navigate it with absolute confidence. The streetwise dumpster rat's patronizingly indulgent, if sincerely friendly feeling towards the church rat began to transform into a wholly new attitude —respect.

"Oh, I wish he hadn't gone away. But I know he's a lot happier," Clancy was saying.

"Who?" said Percy. "Who went away?"

"Reverend DeBassompierre. He was my teacher. I learned everything I know about being a pastor from him. He left here to go to Harvard, which is a place way up North, where everyone is smarter than they are down here."

Clancy trotted over to the bookcase. "I used to spend all day behind here, watching and listening and learning all about the Bible and the Early Church Fathers. Reverend DeBassompierre practiced his sermon every Thursday. He would preach it two or three times and one more time in front of Grace just to make sure he remembered every word—he said he didn't want to preach from notes, he wanted to be able to see his congregation while he was preaching so he could know that he was connecting with them. And that's how I learned about a whole lot of the Bible, and that's important because what the Bible says is what we preach about. I don't think anyone is as smart about the Bible as Reverend DeBassompierre. He said that the Bible isn't just a book, it's a living word, it's God's word, and just like anything else that's alive, what it says depends on what it needs, and you can tell that at different times it wants and needs different things from us. Why, just like the community garden! Sometimes it needs seeds, and sometimes it needs manure, and sometimes it just needs the sun and the rain! That's right! The Bible is like a garden! I wonder if Reverend DeBassompierre ever thought of that! Oh, I sure wish I could see him and talk to him about the Bible and preaching....He was so smart, and so holy...." And the Reverend Clancy took a deep, deep breath, and sighed as if he were giving up the ghost.

What Percy understood between the lines of this passionate paean to an absent hero was the lonesomeness of a rodent out of touch with his own nature and his heart was strangely warmed.

He finished exploring the musty area behind the bookcase, from where Clancy had for countless hours observed the human clergyman at work. He came up alongside Clancy, once again so close that he could feel the church rat's body heat, and again tried to demonstrate his concern the only way he knew. "You're not so bad yourself," he said.

Clancy was so lost in nostalgia for the way things used to be that the dumpster rat's vamping made no impression. "Oh, I'm nothing like Reverend DeBassompierre," he said. "I'm just a rat."

Percy, his characteristic spontaneity pushed aside by his realization that the feelings that the church rat had for the absent human were deeper and more complicated than any feelings that he, Percy, could ever recall having, searched his mind for an encouraging word. "That lady buzzard doesn't think you're just a rat," he heard himself saying. "Baby, she thinks you're the cat's meow. I thought she might rip me to shreds the other night."

"Oh, Sudie Mae," Clancy said. "She's just real sweet. She's just got growing pains. She's been through a lot, poor thing. But that's what the church is for. To help those among us who are struggling.... We've got to be real patient with Sudie Mae."

Clancy moved across the room, to the corner where Macrina's favorite napping spot, the cushion of the prie-dieu, had stood. "Speaking of cats.... I wish you could have met Macrina," he said, "or gotten to know her. She was the cat, you remember, that you thought was going to hurt me. But Macrina would never hurt one of us. She was domesticated, she said. And she and the Reverend were good friends, and the Reverend took her in when she didn't have anywhere to go, and he took her to Harvard, too. That's just the kind of Christian he was...."

Percy perceived the sincere regard for both human and cat, as well as the unspoken sense of injustice and sorrow, that it had been a cat, and not a rat, that the human clergyman's Christian charity embraced.

But before Percy could respond with some encouragement or

sympathy, Clancy was on the move. "Let's go to the Sanctuary," he said.

⚜

FOLLOWING CLANCY over the threshold from the hallway into the dim and empty sanctuary, Percy was again impressed. Never had he been in such a large, enclosed space. It was enormous, with high vaulted ceilings and, as always, faintly redolent with the spicy sweet odor of frankincense. Clancy scampered right down the center of the crimson aisle carpet to come to a halt just before the altar, bold as a lion, as if, in the absence of the humans, he owned the place. Percy, for his part, normally without fear in the presence of even the most hostile or reactive human that he might encounter along the waterfront, had to resist the impulse to lurk in the shadows of this generous yet enclosed space. Perhaps for the first time in his rollicking life, he felt out of his element entirely. He trotted up right beside Clancy, facing the altar, above which a large wooden crucifix hung suspended from a rafter. He was vaguely yet unabashedly aware that he was drawing close to the church rat for his own reassurance.

"Oh, I just love it in here," said Clancy, gazing up at the dangling crucifix, rather as if he were speaking to the impaled human figure as well as to Percy. "Even though Reverend DeBassompierre is all gone, and he probably won't ever come back, whenever I'm in here, where he used to celebrate the sacraments and preach the Gospel, I still feel close to him. I guess because, even though we're about as different as we can be, and he couldn't even know about me, we shared something bigger than both of us. God called us both to spread his Love. I feel so blessed, even though it isn't always easy, and I miss him so much...."

As the Reverend Rat trailed off into silence, Percy regarded the harassed looking, open armed humanoid figure on the dangling cross above. Not knowing any different, he assumed vaguely that it represented somehow the human whose departure had left Clancy bereft. The human body was to Percy deeply unappealing—so furless, always swaddled in cloying fabric, and exuding an anxious vulnerability in spite of their great size and uprightness. The figure above was no different, apart from its near nakedness, which in fact served to make it seem all the more pathetic and grotesque. It was incomprehensible to him as an object of desire. The longer he looked at it, the more he felt he wanted to get out of this cool, empty, austere, and unnatural space, where nothing seemed real. His vigorous, vivacious flesh was clamoring for warmth and vitality. But at the same time a novel impulse—not a little exciting—was awakening within. It might be good, he discovered, to wait. It came as a real surprise to him, that, though he wasn't having what he was used to thinking of as a good time, it nonetheless felt good just to be close to Clancy, even though Clancy's heart was a thousand miles away.

Soon enough, however, Clancy became aware again that he had company. "I'm so glad I didn't just imagine you," he said. "I'm so glad you've decided to join my church."

Not so fast, there, fella, thought Percy. *Percy doesn't make any promises.* But he held his tongue, for the time being.

❧ 7 ❧
GULA (GLUTTONY)

"SO WHAT DO YOU ALL DO FOR fun around here?" inquired Percy.

"Fun?" Clancy was genuinely puzzled. Wasn't it obvious, to his newest friend and member of St. Aloysius Jr., that among other things, attending services and enjoying the company of fellow Christians was the very epitome of fun? But maybe Percy had something else in mind.

"What do you mean?" said Clancy.

The two rodents were sitting side by side in the shade of the composter. It was a brilliantly sunshiny early afternoon, and the churchyard as well as the church itself was peacefully devoid of any human presence, it being Saturday. It was a day of the week particularly sacred to Clancy, for usually by Saturday he had his Sunday sermon plotted out if not completely memorized, and he was able to look forward to the next day's liturgy with a sense of delicious leisure. It gave him the opportunity to simply be available for his parishioners to catch up on things, and he was happy, though not surprised, to find that Percy seemed eager and willing to pass the time with him.

"What do I mean?!" Percy said. "I mean fun! I mean kicking

it! Letting loose! Living your best life! Eating! Drinking! Making...merry!"

"Well, we worship!" said Clancy, with the air of someone stating the obvious.

"Worship!" Percy groaned before collecting himself. Having attended a few services, he thought that all the preaching and singing and praying were a lot of things, but fun wasn't one of them. But of course, he realized that church meant a great deal to Clancy, and he did not want to be unkind. "Well, okay," he said. "But you know, there's lots of ways to have fun, and they don't all have to be so...fancy. You can have fun just...hanging out!"

"Like we're doing right now!" said Clancy. "You're right, Percy. It's a lot of fun spending the afternoon with you!"

Percy suppressed the urge to nip Clancy's ear. Certainly, he was enjoying the afternoon, but again, he didn't exactly consider passing the time, doing nothing more than talking, tons of fun. He wondered how best to explain what he meant.

"Listen," he said, "don't you ever feel like...cutting loose?"

"From what?" said Clancy. He wasn't at all conscious of feeling the least bit bound. He couldn't imagine, in fact, feeling freer.

"You know," said Percy, "from the old rat race. Don't you ever feeling like getting away from it all? Going a little wild and crazy?"

Wild? Crazy? For Clancy, growing up as he had with Aunt November, whose manner was nothing if not disciplined, the terms had pejorative connotations, bringing to mind scenes of strife and squalor, of chaos and discord. But again, maybe that wasn't quite what Percy meant, Percy, whose life after all had been as different from Clancy's as his form was similar.

"I don't know if I'd like to go wild," said Clancy, with real simplicity. "I've always been tame."

Percy turned his snout and regarded the rat beside him. There was about the funny little fellow, something at once so naïve and yet so remarkably self-possessed that Percy still had a hard time resisting the urge to bedevil him—not so much out of malice as out of a sheer urge to make an impression. And so, in response to Clancy's blithe and cheerful self-revelation, Percy let himself go and stepped up upon his hindlegs, then hopped on Clancy's back, pinning him and nipping his ear before rolling him over and pinning him so that they were belly to belly. 'EEEeeek!" cried Clancy.

"We were born to be wild, baby," said Percy, rolling off his friend but not without a few well-aimed nips and pokes. "Listen. Come along with me tonight. I'll show you what you've been missing being cooped up in this church."

"Go where?" said Clancy.

"Down to the waterfront! The old country! Where else!? Haven't you ever wanted to go see where you come from?"

"The waterfront!" Clancy was truly aghast. He felt something in himself shrivel, as if touched by an icicle that at once froze and burned.

"Percy! I can't go down there! It's dangerous!"

"Not with me around," said Percy. "Come on. It'll be good for you. Trust me! Would I let anything happen to my best buddy?"

Clancy flushed. The shriveling, icicle feeling was soon lost in the warmth of being referred to as a best buddy. "No," he said. "I know I shouldn't be so uptight. You're right, Percy. I think it would do me good to see where I come from. I wonder if anyone there will remember me and Aunt November...?"

※

OF COURSE, the two rodents did not set out on their journey to Clancy's native ground right away. The middle of a sunny Saturday afternoon was not, after all, the most opportune time for a pair of rats to visit a busy waterfront business district. They decided to spend the afternoon and evening taking it easy and resting, and then leave the church sometime around midnight.

By the time they got to the waterfront, Percy said, most of the human crowds would have dispersed, leaving behind only the most hardcore weekend revelers, who would be too intoxicated, for the most part, to pay any attention to the presence of what they thought of as vermin.

"Lord, it's late!" said Clancy when they met at the composter at the appointed time of departure. "But I was able to take a little nap, and as long as we're back in time for me to get a little more rest before church tomorrow, it'll be okay."

"Sure we'll be back early," Percy said, hurrying Clancy along across the front yard of the Church to the curbside of the boulevard. "Nothing good happens after sunrise, as my old friend Bart used to say! I promise, I'll get you back in plenty of time to get your beauty rest, Preacher! Now, listen good to me. I take this route all the time, and there's nothing to it, but you're a virgin, I know, so we're gonna be extra careful. The thing to remember, when you're in human territory, is stay close to the edges and in the shadows. And when we're on the road, that means stick to the curb —chances are no one will ever see you. This big stretch here is pretty much a straight shot all the way downtown, and there we just have a few side streets to get down to make it to the waterfront. *That's* where you're really going to have to watch out, until we're way back in the alleys, where the humans don't go except to piss and shoot up. Like I said, the humans down there this late are usually too plastered to know us from a couple of squirrels, but you still don't wanna get too close to them when they get drunk. They can get crazy—so just try to stay out of sight. Plenty of things to hide under down there...parked cars, wastebaskets, bushes...the thing is, just don't get antsy; bide your time and only move out in the open when the coast is clear. Stick with me, and do what I do, and you'll be fine. Nothing to it, once you know what's going on. All right! You ready for a night you'll never forget?"

"Ready!" said Clancy gamely. He was still, of course, more than a little apprehensive, as he had been all day, at the prospect of going all the way down to the waterfront—in the heart of human territory—on foot. But the knowledge, if not the memory of his journey thence with Aunt November long ago was somewhat reassuring. And after all, Percy would be by his side and looking out for him, and if he couldn't count on Percy, who'd rescued him from the perceived (if not the real) threat of a cat attack, who could he count on? Apart from the Lord, of course.

And so the journey out proved, for Clancy at least, more exhilarating than terrifying. Automobiles whizzed by intermittently as the two rats loped along the roadside, unseen in the darkness against the concrete curbing. In the dark sky above, a pale quarter moon shone among a panoply of seemingly random scattered stars. Every few yards or so Percy would pause and look behind himself to make sure that Clancy was keeping pace. This increased Clancy's confidence that all would be well.

As Percy had explained, for the most part the way to the waterfront was a straight shot. Then they navigated a number of sharp turns down a labyrinth of side roads that were blessedly devoid of human or vehicle activity. It was only once they reached the relatively vast open pedestrian plaza of shops and bars and restaurants abutting the gently rippling dark water of the sound that Clancy began to feel uncomfortably exposed. Even though the humans were not, as Percy had assured him, as thickly converged as they would have been earlier in the evening, there were enough of them staggering about or gathered in tight constellations around the entrances of establishments for Clancy to find it hard to imagine that two rats out in the open wouldn't be noticed. But just as Percy had promised, they made it across the plaza in a series of dashes from cover to cover to finally find sanctuary in a narrow alley between a crab shack and a gift shoppe that was apparently Percy's home turf.

"Here we are, baby!" said Percy, reaching his forepaw proprietarily across his friend's back. "Told you nothing would happen! You made it. Come on—I'll show you around...." And so saying, with his ropy tail he gathered Clancy to himself in an embrace that was more like a bump, and a rather rough bump at that, but it was meant to be bracing. Clancy was in fact so overcome by the darkness and the noise and the haunting familiarity of the atmosphere of the alleyway that he had the wherewithal neither to proceed or resist, and so Percy fairly dragged him along into the recesses of the alleyway, until a huddle of moving shadows resolved itself into a group of rats wrangling over a discarded crab cake.

"Some welcome home," said Percy. "Don't you bastards have any manners?"

"Percy!" The rats disengaged from one another and greeted Percy in a chorus of gravely squeals. "You're back!" One large and particularly mangy individual launched himself toward Percy and the two tangled and jostled one another about for a while before separating and regarding one another cheekily. "Where've you been, Perce? What've you been getting yourself into?"

"Nunya," said Percy, not antagonistically. "Just taking care of business. You know I like to keep moving when things get a little hot around here. How've things been with you losers?"

"Same old dung," said the rather mangy rat, casting a curious and rather bleary eye at Clancy. "Who's this?"

Clancy endeavored to overcome his instinctual, or at least deeply inculcated aversion to the attention of such a very ill-comported group of rodents. It seemed to him that there wasn't one rat among them, including this apparent ringleader, who did not possess some scrape or scar or scab or missing tuft of fur or other stigmata of a wayward lifestyle. *It's not their fault*, he told himself silently. *Not all of us are blessed to have an Aunt November around to show us how to do right and stay out of trouble.* He swished his tail in welcome as Percy introduced him. "This is Clancy. He's a church rat, living uptown, but he's cool. Used to live here, so I thought I'd bring him around and show him a good time. Clancy, this is Winston—" The mangy, wrestling rat bared his incisors. "—and Cruddy, and Jim, and

Rebus, and Ferston. They're a bunch of lowlifes, but they could be worse."

"Nice to meet ya'll," said Clancy. "It sure is something else down here! I haven't been down here since I was just a baby. My Aunt November took me away to live in the church. Maybe ya'll remember a female named November? Older, kind of stout? But sweet as she could be, unless you crossed her.... Anyway, I don't remember much down here at all. Aunt November said it just went downhill when the humans put in all these places where they drink and dance... she was real strict."

"Are you for real?" That largest and most mangy rat said, and before Clancy could respond, Percy stepped forward warningly.

"Watch yourself, Winston," he said steelily. "This is my friend. Maybe he's a little wet behind the ears, being out in the burbs all this time, but he's one of us. He just hasn't had much of a chance to live life. So I expect you bastards to help me show him a good time and keep him out of trouble. You dig me?"

"All right, all right...." said the chastened Winston. "No worries." He turned to Clancy with an amplified air of gutter graciousness. "We just like to break each other's balls around here. It's all good. Listen—you want some grog?" Clancy looked to Percy for guidance. Percy nudged him encouragingly. "G'head," he said. "Give it a try. Who knows, you might like it. Might help you relax. Hard to know how you'll like it—but a little nip never hurt anyone...." He darted a glance at Winston. "It better not...."

Winston sidled up to Clancy. "Nothing to worry about! Look at me! I don't miss a night and I'm as healthy as a horsefly. Drinks on me tonight....Right this way."

"You go on, Rev," said Percy to Clancy. "I got a little business to tend to. Let these guys take care of you. I'll catch up with you in a few."

Clancy's eyes bulged. Percy was going to leave him with these.... A jumble of derogatory terms came to mind unbidden, and Clancy felt ashamed of himself, for he knew he was judging them by surface appearance and not by the knowledge that they were made in God's image—every bit as much as he. Surely Percy would not leave him to their company if he was not sure that they could be trusted...and neither would God. "All right," he said, a little breathlessly.

Percy seemed to hesitate, then took off toward the front of the alleyway. With Winston at his side, Clancy made his way into the *demimonde*.

❦

"So—" said mangy Winston, giving Clancy the once over, "you say you used to live down here? Can't say I've seen you around, and I've been here all my life."

"Oh, but I was just a little thing then," said Clancy. "My Aunt November took me off to stay with her at the church. She didn't want—" Clancy stopped himself just in time before potentially offending his host by informing him that, as far as Aunt November had been concerned, the rats of the waterfront were hopelessly degenerate. "—She didn't want me getting sick. I was real puny back then."

"You sure ain't too puny now," said Winston. "You look pretty healthy to me. Anyway, welcome back. There's nothing like the waterfront on a Saturday night! Anything a rat could ask for— grub, grog, and girlies. Perce sure thinks a lot of you, or he wouldn't have asked me to show you what's up. He knows he can count on me. Whatever you want to try, just ask...."

"Okay," said Clancy agreeably, eager, despite his bewilderment and disorientation, to make a good impression upon his dear friend Percy's admirers. He was getting used to the sights and sounds and smells of the dark alley, along with the overall frenetic quality of the pervading atmosphere. He'd certainly never seen so many of his own species in one place in his life, and they all seemed to be observing him with guarded curiosity from their perches atop garbage bags and milk crates and stacks of wooden and cardboard pellets. He scampered as close as he could to stay beside Winston as the two of them made their way in the wake of the other rats that Percy had introduced him to towards the back of the alley. There stood a metal container, much like the dumpster back at the convenience store that Percy stayed in, but smaller and of a lighter green color. Even from many yards away Clancy could smell a sharp, yeasty aroma emanating from it. The rats leaped from the concrete to the edge of the access window near the top and disappeared inside. "Party time!" said Winston, and he scrambled up and in. Clancy took a deep breath and followed.

Looking in from the edge of the access window, Clancy could see, towards the front of the container, a heap of glass bottles, mostly intact but some broken into jagged treacherous shards. Seeping from the bottom of this heap of glass he could make out, even in the darkness, a sheen of liquid that Winston and the others were eagerly lapping up.

"Lord!" exclaimed Clancy. "What is that stuff?! Is it sanitary?"

Winston stood on his hind legs, peered up, and beckoned Clancy down with his forepaw. "Clean as your mother's milk!" he said. "Fresh dregs. This is some of the best liquor on the waterfront. Here—just have a taste." And Winston sloshed the tip of his tail in the seeping, sharp smelling liquid, and held it out to Clancy. Clancy was more than a little reluctant to put his tongue to this strange, unkempt rat's tail, but he certainly didn't want to offend by being too squeamish. The taste of the dripping, course-haired and scaly-skinned tail was at once sharp and fruity and yeasty, but not bad. And as he swallowed, his gullet burned not unpleasantly, as the heat of the substance slowly unfurled in his flesh to reach every extremity. "Wow!" he exclaimed, reminding himself of Bertram.

"See?' said Winston. "Only the top shelf for Percy's pal."

Clancy was intrigued. He knew that this stuff was alcohol, and that alcohol had the curious, seemingly supernatural ability to change the mood and often the behavior and even sometimes the personality of the creature who indulged in it. He'd seen it, on a few alarming occasions, reduce the Reverend DeBassompierre from a respectable, articulate priest to an incoherent zombie. But, he told himself, that was because the Reverend DeBassompierre, by his own admission, had a tendency to drink too much when he felt stressed. Clancy didn't feel the slightest bit stressed; on the contrary, he felt unexpectedly relaxed in this new and alien, if hauntingly familiar environment, among his own species, even though they were strangers. As the warmth that had suffused his flesh faded, he wondered if another little taste might restore it. He bent his snout to the floor and licked, and gulped, and licked his clefted palate and licked up some more.

"This is yummy!" he said. "Thanks, Winston!"

"Drink up!" said Winston encouragingly. "There's plenty, and there's always more coming, except on Sunday, as long as there are humans coming down to the waterfront. Do they love their grog! Have all you want! You only live once!"

As ever, that clichéd statement struck Clancy as being demonstrative of a pitiable eschatological ignorance, but he figured it wasn't the proper time to share the Gospel of eternal life with these fellows. There was a time and a place for everything, and he would repay their hospitality by inviting them to St. Aloysius. But that could wait. The warmth was already fading. He lowered himself again and licked the floor of the dumpster.

❦

PERCY HAD personal business to take care of; that was an unspoken reason he'd had for returning to the waterfront. Since becoming involved with the church, and by extension the families within, he couldn't help but come to a sharper awareness that his relationship with his own offspring was nonexistent.

This was, he told himself, not his fault alone. His eldest set of kids— and there were three of them, if he remembered correctly —were begotten on the body of a female rat named Rowena who, in spite of all he'd done to make her comfortable if not happy, had refused to let him see them until, as she said, he "got his act together." But every time he tried to get her to be more specific about what he could possibly do to please her, she would simply clam up and feign distress. He'd arranged for her to possess—inasmuch as a rat could be said to possess—a prime piece of waterfront property consisting of the enclosed delivery and maintenance area behind the waterfront's most luxurious hotel, by chasing away all the other rats inhabiting the space. After that he'd attempted on various occasions to visit his offspring and present them with the choicest morsels from around the promenade. At one low point he'd even sworn to Rowena, with as much sincerity as he could manage, to try to be faithful to her. But for Rowena, apparently, "getting his act together" meant something beyond providing for her and their offspring. But exactly what it meant she consistently refused to articulate. "You should know," she always maintained. "If you really loved me, you wouldn't have to ask."

"She's never satisfied," he reminded himself as he made his way from the alley to the hotel. But he couldn't help but imagine that once he told her he'd become involved with a nice set of creatures, and was learning something about what it might mean to raise a family, she might consider that at least a step toward "getting his act together." At the same time, the prospect of taking back up with her if only in the interest of the offspring filled Percy's soul with an amalgamation of excitement and dread. She was a very difficult female, full of mystery and caprice, and as moody and changeable as a coastal summer sky. But she had been his first love, if love it had been, and no matter who else had come along, he would always have a soft spot for Rowena.

"SLOW DOWN, SON!" Winston sounded at once amused and alarmed. "Go too fast, you might get sick. You could even shit yourself. Told you you'd like this stuff!"

Clancy lifted his snout out of the seeping puddle of intermingled liquors and nodded his agreement with such vigor that he lost his balance. In light of such clear evidence of overindulgence, he had to agree with Winston that he ought to slow down, but the warmth and the bite of this fascinating concoction were unexpectedly compelling! "I feel..." he began to say, pausing because he found it slightly difficult to form his words, "...so free!"

"Good!" said Winston. "Party on! I knew you were one of us! You can take a rat out of the wharf, but you can't take the wharf out of the rat!"

"Amen!" said Clancy, Winston's affirmation of him causing him to feel all the freer. Forgetting himself, he lowered his snout for another gulp. Winston observed this with indulgence, then took him by the ear with his own snout and nudged him gently towards the edge of the dumpster, where the liquid was less deeply pooled. "Listen, let's find something for you to put in your stomach. That way you can pace yourself a little better."

"...'m'kay...." said Clancy thickly. It took some effort, and he had to squeeze one eye shut in order to see straight, but he followed Winston up and out of the dumpster, and across the narrow dark alley to where a number of loose plastic bags were placed against the brick wall. One of these bags, having been gnawed open earlier by Winston and a few of his crew, was spilling its contents onto the concrete. These bags consisted of scrapings off the dishes from the crab shack: half eaten, richly seasoned crab cakes, heaps of coleslaw, damp but delicious fried potato wedges, and even some crusts of key lime pie. "Yum!" cried Clancy as the aromas reached him, and he dug right in, forgetting for the moment his vow to reduce.

"Dag!" said Winston. "Don't they feed you uptown?"

For the moment Clancy was too busy gobbling to attempt to answer. *Not like this....* he found himself thinking, for it was true that the community garden and the food pantry and Grace's wastebasket notwithstanding, St. Aloysius hardly provided the variety and succulence of the waste that was on offer here. He wondered how on earth these alley rats like Winston and his chums managed to stay so lean and mean! He supposed it all came down to genetics. Aunt November, after all, ate like a bird and yet was forever trying to slim down.

Aunt November. Out of nowhere, seemingly, a great wave of maudlin emotion swelled up within Clancy, and his appetite suddenly dissipated like a morning fog. He wondered if she could see him from her figurative cloud in heaven, here in this waterfront alleyway, precisely the place from which she'd rescued him from a life of delinquency and squalor. What would she think? Surely she would be horrified, even in Glory.

In his mind's eye, the image of his beloved and exacting great aunt gazed down upon his current situation with beatific disappointment. Clancy wanted to die. The potato wedge, which a moment before had been so delectable, turned to a foul mush in his mouth. It was all he could do to spit it out. But there was also, within this sudden descent into melancholy and shame, a certain exhilaration. Oh, how he'd let her down! And not only Aunt November, but the church, and his flock, and Reverend DeBassompierre, and even Jesus and God Himself! Surely this behavior, guzzling liquor and gorging himself on rich food, was conduct unbecoming a minister of the Gospel! And yet again, did not Jesus Himself turn water into wine, and sup and sip with sinners and tax collectors? With this recollection, which seemed to come to him unbidden and thus from beyond, Clancy's spirits rose again, and he slurred aloud a hallelujah. Aunt November's potential disapproval—for the moment, at least—forgotten, Clancy's appetite returned. He seized and devoured the remainder of the potato wedge, and then found that he was thirsty. Remembering that he was not unaccompanied, he turned to Winston and asked if there was more of what that rat referred to as grog.

"Sure!" said Winston. "What, do you think we drank it all? There's still plenty, back in with the bottles. But listen—don't you think you better slow your roll...?"

But Clancy, unfamiliar with the argot of the alley, didn't understand, and didn't take the trouble even to wonder, what Winston meant by that curious phrase. Up he leapt, through the access opening of the bright green dumpster, landing on the pile of empty bottles with a clatter and an "Oof!"

"Better keep an eye on him," said one of the alley rats to Winston. "If he gets sick, Percy'll have your hide."

"Dadgum tourists," grumbled Winston. "Nothing but trouble." And with great reluctance he followed Clancy back into the glass recycling container.

৩৲৶

"WELL. Look what the cat dragged back...." was the wry and sour statement the female rat drawled by way of greeting Percy. "What brings you around? Worn out your welcome with whoever you've been shacking up with uptown? Guess you're gonna hafta hop a boat before long if you want to keep trying to outrun *your* rep..."

Percy gritted his teeth and prayed, in his novice way, for patience. Rowena had a right, he supposed, to be snarky with him, since she had, after all, been the one he'd left with three offspring to raise. *But*, his internal advocate stood to object in the courtroom of his conscience, *she said she'd had enough of you as soon as you chased away all the squatters and got her set up nice here in the service entrance behind the Ritz Hotel, and besides, she is as bad as I am about fooling around. How do I really know those three babies are mine after all?*

"Fair enough, Rowena," he said, as serenely as he could. "I

know...I'm a bastard. I don't want to argue with you. Let's just let bygones be bygones, huh? I just wanted to stop by and see you and the kids, that's all."

"Me and the kids!" Rowena roused herself from where she was nesting quite luxuriously on a pile of towels within a discarded old laundry hamper with a hole in its canvas near the bottom. "Well, what a doting father! Aren't we lucky...." She yawned and stretched herself toward him and sniffed. "And you're not even drunk...at least not so I can tell...." She withdrew swiftly and pointedly backed into her hamper, and when she spoke again her vocalization was clipped. "The kids are asleep. I don't want them disturbed. They need their rest. And so do I."

"Rowena, gimme a break!" Percy could not keep the exasperation out of his own vocalizations. "You've got it pretty cushy here, and I ought to know. Look, I won't wake them up, if you're gonna be like that. I just want to see them. Okay?"

Rowena, having curled back onto her towels as if to sleep, opened one dark eye and regarded him, and once again thrust forward her snout and sniffed, then turned away as if to avoid his odor before rearing up again to hiss in his face. "You're up to something," she declared. "I don't like this. You're in some sort of trouble, aren't you, and you think you're such hot stuff that I'm gonna just take you back like nothing ever happened...."

"I'm not in any kind of trouble, Rowena, and if I was, do you really think I'd come to you for any help? Gimme a break. Look, as a matter of fact, I'm doing just fine, and that's why I wanted to come by, and just...let you know I want to be more...around for the kids. I know I could have been more help to you when it counted, but the past is the past, and all I can do is say I'm sorry...."

"Sorry!" Rowena spat the word back at him as if it burned her tongue. She scrambled out of her soft bedding and thrust her snout in front of Percy's. "You bet your *tail* you're sorry. Because of you, none of my old friends even remember who I am, much less come and hang out with me. Because of you I'm stuck here all the time with three squalling babies and can't have any fun! Because of you I'm all washed up while you just go on with your life and do whatever you please!"

"Rowena...." A truly sympathetic note entered Percy's tone. It wasn't the first time he had heard this tirade. But it was the first time, he supposed, that he listened. He couldn't deny that he'd left Rowena with all the responsibility. He couldn't deny that if he were her, he'd probably be just as nasty. But what was he supposed to do?!

"Rowena, I really am sorry. I know I've been a turd. But can't we just get along? I'm here now, aren't I?"

"You ain't the only one."

The voice, crepuscularly deep, gravelly, and at once restrained and fur-raisingly confrontational, came from behind him. Percy, his system flooded instantly with adrenaline and testosterone, spun around, incisors bared and ready to fight. He was, as a matter of fact, one inch away from pouncing upon this unexpected adversary when he perceived that, in spite of its height and girth and evident ferocity, his challenger was a female. A female who was, in fact, well known to him from his nights on the streets, though not as a paramour. Far from it. This was the only other rat, apart from old Bart, that he would never wish to cross.

"G'head," the big female said. "Try something."

"Big Cindy!" Percy's jaw dropped and he fell on all fours. "What're you doing here?"

"Looking after my lady," said the rat named Big Cindy. "Not that it's any business of yours. Want me to get rid of this chump, Rowena? He bothering you again?"

"Not right at the moment, hon," said Rowena, with a pointed glance at Percy. "But give him time...."

The residue of the adrenaline rush had left Percy's tail switching and coiling with nervous energy. He held it still lest Big Cindy take the motion as some sort of provocation. Rowena and Big Cindy? He couldn't quite believe it. The Rowena he had known had only ever expressed contempt and disgust for females of Big Cindy's persuasion. But of course, Rowena had never made a virtue of consistency.

"Listen, Big Cindy, I don't want any trouble. I just came by to see my kids...."

"*Your* kids?"

In the vast concrete landscape of the service entrance of the waterfront luxury hotel, lit around its perimeter by security lampposts, Percy was crouched quite literally in Big Cindy's imposing shadow. "*Your* kids? *You* the one that's been feeding them? *You* the one's been teaching them what they need to know? *You* the one's been tucking 'em in at night and lettin' 'em know they got someone watchin' over 'em? *You* the one helpin' their mama make ends meet? You?"

Percy hung his snout; his whiskers, normally stiff and twitching, drooped.

"Damn straight," said Big Cindy. "Rowee told me how you were. All talk. And when it comes to taking care of your own, you hightail it off somewhere. Typical male. Well, I got news for you: I been more of a daddy to those kids than you'll ever be, and I don't think I want you coming around here getting them all mixed up about who they belong with. I love 'em just like they're my own, and no one's gonna take that away from them. I mean nobody. So if I was you, chump, I'd get to scramming. You hear me?"

Percy wasn't always aware that within him there was a tender heart, but as he listened to Big Cindy claiming her rights and expressing what he knew was a hopeless devotion to Rowena, he felt that tender heart sink and then swell with a terrible compassion. *Oh, Big Cin*, he thought. *Rowena's got her claws in you deep.*

But there was nothing to do but hope that in the end Big Cindy was more right than she knew, and that no one—*including* Rowena—would separate those innocent baby rats from the love of the only truly protective and devoted parent they knew: Big Cindy.

"I hear you, Big Cindy," said Percy. "I'll make myself scarce." And with that he cast a parting scowl at Rowena and scuttled off to rejoin his friend.

⚜

CLANCY COULDN'T PUT his claw on what, exactly, it was that had changed. It seemed to him that one moment he was on top of the world, and the next, quite literally down in the dumps. This sudden plunge was just as much physical as it was emotional. He was finding it increasingly difficult to move with any coordination, to speak with any coherence, and even to think straight. What had happened to the wonderful sensation of liberation, of confidence in his capacity to fascinate, that he'd begun to experience after the first few swallows of spilled alcohol? He'd had more than a few more swallows since returning to the green dumpster, but while the warmth had returned to his blood, he no longer felt light, but heavy. He felt, in fact, as if all he wanted to do was lie down in the puddle of liquor all around him and let himself dissolve. "I don't feel so good," he moaned, as he collapsed with a splash.

"I told you to take it easy! Don't you dare pass out! Percy'll have my hide!"

Clancy raised his snout and managed to open one eye, and his tail sloshed weakly in the puddled liquid. "Percy!" he moaned. "I feel awful."

"I'm not Percy, you flea-brain!" Winston shouted right into the delicate, convoluted cavern of Clancy's right ear. "Percy ain't here, you nincompoop. No telling what he's up to. But I know one thing, you better get yourself together before he comes back looking for you—*if* he comes back. Knowing him, he's off getting himself some tail, like *I* should be doing. Now listen. Get up, and let's get out of here, before you drown your crazy self. I've seen it happen. Hey, losers!" Winston shouted up in the direction of the access door. "You guys get in here and help me with this lightweight!"

By that point, Clancy had lapsed into a state of bleary, queasy, and limp incomprehension. He heard what Winston was saying, but only through the dumb, insistent throbbing of his heartbeat. He then felt himself being rat-handled rather roughly, lifted from below by unsteady and thoughtless and sharp-clawed rodent paws, one of which gripped him in a most sensitive spot on his underside. Too mortified to resist, he could only let himself be hoisted, then pulled up by the tail and pushed up by the nose to the access window of the dumpster, and then lowered down in this same manner to the concrete ground of the alleyway.

"There," said Winston, breathing hard. "That'll do. Now he won't be getting any more grog in him, at least."

"Hefty little bastard," said one of the other rats. "You'd think he could hold his liquor better. We just gonna leave him here?"

There was a pause, as Winston regarded the prone and sopping form of Clancy with not a little disgust. "Just leave him," he said. "We've done enough."

"You sure?" came a dubious response. "He's in bad shape."

"No duh," Winston said. "Let Percy deal with him. I'm not a damn babysitter. I got a female waiting. Percy can shove it. He ain't the boss of me, anyway."

Notwithstanding this bravado, Winston cast a glance toward the front of the alley as if to make sure the coast was clear. "C'mon," he said to his lackeys. "Let's get out of here."

And off they went, leaving Clancy to the mercy of the underworld.

۞

PERCY WAS IN A HURRY, as the horizon steadily brightened, to get back to the alley where he had, perhaps foolishly, left Clancy in the care of his friends— if friends they were, for in light of this business with Rowena and Big Cindy, how could he be sure what was really going on down here anymore?

As he skittered along the waterfront in the pearly light of dawn, he couldn't stop marveling at the way things turned out sometimes. Rowena and Big Cindy! Never would he have imagined. Once again, he felt his heart go out to Big Cindy, who, despite her forbidding reputation and gruff manner, had always struck him as a decent sort, deserving of respect simply for being herself. And if he was completely honest, even though his desire to be a better parent to the triplets had been sincere, he wasn't at all sure that he could have sustained for long any sort of rapprochement with Rowena. She knew too well how to get under his pelt with her scornfulness and recriminations. He imagined, though, that she was too savvy to lay the same trips on Big Cindy. As a matter of fact, she might just have met her match with Big Cindy, and that would serve her right. And as for the kids, Big Cindy was a godsend. He figured that things might have been different for him if there had been a Big Cindy around when he was their age. But at least he'd had old Bart...

"Well, look who's back! Hey, handsome!"

Percy was so embroiled in his reflections that he was practically on top of the pale little rat before him before he realized he'd been greeted.

"Oh hey, Smoky," Percy said. "Sorry, I didn't even see you...."

"Didn't see me!" the small pale rat replied with affected indignation. "Well, we can't *all* be big handsome hunks like you! Where've you been lately? Last I heard you were all shacked up with that shady Rowena."

Percy shuddered. "Don't believe everything you hear," he said. "It's good to see you, Smoky, but I'm in kind of a rush...."

The small pale rat executed a cunning little snap of his tail. "Always on the prowl," he said, not without a saucy admiration. "Well, don't let me keep you, then. We were just wondering if you might like to join us for a little snack." He indicated the space underneath the front porch of the flower shop. Through the latticework a group of rats similar in size and appearance to Smoky himself were gazing at the two of them with languid amusement.

"The humans who run the place brought in some brownies and left a few of them right in the storeroom. And darling, you've never had anything like them! I don't know what's in them, but one little crumb and in a few moments, you're just as relaxed as can be and walking on air! It's marvelous! Better than you know what...." Smoky purred. "And you know how much I *love* you know what.... But if you've got other plans...."

In spite of himself, Percy felt distinctly intrigued and sorely tempted. He was by nature an adventurer, after all, and with a new experience on offer, he wondered reflexively what it would hurt to take a few minutes to give it a whirl. Better than "you know what"! Could anything be better than that? Percy's experience of Smoky was that the crazy little creature was prone to dramatic exaggeration, but he wasn't a liar, and really, what was there to lose?

He looked at Smoky, whose eager, winsome expression reminded him of Clancy, and as the burgeoning sunrise shone in the little rat's sprightly, somewhat bleary pale eyes, he knew that there was no time to waste. "Some other time," he said to Smoky. "I have to get going. But it really is nice to see you."

And before his curiosity once again got the better of him, Percy scampered off.

🐁

HE FOUND CLANCY, as he knew deep down he'd find the hapless uptown rat, alone, unconscious, damp, sticky with liquor, bedraggled, and what's worse, exposed to any threat or predator that might happen to come upon him as the night turned into day over the sleepy waterfront. "Those bastards!" he growled, thinking of Winston and his worthless lackeys, but he knew he was just as much to blame for any harm that had (or could have) come to Clancy in these mean streets. He scurried over to Clancy and, taking the prone rat by the base of his tail, began to drag him toward the green bin, with the object of getting him underneath, hiding him at least from any large potential predator.

"Oh, Aunt November," moaned Clancy. "I feel awful...."

Percy continued to drag poor Clancy by the tail along the concrete.

"Ooowww!" Clancy moaned. "My flesh is burning! I'm in hell! Jesus, save me!"

Percy had to pause for a moment to relax his jaw and catch his breath.

"I'm dying," moaned Clancy.

"No, you're not." Percy reached over and opened one of Clancy's eyes. "You're hung over. I'm going to kill that worthless Winston. I'm going to tear him limb from limb."

It took Clancy a moment, as Percy's voice and image penetrated his consciousness, to come to some measure of his senses. Shards of memories of the previous few hours descended upon his psyche, lacerating it with embarrassment. "Oh, Lord!" he cried. "I got drunk! I got sloshed! Oh, Percy, I made a fool of myself!"

"Welcome to the club," said Percy. Now that Clancy seemed reasonably conscious, he squeezed himself under the green bin, and beckoned Clancy to follow. "Get under here, before something sees us. I mean it! I'm going to make Winston wish he was never born. I told him not to let you get too out of paw...."

Clancy squealed as he squeezed underneath the bin, for every inch of his hide really did feel as raw as if he'd been burned. "Shhhh!" Percy warned. "It's getting light...you don't want some alley cat to hear us!"

"I'm sorry," moaned Clancy.

"Don't be sorry. Just be quiet. This is as much my fault as anyone's. I knew I shouldn't have left you with those losers. Live and learn. Just go back to sleep, and you'll feel better. We're stuck here anyway.... The cats'll be along soon looking for all the leftovers. They always have a feast down here on Sunday morning...."

"Sunday!" The word pierced Clancy's torpor like a thorn. "Oh! Lord!" And the sound and the effort of his own exclamation caused his head to throb and his bowels to expel a copious amount of loose stool. He moaned and writhed with anguish, then began to squeeze himself out from under the green bin.

Percy grabbed him by the tail. "Don't even think about it!" he said. "It's too late. And you're still half drunk. You can't *preach*!"

But Clancy could not be held back. He thrashed until Percy loosened his grip, and emerged, not without a moan, out into the open alley. There he had to pause while he expelled yet another gout of diarrhea. "Oh, Lord," he said, "strengthen me."

Percy stifled his own moan of exhaustion and dismay. The silly rat didn't have a prayer. He'd be some cat's breakfast before he even made it to the boulevard.

"Oh, for God's sake," said Percy. "Wait for me."

※

A LOW-LYING MORNING FOG, like a gift from heaven, served to shroud the two rats as they made their way across the waterfront district to the boulevard that led to the church. And unbeknownst to them, high above that dense yet rapidly dissipating fog flew a guardian angel that had been keeping a sharp eye and keen nose on Clancy throughout his nocturnal adventure. Her name was Sudie Mae.

THE END

www.ingramcontent.com/pod-product-compliance
Lightning Source LLC
Chambersburg PA
CBHW060244030726
47493CB00025B/2160

* 9 7 8 1 9 5 8 0 6 1 0 0 8 *